Highland Skies
Book Three
Highland Treasures

highland skies

highland treasures

book three

by

c.a. szarek

Highland Skies
C.A. Szarek

Highland Treasures Book Three

OtheR books by c.a. szaRek

<u>Highland Secrets Trilogy & Companions—Historical Fantasy Romance</u>
The Princess and The Laird (Highland Secrets Prequel)
The Tartan MP3 Player (Book One)
The Fae Ring (Book Two)
The Parchment Scroll (Book Three)
Highland Valentine (A Highland Secrets HEA Story)
Highlander's Portrait (A Highland Secrets Story)

<u>Highland Treasures—Historical Fantasy Romance</u>
Highland Oath (Book One)
Highland Essence (Book Two)
Highland Skies (Book Three)

<u>The King's Riders—Fantasy Romance</u>
Sword's Call (Book One)—*Also in Audio*
Love's Call (Book Two)—*Also in Audio*
Rogue's Call (Book Three)—*Also in Audio*
Fate's Call (A Novella from the World of the King's Riders)—*Also in Audio*

<u>Crossing Forces—Romantic Suspense</u>
Collision Force (Book One)—*Also in Audio*

Cole in Her Stocking (A Crossing Forces Christmas) — *FREE read!*

Chance Collision (Book Two) — *Also in Audio*

Calculated Collision (Book Three) — *Also in Audio*

Collision Control (Book Four) — *Also in Audio*

Weekend Collision (A Crossing Forces HEA Story) — *FREE read!*

Superior Collision (Book Five) — *Also in Audio*

Incendiary Collision (Book Six) — *Coming Soon!*

<u>The Giovanni</u>

King of Hearts (Book One) — *Also in Audio*

Queen of Diamonds (Book Two) — *Coming Soon!*

Dedication

For Kylie. You always encourage me to fight for what I want, and I need that in my life. We might have met at work but we're so much more than just coworkers. Love you, girl!

chapter one

Liam waited until Dunvegan was quiet, like he always did when he wanted to sneak over to the Fae Realm. It was just before midnight, which was the latest he'd ever had to wait, but his father, a former Fae Warrior had been especially…nosy…all evening.

He'd had to reinforce his magical shields with a spellword multiple times, because his father could read minds. It was his gift—or his curse, as the man always declared—and Liam tended to agree, considering he didn't want his da anywhere near his thoughts.

Especially when he was planning something against the rules.

Dangerous. Life threatening.

Forbidden.

Liam had heard it all his life.

It didn't matter.

In the Realm of the Fae, he had wings.

He *needed* to fly.

Liam quickly made it down the beach and to the cave that held the Faery Stones. He couldn't chance bringing his beloved roan stallion, Treun, because leaving his horse while he was gone would pretty much shout that he'd done something all his family—Clan MacLeod—deemed foolish and childish.

He'd also left his favorite claymore in his rooms.

Because of its size, he'd opted for his dirk, which was sheathed in his boot. The Fae-forged blade had been a gift from his father when he'd turned eight and ten and could still inflict any needed damage. He was equally skilled with it, as he was with his sword.

A part of Liam protested leaving his main weapon, but he didn't plan to be gone long, and his long dagger would have to do.

He needed to draw on any knowledge of stealth—magic and skill alike—he was ever capable of. His cousin by blood—and aunt by marriage—Alana, had a strong tie to the Faery Stones and would sense when they opened. She was a former Fae princess, and his father had been her bodyguard. They'd been exiled from the Fae Realm before he'd been born.

Of course, he wouldn't have to deal with *those* consequences until he returned.

Liam didn't have much time, and he could only hope the spell he'd used the few times he'd successfully sneaked over to the other realm unseen would work to keep him hidden and safe.

His favorite cousin, Lexi, had helped with her magic in times past, but he couldn't rely on her now. She'd been living in the far future, blissfully happy with her husband in the twenty-first century for almost five years now. At least, that amount of time had passed for them, in the seventeenth century.

He'd just turned five and twenty, and his actions tonight would be far from appreciated if he got caught.

Liam could hear his father, Xander's voice now, *"You're not a laddie anymore, Liam. You're a man. You need to stop making foolish choices that put our whole family at risk."*

He sighed.

His family was always smothering him, but he loved them — even his trouble-prone raucous cousins, two of which — Lachlan and Rory — were close to him in age. Iain was the bairn, at seven and ten, but they were all as close as brothers, even Angus, who was more than ten years older.

None of them would ever understand. None of them knew what it was like to fly.

Only his father could, but the man often refused to talk about the past.

When Liam had sneaked to the Fae Realm and his wings took him into the purple and gold skies, so he could soar — that was the only time in his life he recalled true freedom.

Aye, it was dangerous.

The tales he'd heard from his father and aunt had always resonated, but a part of his mind denied it could be wholly true.

After all, he'd survived several trips without a scratch.

He and Lexi had never successfully gone to the Fae Realm together, but he had on his own several times, using stealth magic he'd gleaned from his former Fae Warrior da, as well as an invisibility spell he'd learned as a laddie to compete with his cousin Rory's famous pranks.

Liam admitted he'd been lucky to get into the realm and away from the Fae Warriors who guarded the Faery Stones, usually with a small magical distraction of some sort.

Like him and his father, they were winged and fierce. Skilled and highly trained soldiers.

The Fae army.

His father had once been one of their elite numbers.

They wore green armor and kept their hair fashioned in long thick plaits. It was said, the longer and thicker the braid, the more power and magic the Warrior possessed.

He was also told the Fae could smell—or sense—human blood and would kill anyone who suffered such an affliction on sight.

People like him were considered an abomination.

Liam—like his cousins Angus and Lexi—were half-Fae. His mother was a MacLeod by birth, sister to the laird, their father.

Had he been born fully Fae, he would've been raised as a Fae Warrior, too. Like his father before him, and his grandfather, who was Captain of the king's guard, and leader of all the Fae Warriors.

Liam loved his mother dearly, as well as respected her, and his parents both believed they were fated to be together, but part of him had always mourned that he couldn't be who he was supposed to be, since he was half human.

Guilt would always swirl low in his gut when he contemplated that, and he'd been told how he was better off with Clan MacLeod, who were his blood, too. He and his half-Fae cousins were the best of both realms, according to his aunt.

You want nothing to do with my people, his father always admonished.

Fae didn't have surnames, so he'd always been Liam MacLeod, instead of Liam, Warrior of the Fae, son of the great Fae Warrior, Xander.

Liam had heard tales of Alana's sire, the king, about how bloodthirsty and ruthless King Fillan was. The same was said of his father's father, Daegus.

All the Fae couldn't be vicious and evil, could they?

They loved and lived just like humans, didn't they?

Liam shook the idea, the guilt, and the doubt from his head.

He needed to go now, if he was to take to the air, feel the wind in his hair and flowing over his body as his wings took him higher.

Liam shot into the cave of the Faery Stones through the mostly hidden narrow opening. The Stones were the key to the portal that would carry him to his desired destination.

The space widened as soon as he was a few feet in, forming a natural room, but the place lit up *unnaturally*, by the magic of the Stones, no torches or candles needed.

Five clustered natural formations created the Faery Stones, rising from the small cavern's floor, perfectly spaced from each other in a loose semi-circle. One was centered with the other four surrounding it.

The crystals glinted off some light source, but the

radiance came from inside them. They gave off enough light to illuminate the cave, but they were hidden well enough to prevent unexpected guests.

Liam felt the magic vibrating from the Stones and across his torso. Alana had placed a spell on them meant to discourage, and even repulse, unwanted humans from finding the cave and Stones.

The magic didn't make him want to run away, as intended. He was aware of it, and it made his skin prickle, but it wasn't the desired deterrent. Perhaps because he was half-Fae.

The main crystal—crucial to making the others work—hummed in welcome.

He smiled and blew out a breath.

Liam's tie to the Faery Stones wasn't as strong as Lexi's, but he could usually open them on the first try, if he was calm and focused enough.

He closed his eyes and the melody of the magic washed over him, settling him, and almost convincing him he wasn't doing something wrong.

Three more steps brought Liam to the Stones, and his body thrummed with magic and anticipation as he reached for the center gem.

Each crystal sat atop the five naturally formed pillars, pulsating with power, which increased with the first brush of his fingers to smooth Stone.

The semi-circle the Faery Stones sat in was perfect, as if it had been placed there, not grown. Their complete origin story was unknown, according to his former princess aunt, but they'd been put in this small cave a millennia ago by the Fae, to link the two realms.

Liam initiated the pattern, and magic swirled, bringing him in for a warm embrace. The main crystal called to him, the volume of the melody louder with each note dancing over his skin.

Warmth shot through him, darting up his fingers, into his arms and legs.

The first pop was born, indicating the portal's advent.

Then the familiar sound of tearing parchment.

The following *pop-pop-pop* was each louder than the last, and a magic-born gale swirled around him, making his plait dance around his shoulders.

Liam had braided his long hair in hopes of passing for a Fae Warrior if he was caught on the other side and his magic failed him. He had the height and breadth of his father, and all the MacLeod males, so he looked the part, and carried a muscular frame. His wings finished the picture of what could've been.

The flow of power worked up more heat inside him, and the moving air was like a caress, offering blissful coolness and calmness that evened his breathing.

White light shot straight up to the cave's ceiling from the center crystal of the Faery Stones, the last indication before the portal's birth.

An iridescent orb appeared, and the whole interior of the cavern shimmered and wavered, as the glowing bubble grew.

The opening hovered above the stark white sand littering the floor of the cave, and the light reflected off it, like the surface of a lake in the sun.

As it grew larger, the opening hovered and lowered at the same time, coming to rest only an inch or so from the floor of the cave. The portal was opaque, like a foggy looking glass, but it started to clear, like multicolored clouds sliding away, revealing the other side.

Liam couldn't make out much since it was so late. The day and night cycle were the same in the Human and Fae Realms alike.

The doorway would be large enough to step through in a few heartbeats.

The Fae Realm.

Over there, his magic flowed more easily, as if it was constantly at the tip of his fingertips at the barest wish, instead of the normal firmness he had to put behind each command, each spellword, to get magic to obey. Over there, his powers were always right beneath the surface of his skin, ready for his beck and call, pushing back, making their presence known.

Liam called his magic to him now, trying to wear it like a cape, as it played with the swirling energy of the Faery Stones.

He put his palm out and conjured a small bright red, tweeting bird, with a wild vivid yellow comb and deep blue eyes. The bird was Fae, like nothing in the Human Realm. It was called a *josta* and known for its loud nuisance calls.

The waiting portal glimmered, compelling, summoning.

He tossed the bird into the opaque opening, waited two breaths, then stepped through behind it.

The portal snapped shut behind him, with a *pop*.

Liam's conjured bird was nowhere in sight, although it was late and dark, so his visibility was limited.

It was quiet; maybe too quiet.

Where are the Fae Warriors?

The Faerie Stones on this side were not in a cave.

They'd been placed on a raised wooden platform, and the area consisted of a large open clearing in the middle of a thick forest full of maroon and blue-barked trees.

The Fae referred to the place as the Field of Light, because of the illumination the Stones themselves gave off, like their sisters in the Human Realm.

It wasn't daylight radiant, but Liam could make out the area around the dais, as well as the stairs to dismount it.

The night was much warmer than in his realm, and the blue and orange grass swayed in a breeze his powers told him was magic-born.

His da had explained that the weather was controlled by the king's mages, and kept mild, instead of being left to nature's chaotic desires.

He needed to get off the platform so his invisibility spell would hold, keeping him hidden and safe, like before. He was foolish to stand there and question his stroke of luck that the Faery Stones had been left unguarded.

Liam scanned the area as he cleared the dais, moving out of the circle of light the crystals gave off.

He flapped his wings, testing them, smiling when

the strong muscles above his back responded at his mental order, as if they hadn't just rejoined his body. He wrapped the large iridescent appendages around his torso. Needed to reassure himself that they were back, and not something he'd imagined.

Liam hadn't felt his wings reappear with any kind of noticeable surge of magic, but the power was there, all around him, thick in the air of this realm, for the taking.

He caressed the tip of one of his wings, and shivered at how normal it felt, just like any of the other skin of his body, despite being nearly transparent with colors dancing over the flesh, playing in the light the Stones emitted.

In the sunlight, Warrior wings were like living, moving prisms, all colors of the rainbow visible. He almost regretted the lateness of the day; he wanted to see the full spectrum.

His wings appeared fragile, but the sight was deceiving. Despite his lack of them in the Human Realm, they were strongly honed muscles that would carry him wherever he directed, as if he flew every day.

He wished he could.

Always.

Liam pumped them twice, staring up at their size; they were large and likely double his height. He lifted from the ground, hovering before two more great sweeps to take him higher, away from the Field of Light.

He grinned and resisted the urge to twirl in the air, his arms extended like a laddie. Or dive up and down, making loops. He needed to make some distance from the Stones and get to the safety of the forest.

The air was warm, and he soared forward on a thermal. He wanted to go higher, explore the sky, go farther into the realm than he had before.

Liam sensed the magic before he saw the blue ball of light coming at him, but when he dodged to the left, the magic followed his movements, as if he were a locked target.

Two more blue balls came at him from below and to the right.

He pumped his wings harder, trying to rise, but there was resistance around him, and he couldn't move.

All three of the blast spells smacked into his chest at the same time.

White-hot agony exploded all over Liam's body.

His limbs froze, refusing mental commands, and his wings crumpled.

He plummeted to the ground, and a new round of pain swallowed him whole when he slammed into the blue and orange foliage.

chapter two

Liam's body was made of pain. Shooting through every inch of his skin, claiming even his bones, matching the kicks and punches he was enduring. Consciousness smacked into him, as sure and severe as the agony contorting his form.

He groaned and rolled to his side, wrapping his wings tightly around his middle, but they too suffered abuse, and torment rocketed all over them.

Liam curled into a ball, as small as he could make his large form, but the Fae Warriors continued taking out their fury on him.

Fury he hadn't earned.

His father had been right, after all.

Liam's luck had run out.

"Halfblooded filth," one of the Warriors spat, punctuating his insult with a kick to Liam's chin.

His head flew back of its own accord, snapping with a jolt of fire down his spine.

He tried to call his magic, which only resulted in more torture, as if he'd been engulfed in real flames, burning its way down his limbs and into the tips of his wings.

Whatever magic the blast spells had contained made it impossible to muster even the smallest defense and turned his powers on him.

"Tryin' to pass for one of us!" This voice was

deeper than the first, and no less full of anger.

"I can smell human shite comin' off him!"

One of them kicked him in the chest, whooshing away the little air left in his lungs.

He couldn't even cry out.

Liam's head spun, and he fought against a wave of unconsciousness. If he passed out, they would surely kill him.

Although, that was probably already their plan.

"Gris! Hogarth!" a third male shouted from farther away.

Blessedly, the kicks stopped, but Liam still couldn't move.

The rustling of wings settling grabbed his attention, as well as the thudding of heavy boots landing.

A third Fae Warrior must've joined them.

His focus was going in and out, and his temples throbbed as he tried to concentrate on what was being said above him, about him.

Liam's instincts shouted for him to move, to flee, but even if he could get to his feet and make his wings work, his magic was down. He would be even more defenseless against their spells.

They would pluck him from the sky, again.

"What do you have here?" the newest arrival asked.

"A filthy halfblood!"

The swoosh of a sword clearing a scabbard shot ice down Liam's spine.

"Why haven't you reported it? Where's the rest of

your Wing?"

Feet shuffled too close for comfort.

"Rance—"

"You great fools. I can smell the ale on you. Captain Daegus will have you beaten—or worse. The mages will sense the Stones were opened, and what will you say? They're probably already gathering to storm the Field."

More boots shifted, and another kick to Liam's gut.

A new star of pain exploded. He tried to grab his knees, but his arms wouldn't obey his command, and his world spun, as if he'd been sucked into a cyclone instead of lying prone. He could no longer feel the ground beneath him.

"We caught him, didn't we?"

There was a bitter laugh. "None of that will keep you from the dungeons—or the gallows."

An argument ensued, but Liam couldn't concentrate on their words.

Darkness encroached, threatening to swallow him whole, but he fought to remain aware, and it receded, only to reassert its demands.

He lost the battle, and woke, half-aware because he was being stretched wide by his limbs.

Agony dominated his body.

It was still dark outside, giving him no clues as to how much time had passed.

"Grab that leg!"

"What does it matter if we drop him? He's dead, anyway."

Liam dangled high in the air between two Fae Warriors. His wings hung limply from his back, and when he tried to move them, pain answered the order, and they didn't even twitch.

"I think he's awake."

"He won't be for long."

Their thick Fae Scottish accents spoke of their low rank—and likely low birth. The Fae Realm followed a caste system guided by how much magic lived in any given bloodline. It extended even to the Warriors, so these two, and perhaps the third were likely low-ranking. Unlike his father and aunt, who were both highborn and sounded like it, royal and refined.

Liam drifted out again to the blessed peace where nothing hurt.

His body slammed into something, and his shoulders and wings shot a painful protest into his arms and legs, trapped beneath him. He couldn't move.

The earthy musk of wet rocks and moss tickled his nose, but the ground under him was loamy and gritty; rough. The sound of trickling water danced over his abused senses. He could smell it, too. The water couldn't be far.

"No one will find him here," one of the Fae Warriors said.

The other grunted—probably an agreement.

"Finish him."

"Nay, this is all your fault. You do it."

They bickered back and forth.

Liam swallowed, but his throat burned, and he

couldn't speak.

Nor could he move.

His head was wrenched back, in a large rough grip. "You have no business having this braid, you halfblooded filth. And how dare you carry this blade?"

A weapon flashed into view, surrounded by an eerie magic glow. It wasn't a huge claymore, only a long-handled dirk.

His father's dirk.

The Fae Warrior yanked his braid.

New pain shot into his scalp, as if a giant claw had grabbed his head.

The Fae soldier sawed through Liam's hair, then held up the long dark plait no longer attached. He spat in Liam's face, cursed in Fae, and tossed it away.

The word was close to Gaelic, so it didn't require translation.

"Let's get out of here. I hate this place," the other warrior said.

"Grànnda Falls is no place for us," the Warrior who'd cut his hair agreed.

"We can't leave until he's dead."

Liam shuddered and everything inside him screamed for him to fight, but he couldn't move.

Nothing responded to his desperation, muscle, and magic alike.

The Fae Warriors must have him under a spell that wouldn't allow him to shift even a finger.

He called to his magic again, but nothing happened.

Liam couldn't even feel it.

Worse than when he was at home in the Human Realm.

For the second time, a sword cleared a scabbard.

His vision went in and out as he struggled to focus.

He wanted his mother; he wanted his father.

Liam prayed he was not about to die.

The Fae Warrior slid his sword into Liam's gut.

Agony swallowed him; he couldn't even cry out.

Sienna shoved the oar into the reed-filled shallow water and guided the small skiff to the loamy grassy bank of the stream, going for a relatively clear spot. She didn't want to sink into the muck before she pulled herself to dry ground.

Her trek this morning had been successful. Her satchel was full of all the herbs her *mórai* had asked her to harvest to refill their stores.

They couldn't rely on magic if someone needed healing, so they had to make do with what nature offered. Good thing her grandmother was an expert in herbs and roots.

The bogle rushed to the edge of the small bank, making barking and growling noises, all his bright ever-changing furry hair standing on end, up to his tufted ears. Even his fur-covered tail was vertical, and his bright red coat displayed his anger.

She rolled her eyes and hefted the skiff up and out of the water, settling it on the brown grasses where it would be safe from getting swept away. She straightened and opened her arms as soon as her boots were on solid ground a little further from the stream. "I wasn't even gone that long, Triobloíd."

Sienna's little companion flew up and burrowed into her chest, his ball-like body softening, and his fur, which changed colors with his emotions, settled to a contented bluish-purple.

Trio made a trilling purring sound that had her smiling.

"You don't like water, so why would I bring you with me?"

He harrumphed and glared up, but he only had one over-large eye open, and like his hairy body, colors darted across his iris, not settling into any particular hue.

Since she'd found him as a tiny little fluffball a few years before, the bogle hadn't been far from her side. Sienna smirked and ran her hand over his rough fur, scratching behind one tufted ear until he was thrumming with pleasure.

Most Fae considered bogles a menace and would kill them on site, but the little creatures were typically harmless. They did have sharp teeth but were known for being defensive more than attacking unprovoked. They had minimal magic, and their fur was deceiving—it appeared as if it would be soft to the touch, but it was rough, like unkempt hair.

At Sienna's best guess, Trio had only been a few days old when she'd found him beneath an Acana tree at the edges of Grànnda Falls, where the foliage lost its bright oranges, blues, purples, and pinks, settling into greens and earth tones that made most Fae shudder.

Her little bogle had been all alone, no parent or littermate in sight, and he couldn't tell her what had happened. She'd raised and kept him—much to her family's chagrin.

Her *móraí*—her father's mother—and her siblings always said she brought too many strays home. Perhaps, but Trio was the only creature she'd kept. The rest of the birds and small woodland animals she'd healed had been released and left to their own devices. In truth, it was more like her bogle had kept her, instead of the reverse.

Trio jumped down from her grip, sniffing the green and brown grasses around her feet. He swished his long tail around and lifted his head. One of his ears twitched. His flat little nose followed suit, shifting as he seemed to catch the scent of something.

Sienna frowned and scanned the area ahead of them, opposite of the direction she should be going—back to the huge hollowed out tree her family called home, on the forested far side of the giant waterfall the whole area had been named after.

Unlike most Fae, they lived in the base of the gigantic tree, instead of up in its large branches. Her family didn't have the magic required to gain access to a lofty home.

Her family didn't have any magic at all.

Among the Fae, magic was valued more than anything else. As a result, her family had been cast out of what *Móraí* called, "polite society."

The whole area surrounding Grànnda Falls was void of all magic and avoided by most Fae. Its muted colors and lack of what her people valued most was of mysterious origin since it was so different from the rest of the realm. It was a place only occupied by outcasts and exiles.

Trioblóid made a chuffing sound and darted toward the grasses.

"Trio, come back here! Home's the other way!"

The bogle ignored her, locked onto whatever held his focus, shuffling along the pebbly grassy ground, as fast as his stubby little feet could carry him.

He rarely disobeyed, despite his name, which meant *troublemaker* in Fae. Perhaps her *móraí* had properly named him, after all.

Sienna didn't bother shouting after him again, he wouldn't respond.

His coat was a dark green of concentration, and his short snout practically scraped the ground.

A warm wind tickled her cheek, shifting her hair over her shoulder. Her long loose locks brushed the back of her neck, shooting a shiver down her spine.

She startled.

The metallic scent of blood made its way into her nose.

It had to be what her bogle had smelled first. Bogles ate meat and plants, so Trio would be tempted to take advantage of an easy scavenge.

But what's bleeding?

Sienna lifted her skirts—cursing herself for not donning trews that morning—and hurried after her wee creature.

Trio trilled an alert of danger and snarled, skidding to a halt a few feet ahead of her.

She gasped and swept him up into her arms.

He was bright red again, but there was a tinge of dark brown, and stark white at the tips of all the hair standing on end.

Her bogle was petrified.

"Trio, calm."

He shivered against her but made a mewling whimper of reluctant acquiescence.

She ran her hand over his rotund shape and gently put him down. Sienna approached the large, crumpled form on the banks of the stream.

A man.

He lay at the edge of the widest part of the waters on this side of Grànnda Falls before the brook wended into a river farther than she'd ever ventured from home.

The burn.

Beyond the vivid orange and blue grasses, the foliage merged into browns and greens. Like a straight line dividing the lands, a visible border between the Falls, and *his* world.

Her eyes landed on crumpled iridescent wings, half-protruding from under the man's large body.

Sienna swallowed and trepidation shot all over her, making her belly quiver. "A Fae Warrior?" she breathed.

No wonder Trio had called a warning.

The pool of blood caught her attention next. So

much blood the loamy ground wasn't absorbing it anymore.

Is he dead?

Her bogle made a sound of answer, as if she'd spoken aloud.

When their eyes met, Trio's irises were a bright yellow of caution and his fur matched, but other colors of mixed emotions danced over his coat, as if refusing to settle.

"I know how you feel," Sienna whispered.

Instead of fleeing the banks of the stream, she inched closer to the Fae Warrior.

Trio stayed so close his tufted fur brushed her calf.

The man lay with his shoulders touching the ground, and his lower half twisted hips up, one leg over the other, and his wings pinned beneath him. As if he was broken and boneless.

He had to be dead because the position couldn't be comfortable or painless.

His head was to the side, facing away from her, and his hair was dark, curly, and messy. He was also absent a thick Warrior plait—one of the most valued traits of a winged soldier.

Instead of the green armor that usually adorned Fae Warriors from head to toe, he wore an odd, saffron leine torn and covered in blood at his waist. Instead of trews, he wore a patterned fabric, which seemed belted on and left his legs bare. Almost as if it was a short skirt.

Sienna stared, unable to move, until Trio bumped her shin, and she jolted back into her skin.

Her bogle was no longer red or yellow, his coat had settled into a bright orange. It seemed her wee creature was as curious about the Fae Warrior as she.

But is he a Fae Warrior?

Sienna scanned his whole form.

He was huge, as were most winged Fae. His face was obscured by his sable curls, so she inched closer, within touching distance.

She'd never known of a winged Fae man who wasn't a Warrior for the king.

What had happened to him?

Had he been cast out of the soldier's ranks, and his braid cut off?

Maybe he was banished, like the others of her small, exiled community?

Or had he simply been left here to die?

"That's a lot of blood." The whisper fell from Sienna's lips.

He had to be dead.

She nudged him with her booted foot. When there was no response, she did it again, this time harder.

He groaned.

She jumped back.

Trio yelped.

Sienna had tromped his tail, but she ignored her bogle and moved back to the Warrior. "He's alive!" she breathed.

How could he be alive?

She hit her knees without hesitation and reached for his face, shoving his hair away so she could see him. Maybe wake him.

Her *mórai's* voice manifested in her head, calmly instructing her to assess the damage first.

Sienna mapped his form again, her gaze landing on his waist where most of the blood seemed to be. She grabbed his sides and tried to shift his body so she could have a clearer look but moving him was like hauling a boulder.

She applied more force, and the Warrior cried out.

Trio trilled his worry, but she didn't spare a glance for her bogle.

She grabbed the edges of the man's yellow leine. It was already torn and dirty, so she ripped it away from his body, and it parted down the middle, exposing his bare flesh.

Sienna gasped.

His chest and stomach were swollen, glaring red, black, and blue with bruising. That wasn't the most disturbing of his injuries.

A three or four-inch-long puncture wound dominated his left side.

A sword wound.

Bleeding steadily.

Someone had run him through.

How had he survived that?

Her grandmother's lessons demanded focus, but was it worth trying?

Could she even save the Warrior?

Sienna dug in the satchel hanging across her body and latched onto a clean cloth. She shook out the drying herbs it'd been wrapped around and let them fall to the bottom of her bag.

The first thing she needed to do if she hoped to save him was stop the bleeding.

She covered the ugly gash and leaned forward, putting her weight into her hands, applying pressure to the wound.

The man screamed.

Sienna looked up from her bloody hands, her gaze colliding with a pair of agony-filled, violet eyes.

chapter three

"What're ye doin' ta me?" The voice was deep, thick with pain, and the accent odd.

Sienna startled and lifted her fingers from his pallid flesh. "Trying to save your life, of course." She was covered in his blood up to her wrists.

"Thought I was already dead," he muttered. The man's big shoulders hit the ground again, and he closed his eyes.

"You will be, if I can't stop this bleeding." She couldn't look away from his face.

It, too, had been abused. His lip was split, and one of his cheeks was swollen and bruised, but it didn't detract from the appeal of his features. His jawline was strong, sculpted, his cheekbones high, and nose straight, fitting his countenance.

All Fae were beautiful, but he had a ruggedness Sienna was immediately drawn to. So fast she didn't know how to question it.

This Warrior was…different.

Violet eyes were common enough among her people, but because his hair was so rich and dark, they were more striking.

She wanted to beg him to open his eyes and caress his bruises away. She wished for the thousandth time her healing ability was magical.

Sienna could've fixed him in moments instead of having to rely on the remedies her *móraí* had taught her. Remedies that were much less of a guarantee.

Her fingers made quick work of the small bundle of herbs she smashed together, massaging the yarrow root to activate it. It would help staunch the blood, and the Acana leaf would ease his pain. The earthy scents washed over her, and she sent a prayer to the Goddess her plan would work.

He jerked away when she pressed the poultice into his wound.

"Stop moving," Sienna ordered, then bit her bottom lip when she read the agony on his handsome face.

"Stop makin' it worse," he retorted, throwing her a glare.

She was torn between amusement and irritation. She didn't know this man, and she *had* yelled at him first. Sienna couldn't command him about like her brother.

The idea made her frown.

She was *glad* he wasn't her brother.

Sienna had never wanted to run her thumb across Ealeric's bottom lip to see if it was soft, or kiss the hurt away.

She startled.

What, for the Goddess' sake, had just darted across her mind?

The Warrior was staring.

She could feel it, and she didn't dare look at him, or the heat already burning her cheeks would intensify and Sienna would be as bright pink as fresh Acana leaves ready for harvesting. She needed a distraction. "Can you sit up?" She pushed the words out, studying his poultice-covered wound instead of his face.

"I…dinnae."

"I need to wrap this around you to hold the poultice in place." Sienna ripped his leine into strips as she spoke.

Trioblóid, who'd been quietly watching them, chirruped.

It was a curious sound, and not one she'd heard him make before.

His hairy coat shifted colors in waves of yellow and orange, mixed with more calming tones of blues and purples.

The wounded Warrior stared at her bogle, mouth half-agape.

Trio moved closer.

The big man tried to scoot away on his elbows, but he cried out in pain and collapsed to the ground.

"Be still!" Sienna barked.

"Wh-what is *tha*?" He demanded; his pretty violet eyes wide.

Sienna frowned. "That's Trioblóid. He's my bogle."

"Bogle? Bogles dinnae be real."

She cocked her head to one side, letting the rolling way he spoke wash over the little space between them. Despite his odd accent and even odder reaction to Trio, she was still drawn to the broken Warrior.

"Bogles are as real as you and me. I need to make

sure your poultice stays put. Can you help me get this around you?" She held up the remnants of his shirt.

Liam tore his eyes from the strange brightly colorful creature and looked back at the lass. So many questions and demands battled behind his lips, but she'd said she was trying to save his life, and his gut ordered him to let her. To listen to her.

His cousin Angus' wife, Lila, was a healer from the far future, and it seemed this Fae lass was one as well.

Perhaps luck was with him, to be left for dead by Fae Warriors, only to be found by a healer.

She didn't seem to be bothered that he wasn't fully Fae...unless she couldn't tell.

How could that be?

Liam's father had said all Fae sensed human blood. The Warriors in the Field of Light certainly had.

That didn't seem to be the case with this lass, and she was literally covered in his blood.

His wings ached as much as the hole in his side, and he wanted to sit up as she'd suggested. However, his pain-filled failure to move away from the creature wasn't something he was eager to repeat. More hurt he didn't want to chance.

A bogle?

Childhood stories from his now-dead grandfa, Iain, danced across his mind. A plethora of mythical creatures, selkies, kelpies, banshees, changelings, and goblins that punished wee laddies' and lassies' mischievous deeds.

Were they all real, too?

Perhaps Liam's realm had been wrong?

Did they simply all reside in the Realm of the Fae?

His father and aunt had never spoken of such things.

The bogle was so ugly, it was kind of cute. Round, like a child's ball, but hairy with a long tail and tufted ears, like a wild cat. Its wee face was flat, but its nose, too, was feline-like. Its eyes were oversized, too big for its body. Four short feet stuck out as if they'd been attached to its rotund body, as an afterthought.

"Trioblóid," Liam breathed.

The lass paused and cocked her head. She still held the strips she'd made from his ruined leine.

She had long, red locks, but the hue was too bright to be the natural red tones he'd seen on human lasses.

The hair danced with her movements and somehow, he wanted to reach out and touch it. Run his fingers through it to gauge its softness.

"Aye, Trioblóid," she said, a question in her expression.

The creature trilled as its name was repeated. It shifted closer to them. The hairy fur coat was bright orange now.

"Troublemaker." Liam must really be dying, because he could swear the bogle had changed colors several times since he'd laid eyes on it.

How was that possible?

All he'd known of bogles from Grandfa's stories

was they were a nuisance, multiplying like rabbits and stealing food from stores.

"Aye," the healer whispered, the barest hint of a smile curving the corner of her mouth.

His savior was beautiful, with fair freckle-kissed skin across high cheekbones. Curiosity as to whether she had them anywhere else on her body darted into Liam's mind.

How could he venture such a thought when he was in so much pain?

He smirked.

She was staring, and her unusual, but gorgeous eyes bored into his. They were a reddish gold color that went perfectly with her hair, like burnished bronze.

No human could ever have such a hue, and he was drawn next to studying her shapely mouth, unable to tear his gaze away.

Her face was heart-shaped and gave her a youthful edge, but she appeared to be around his age. Although, appearance was not a true indicator of age for any Fae, because they lived much longer than humans. His father was nearly eighty, as was his aunt Alana, but neither looked over forty or fifty in human years.

Several heartbeats passed, and neither Liam nor the lass spoke, they only stayed like that, gazes locked.

She broke the spell by clearing her throat and waggling his ruined tunic. "We need to do this. Please try to sit up. You can't lose any more blood."

Agony rocketed through his whole form as he tried to obey the lass and pushed up on his elbows.

Even that minor elevation made his whole torso burn and ache.

Liam hurt…everywhere.

The vision in one of his eyes was blurry, he had to blink to clear it several times so he could focus on anything, or on what she was saying.

Her lips moved, and he could only watch, he didn't comprehend the words coming out.

Evidently, she was explaining what she was trying to accomplish, so Liam tried to allow her more access, pushing up with his arms, until his wrists were bent, and his palms sank into moist dirt and grass.

It took all the strength he could muster to remain in that position. His forearms and biceps shook, threatening to fail on him.

The healer went to work, sliding the thin fabric around him in seconds, and he was able to free one wing then the other with careful movements.

He extended each iridescent appendage, every muscle screaming a protest from being crushed beneath his body weight for what had to be a whole night. The sun was now high in the pink and gold sky, so he guessed it was mid-morning.

Liam grunted through it, gritting his teeth until they too ached. He'd cried out several times already, and now that he was back to full consciousness, he wouldn't do that again. He wasn't a wee lad with his first blemish.

The healer tied the strips of fabric around the poultice, firing a new arrow of pain across his abdomen and chest.

He cursed under his breath, and when their eyes met, his savior had one delicate burnt auburn eyebrow arched.

She wore another tempting smirk, and Liam was hyperaware of their physical closeness.

If he could manage to lean forward, he could taste her delectable mouth.

The healer averted her pretty bronze eyes, her cheeks tinged pink, as if she'd read his mind and caught the inappropriate thought.

Even that was tempting.

He cleared his throat. "Sorry. My mother has tol' me many times nay ta speak such around a lady."

She flashed a smile and shyly met his gaze again. "Then no harm done. I am far from a lady. Besides, I've a brother. That was not the first time I've heard such words."

Suddenly, Liam needed to touch her. He grabbed her hand, still covered in his blood. "What's yer name?"

She jolted but didn't break their physical contact.

He stared at where his much larger hand connected with her skin. No magic greeted the touch, and usually he could sense magic in someone with the barest brush of fingers on flesh. Even at home, touching his father's hand, or his aunt's arm would induce a magical response.

Here in the world of the Fae, his magic was more awake, more alive, even now in his injured state. Whatever spell the Fae Warriors had contained him with was gone.

Why could he not feel this lass's magic?

Her hair and eye color shouted she was Fae.

Maybe Liam was closer to death than suspected?

He should be panicked, but he wasn't. The pain had lessened, probably from whatever she'd pressed into his wound.

Surely the lass was a healer, but why had she not healed him with magic?

She'd prepared a poultice, like his cousin-by-marriage would have. His aunt had some healing magic, as did his father, and both had used it many times on family members in the human realm. However, they could not heal large injuries, like his current one.

As before, the Fae lass looked away first, and gently tugged her fingers from Liam's grip.

"I'm Sienna," she whispered, but still didn't look at him again.

Her name rolled around in his head, and it seemed to fit her, despite its meaning. In Fae, it referred to a deep brown color, and this healing lass' was much more red.

She finally met his gaze again, and her pretty face was expectant.

Liam got lost in her fiery eyes.

"What are you called?" she prompted, one of those delicately shaped eyebrows arched, like earlier.

A voice in his head screamed caution. "Liam," he said. Fae did not have surnames, so he didn't want to be too honest with her, since she didn't seem to know — or be concerned — that he was half human.

"What happened to you last eve, Liam?"

"Last eve?"

Sienna's burnished eyes traced his body again. Her gaze stayed low, below his waist, on his plaid.

How honest should he be?

How dangerous was it for him?

His father's warnings about the Fae and evil intents for halflings like him dominated his thoughts. "Would ye believe me if I said I dinnae?" he said finally.

She shook her head.

Liam smirked and shrugged, but the responding burn in his chest made him wince.

The Fae healer said nothing, but her expression demanded an answer.

God's Blood, as his Uncle Duncan would say. This lass was so beautiful it almost made him forget his current dangerous situation—or his pain.

"I was attacked by Fae Warriors." This was a truth he could tell.

"They cut your warrior braid, didn't they?" Sienna extended a hand, as if to touch his hair, but then dropped it, her cheeks pink again.

Liam liked the color on her pretty face, and how it made her freckles stand out. He wanted to assure her she could touch him anywhere she wanted to—unless she was pressing a poultice into his side. "Aye," he said instead.

"You're an outcast, then?" She dropped her eyes to the ground as the whisper fell from her lips.

He wanted to cup her face, make her look at him

and reassure her. The force of the desire was difficult to resist; his palms itched with the demand. He blew out a breath and ordered his hands to remain at his sides. "In a manner of speakin'," Liam managed unevenly.

Sienna's whole demeanor seemed to cave in, and sadness dominated her slender form. Her shoulders slumped, and she wouldn't look at him again.

The bogle trilled and lumbered into her lap, mewling, and burrowing into the healer's body. His furry coat was light pink, but he had moving tones of sky blue and lavender rolling through his hair like soft waves on a calm spring day on the beaches of Skye.

Liam couldn't tear his eyes off the wee creature. "How does he do tha'?"

Some of the melancholy lifted from her countenance when Sienna spoke. "The colors change with his emotions. Trio can do more colors than a rainbow."

"Then the wee thing…'tis…intelligent?"

She threw him a frown. "Of course, he is."

Trioblóid chirruped, as if he was voicing agreement.

Sienna smiled softly and stroked his ears.

Liam would've given his best sword to have her regard him with that smile or caress him like that.

The idea jarred.

He'd never been drawn to a lass as he was to this Fae healer.

He didn't know her, she didn't know him, but his instant…emotions…concerning her should be alarming, not a yearning he didn't want to expel, but only explore.

Liam needed a distraction, or his body—broken or not—would start reacting to the fantasies roaming his mind; where he was healed, and Sienna's cheeks were flushed with color and her lips swollen from being ravished.

He cleared his throat. "He makes more sounds than a josta bird."

She nodded and flashed the soft smile he craved. "He has a wide range, and they all have different meanings, as well. I can't believe you've never seen a bogle before. They're everywhere."

"Maybe where ye come from," he wanted to retort, but of course, he couldn't. Liam muttered something about bogles and nuisances instead, earning a glare from the Fae healer.

"Every creature has a purpose," Sienna snapped.

"Aye, yer right. Even wee creepies I s'pose."

She threw him a smirk that had him grinning, he couldn't help it.

"Well, I was able to stop your bleeding, but we need to get you up and home. My *mórai* can help much better than I."

"*Mórai?*" Liam asked.

The lass cocked her head to one side then nodded. "Aye, my grandmother." Her expression shouted that she thought his question was odd. She arched an eyebrow yet again.

The term must be a Fae one, and unlike most Fae and Gaelic, it wasn't close in translation. In human Scottish Gaelic terms, the word for grandmother was

Seanmhair.

Maybe it was a term of endearment?

It wasn't like he could ask. He had to act as if it wasn't the first time he'd ever heard the word. He was trying to pass for Fae, after all. Liam cleared his throat. "Home?"

"Aye, 'tis not far." She gestured to the right, to the west, against the flow of the stream nearby.

"*Toward* Grànnda Falls?" he asked.

Sienna went bright red, up to the tips of her ears and she suddenly wouldn't look at him again.

He'd heard of the place from his parents. They'd sought refuge in a cave behind the great falls before he was born.

Grànnda was Fae—and this time, the Gaelic word was close—for *ugly* and most Fae considered the area more than ugly; they believed it to be cursed.

Unlike the wild unnatural colors of foliage in most of the realm, Grànnda Falls and the lands around it were the same earthy tones of the human realm, so the area was considered unlucky in the least, and magic-damaging at the most. A place to be avoided, by Fae standards.

Some Fae lived there after all?

Not that Liam had ever been told.

Maybe staying there affected magic, and that was why Sienna didn't seem to have any.

Fear tingled the pit of his stomach.

Would his wings disappear, like when he was home?

"Sienna?"

"I am an outcast, like you."

chapter four

Sienna felt the cinch release around her heart, even for just a moment when Liam didn't question her any further regarding the status of her family or why they resided in Grànnda Falls.

He seemed to read her emotions and had immediately dropped the subject.

She couldn't manifest actual words to thank him, but she distracted them both by sharing her plans to get him on his feet and headed to her treed home.

Other exiles lived in the same clearing, in other trees as well as in the nearby forest, and closer to the giant waterfall the region was named for. They weren't exactly a village, but some of the people were kind, and some she and her family avoided.

All the exiles had been banished for societal reasons. Some were dangerous, and ruthless, criminals who'd escaped being put to death.

Luckily, most of the exiled Fae who lived near her family were of the good sort. They did things for each other; sharing meat from hunts and spending time together around bonfires. Her grandmother healed anyone who needed aid, and even delivered a baby on occasion.

Some, like Sienna's family, had been cast out due to no fault of their own. It was not a feat to displease King Fillan; the haughty ruler was easily offended and harsh with punishment. Exile was preferred to execution, even if it meant being thrown to squalor and leaving fine clothing and jewels behind, not to mention a nice home and easy access to markets.

Their community wasn't nearly as large as a true Fae village, but there was a good number of banished folk living off the land, like her family.

Although, most of their neighbors had magic.

"Do you think you can fly?" Sienna bustled around Liam's big figure, Trio on her heels. She'd washed away the blood from his body as well as her hands.

The injured Warrior was huge, even sitting.

"Nay, lass. Truth be told, I dinnae think I can get ta my feet."

"You must. I certainly can't lift you, and if I don't get you to my *móraí*, you could start bleeding again. You'll die if you lose more blood."

The apple of Liam's throat bobbed.

She'd scared him, but Sienna wasn't contrite. It was always best to be truthful. Not to mention, they were too close to the border.

What if the Fae Warriors who'd turned on him came back to see if he was dead and his body was gone?

A shiver of icy fright shot down her spine. Moving closer to the exiles' clearing was the safest plan. Unless ordered, no Fae Warrior would venture closer to Grànnda Falls.

At least, they never had before.

What if they came into her community looking for

Liam?

Sienna shook the ideas away.

Everything would be fine. *Mórai* would know what to do.

Getting him home was the best idea.

"I can help you arise." She offered him both palms.

The Warrior sat up; pain stamped all over his handsome face as he rested his forearms on bent knees. Liam sucked in an audible breath and flexed his wings.

The movement of the prism of warm sunlight dancing over his iridescent flesh captivated Sienna's attention for a few heartbeats. She wanted to touch him there, caress the skin to judge the feel beneath each fingertip.

She hadn't touched his wings, even when she'd slipped the strips of fabric around his waist. The desire to do so was a drive that warmed her palms and made her fingers tingle.

Liam's huge hands covered hers, and the heat of his touch made her jolt, but she didn't pull away. Maybe she couldn't.

Sienna watched in fascination as he pumped his wings once, then twice, slowly rising, inch by inch.

He wasn't pulling on her hands, just holding them in his, and she didn't want to break the contact.

His wings did all the work, but from the agony contorting his expression, he couldn't endure it much longer.

Soon, Liam was on his feet, but his wings were straight and straining, as if he couldn't remain upright without them in that position. He groaned and blew out a visibly tormented breath.

"Liam?" Sienna whispered.

"I'm braw," he pushed out through pale lips.

She wanted to smile. He was stubborn, and he'd need every ounce of that to heal. "Let me check the poultice. I want to make sure it didn't shift with your movements." Sienna darted forward, her hands at his waist.

Awareness washed over her at his closeness, and she could feel his body heat, but she tried to ignore it and let her fingers gently check his wound.

Liam's torso was bruised and abused, but his muscles were defined and beautiful—just like the rest of him. She didn't know him but being this close to him made her want to burrow deep and stay there. He was big and warm, and made her feel safe.

She was afraid that making contact with his pectoral or abdominal muscles would hurt him, so she made sure not to touch him. She tensed, scrunching her shoulders.

Standing upright, Liam was indeed huge, and made her feel tiny, even though she wasn't considered all that short, at about five feet eight inches tall.

This Warrior had likely close to a foot of height more than that, and an impressively matching breadth.

Sienna looked up, and her gaze collided with his very violet one. All available air evaporated, and her pulse thundered in her ears.

Neither of them spoke.

Liam wrapped his wings around her, drawing her

closer, sliding his arms around her waist, holding her gently, and never looking away.

Her mouth went dry. She couldn't help but let her gaze slide to his lips and wonder what he tasted like. Being wrapped in his wings, felt intimate somehow, and Sienna should be uncomfortable, but she wasn't.

His purple eyes were intense.

Was he thinking the same thing?

Would he dip down and kiss her?

Sienna's belly burned in anticipation, and she parted her lips.

"Thank ye," Liam whispered, his breath warm on her face.

"Wh-ha-hat?" Her cheeks seared as the stutter fell out.

"Fer savin' me. Had ye nay found me, I'd a' surely died."

Embarrassment rose up. She'd been fantasizing about his mouth taking hers when he'd only wanted to thank her. The heat in her face intensified. Sienna broke their eye contact and scrambled for words but failed.

Foolish lass. What were you thinking?

She busied herself by tightening the knot of the tied fabric around him. The poultice was still in place and there was no blood staining the yellow leine remnants. "'Tis my duty," she finally muttered, but still couldn't look at him.

Sienna couldn't stay that close to him anymore. She took a step back, forcing his wings to open and his arms to release her. "We should go."

Liam nodded, but even that seemed full of

discomfort.

She slipped her hand into her satchel until she located the correct bundle of leaves. "Here, this is Acana leaf. Chew it and it should help with the pain. When we get home, my *mórai* can brew you a tea that will be even better, but it will likely make you sleep, so this is the best for now."

Liam nodded, but still didn't speak.

His expression was unreadable, resolved about something, but what?

He accepted the pink leaf and popped it into his mouth.

Sienna felt awkwardness settle between them, and she didn't like it.

Why?

They didn't know each other.

She'd saved his life.

Of course, he'd be grateful, but he didn't owe her anything.

Sienna allowed a few moments for the Acana leaf to relieve some of Liam's pain, then she turned on her heel. "C'mon, home's this way."

The first few steps weren't terrible; his side only offered a remote ache, but the Acana leaf made Liam's head fuzzy, and it was hard to focus.

Sienna spoke as she led the way, but he didn't catch most of it.

The bogle hopped along between them, making

the occasional trill or chirrup, and his hairy coat remained a deep blue color. The wee thing seemed happy to be going home.

The brush-covered ground was mostly even, and when Liam felt unsteady on his feet, he used his wings for balance, but he couldn't lift himself into the air.

When he'd pumped his wings to take all his weight and get up by the stream, his side had screamed, and every muscle in his body had protested every second.

He'd distracted himself by holding Sienna's hands.

That, and staring into her beautiful eyes had helped him resist surrendering to the agony dominating his whole form.

Liam had been a fool to pull her to him like that, especially enclosing her to his chest with his wings. He'd burned to kiss her, even more so when that burnished bronze gaze had landed on his mouth, but then she'd pulled away.

What had he been thinking?

Overgrown sod. Lasses ye've just met dinnae want ye all over them.

"Liam?"

His eyes sought hers, but everything spun, and he scrambled for something to hold onto. He only found air.

Sienna dashed to him, grabbing his forearm, and sliding her arm around his waist.

She managed to keep him from toppling over, but agony kicked from the inside out, ruling his left side and blooming like a fresh bud, shooting upward, then down and across his torso.

Liam sucked in air and cursed in Gaelic and Fae.

"Sorry," she whispered, pulling his right arm firmly around her shoulders and squeezing his wrist. "Had I let you fall, you likely would've reopened the wound."

He swallowed and waited for the release of the pain, but it still had all his attention, no matter how many heartbeats passed.

Until he met Sienna's gaze again.

Somehow that made it easier to breathe.

"It's not that much further," she added, offering a small smile. "Can you make it a few more steps?"

Liam nodded. "As if I have a choice, aye?"

Sienna's smile widened. "Aye." She nodded curtly.

Unconsciousness teased the edges of his blurry vision, but he tried to focus on the feel of her warm body tucked into his right side, and how they moved slowly in step.

Blackness kept encroaching and receding, but each time it presented itself, it covered even more of his line of sight, and Liam couldn't hold out much longer.

They arrived at the edge of a clearing and Sienna said something he didn't catch.

A rough, unfamiliar hand seized his left forearm, then his biceps, and it was too big to be his little Fae healer's.

"Steady, now," someone said. The voice was deep, with a highborn Scottish Fae accent, like his father's.

Liam tried to lift his head, but it would not obey the command. His whole body had doubled in weight.

This time when the blackness came, he lost the battle, and it embraced him before he could fight it.

chapter five

"**B**ut *Móraí*, he's an outcast Fae Warrior. He was attacked, injured, and dumped by the stream, right at the edge of our territory. He almost died."

"*Mò ghràdh*, I cannot guess what that young man told you, but he is *not* a Fae Warrior." Her grandmother's voice was firm but held a desperate edge. In a rare show of temper for the elderly woman, she even shook a fist for emphasis.

Trepidation wrapped around Sienna's spine and settled in her chest, before it shot down to her belly, leaving a burn in its wake. She opened and closed her hands at her sides, because it was either that, or wring them in front of her, revealing her fears that she'd made a grave error in bringing Liam home.

Had she just put her family and their closest neighbors in danger?

Feneal, who'd helped her get Liam into the tree home, paced by the door, holding his fingertips to his lips and muttering under his breath.

The man was as big as Liam and had been a part of their community for as long as Sienna could remember. He was odd, even for an exile, and most believed he'd lost his mind years ago. Feneal usually slept outside, even though he had a small hollow to call home.

The man often painted rocks, talked to air—or other unseen creatures—and sometimes seemed lucid, and other times, like now, was more mad and locked within his own mind.

If anyone knew Feneal's story, no one had told Sienna.

She always tried to be kind to him, and *Mórai* often had her or one of her siblings offer him food, but most of the time Feneal avoided people and they avoided him.

Why he hadn't left their home already was a mystery, and despite his pacing and whispering to himself, Feneal seemed to pay close attention to Sienna's tense conversation with her grandmother, so some level of awareness was there.

His appearance was as rough as his life as an exiled Fae. Trews that might have been nice at one time were ragged and had disintegrated to mid-calf. He wore nothing on his feet, and the oversized leine was brown, caked in dirt. It might've been ivory or white when he'd been exiled.

The large man's dark hair was long and wild, as was his beard, tangled and unkempt. He had bright crystal blue eyes that popped out from his craggy face, and he may have been considered handsome at one time.

Sienna tracked his jerky pacing in the front of their home, and she wished he would leave, because an unpleasant smell wafted in the air, stronger with his every turn.

"His presence here is dangerous," her

grandmother said, her voice dripping with even more desperation than before.

Móraí's slight form and lined face drew her attention. Her long white hair was gathered atop her head as usual, and her soft green eyes emphatic, begging.

It was said the older woman's hair had been the same flame red as hers, but not in Sienna's lifetime. Her dress was the same green as her eyes and although it was loose on her petite frame, it didn't hide the tremors.

Móraí was scared.

Petrified.

What have I done?

Feneal froze in his tracks and compelled Sienna to meet his pale blue gaze. "Human."

Her vision wavered, the room danced, and she fell against the wooden table her family shared meals at, clutching at the edge, so she wouldn't slide to the packed dirt floor.

She managed to feel her way to a chair and sit before her knees buckled. "He…he…can't be human. He has wings. I didn't imagine them. I saw him use them."

Feneal and her grandmother exchanged a meaningful, long look that made Sienna frown.

Since when was the crazy man so lucid?

"He's a halfling, *mò ghràdh.* I assume he didn't share that with you?" This time, there was the usual gentleness to her grandmother's voice, and her expression softened.

Sienna shook her head.

"Smell it," Feneal murmured, and resumed his pacing.

"Smell it?" she breathed. She'd heard Fae could smell human blood. It would make sense that skill took magic…and she wielded none. Sienna studied her hands, remembering how they'd been covered in Liam's blood.

A Fae halfling?

Where had he come from?

Obviously, his mixed heritage was the real cause of the Fae Warriors attacking him.

"Dangerous," Feneal spat, turning on his heal, swiveling and marching like a soldier, following the same repeated path he'd been pacing since he'd started.

"I just didn't want him to die," Sienna half-wailed, her eyes burning with tears she refused to shed.

"Oh, *mò ghràdh,* your heart is too full of love." Her *mórai* crossed the small room and wrapped her thin arms around Sienna.

She wanted to bury her face against her grandmother's neck, like she had a million times before…take in the earthy mix of spicy scents the older woman's clothes always smelled of from the herbs she worked with.

She couldn't.

Sienna needed to…

What can I do?

"Magic," Feneal said. He extended one filthy

hand and closed his eyes. He chanted a spellword Sienna had never heard before, and a transparent purple ball appeared in his palm. He looked at her *móraí*, who gave a curt nod.

"Wh—?"

Before the whole word came out of her mouth, Feneal headed into the back of the tree home, to the small quarters Liam had been placed in to rest on a cot. The room her *móraí* treated patients in, and stored all her medicines in.

"What's he doing, *Móraí*?" Sienna demanded, pulling against the woman's hold, when her grandmother refused to release her.

She might be small and old, but she was strong. Sienna had to tug more than once before she got free and darted after the crazy man.

Sienna had barely made it to the narrow doorway when her heart stuttered.

Liam cried out, and his body arched off the cot, his head thrown back, and his legs and arms spread wide. His whole form was surrounded by the same purple glow, like an aura, that had been in Feneal's hand, and the crazy man stood just inside the workroom, chanting with his eyes closed.

"Stop!" Sienna threw her weight into him, wrenching his arms apart and whirling the big man toward her.

"Sienna, *mò ghràdh*, you stop, my lass." Her grandmother's order was quiet, yet firm.

Liam relaxed into the cot, seemingly still asleep, and his wings lay at his sides at rest, not contorted like before. He looked to be in a peaceful repose for the first time since she'd found him, free of pain.

Sienna rushed to his side. "You've killed him!" She threw the accusation at Feneal but didn't wait for an answer. "Liam? Liam!" She cupped his bruised face and shook him.

Her heart didn't slow from its frantic canter until he gave a low groan but didn't wake.

"Thank the Goddess!" She closed her eyes and rested her forehead against his, finally able to exhale. She stayed where she was, touching him for moments that felt like hours. She didn't want to let him go for some reason.

Her grandmother's gnarled hand slid onto her shoulder. "He sleeps, *mò ghràdh.*"

Sienna nodded and tore herself away from the halfling Warrior she'd rescued and whirled on Feneal. "What did you do to him?" she demanded.

"He is Fae." The big man gave a curt nod and retreated.

She shot a look at her grandmother. "What?"

"Feneal cast a spell that will hide the halfling's human blood. But it is not permanent, as such magic does not exist, *mò ghràdh.*"

Relief whooshed up and out of her mouth until Sienna was dizzy. "He can stay? You'll heal him?" Other questions regarding Feneal's apparent abilities and lucidity swirled around in her head, but those things would save for later.

Liam and his injuries had all her attention.

Her head spun and her legs wobbled. She perched

on the end of the cot, next to her halfling's large feet. Sienna hadn't put her family in mortal peril after all, and she could see Liam well again. Her *mórai* would help.

"I will help him, aye, *mò ghràdh*."

"How long can he stay? How long will the spell last?"

"That I do not know."

"I don't want him to die." Desperation clawed at her from the inside out.

Why did she care so much about the fate of the winged man?

Especially since he'd lied to her.

"He won't die. You made a fine poultice. We need to keep him from fevering, and as long as we can, he should be hale, soon."

Sienna nodded.

She wouldn't let the fear of a fever eat her alive.

Fevers killed when one didn't have access to a magical healer, even though her grandmother was renowned for her herbal knowledge.

Sienna shuddered.

A fever had taken her mother only two days after giving birth to her sister, Amalie.

She wouldn't let a fever take Liam.

He would be fine.

He had to be.

Besides, if he wasn't, she couldn't flay him for lying to her.

Her *mórai* studied her silently, but the elderly woman's green eyes were keen, and Sienna wanted to squirm.

She was hyperaware that her grandmother—not to mention Feneal—had seen her frantic display, and her tender touches to a man she didn't even know.

She'd rested her face so close to Liam's. Something a lover would do, not with a stranger.

Sienna shot to her feet instead of giving in to that stare—or blurting something foolish. She rubbed her palms on her apron. "Let's let him sleep. I'll get supper started." She rushed from the room, spilling back into the tidy kitchen and eating area, not waiting for her grandmother to remark.

There was a ruckus at the front door, and her brother and sister spilled inside, practically on top of each other.

"We heard Sienna brought home another stray," Ealeric announced, panting hard, as if he'd run the whole way home.

She shot a glare at her brother and sauntered over to the hearth to stoke the fire.

chapter six

Liam's temples throbbed. He heard voices, but they sounded distant. He was lying on something. It was comfortable, cushioning his weight, and he was covered in a soft white blanket. It wasn't as long as he was tall, and his feet hung off, but it was better than hard ground.

Was he on a cot?

He blinked to clear his vision, and when he glanced up all he could make out was a dark, rough-hewn ceiling. It was dim wherever he was, and a mix of earthy scents, including something familiar, tickled his nose.

Light filtered in from somewhere, but he didn't spot any source, like a fire, or a window.

Where am I?

The scents in the air reminded Liam of his healer cousin-by-marriage's surgery. Lila's large room where she stored all the dried herbs, plants and medicines took up the lower levels of Dunvegan, the castle he'd been born in, the stronghold of his human clan, the MacLeods. Lila was an exceptional healer with the injured and sick, and he could never forget those smells. This place smelled the same.

Had Sienna managed to get him home, after all?

She'd mentioned her grandmother was a healer, but then wasn't she a healer, too?

Liam didn't remember much, other than the desire to kiss her, a painful trek and a Fae man grabbing his forearm before he'd passed out.

His body still hurt, but he wanted to move, sit up and stretch his wings. His sword wound screamed a protest with the barest shift, so he stopped trying, forcing his tight muscles to release, and relaxed into the cot for a few heartbeats.

He sucked in a breath and squeezed his eyes shut, fortifying himself to try again.

There was a shuffling sound. When Liam opened his eyes, his gaze collided with a golden one.

She squeaked and slapped a hand in front of her mouth. She also reddened to the tips of her ears.

"Good day," Liam said, inclining his head and offering a smile.

Those marigold orbs widened further, and the lass fled the room without a word.

However, he very shortly heard a feminine shout, "He's awake!"

"At least I know she's not mute," he whispered, smirking.

She'd been fair-haired and very pretty, but the shape of her face and eyes reminded him very much of Sienna. She was also about the same height with a similar build.

His Fae healer had mentioned a brother when they'd been on the banks of the stream, but there was no doubt she also had a sister, because despite the difference in coloring, the young Fae female looked too much like her to not be kin.

"Liam?" Sienna entered the room, the younger girl, as well as the bogle on her heels. She wiped her hands on a white cloth.

Again, he tried to pitch his torso up, and managed more of an angle than the first time, but he had to suck back a groan.

"How do you feel?"

Her long flame locks weren't loose today, they were piled on the top of her head in a messy knot that was somehow endearing.

His savior also wore trews instead of skirts, and Liam's stare was immediately drawn to her shapely hips and slender waist. He wanted her to turn around to see if her bottom was as tempting as her supple curves.

He opened his mouth to answer, but no words came out.

Sienna frowned.

He cleared his throat and tried again. "I'm braw." Liam was pleased it didn't come out as a croak.

She smirked, and her mouth was also tempting.

He really needed to stop. Needed to get control of his draw to her. He'd had a few lovers, but he'd never been as intrigued with any of them as he was with this stranger of a Fae lass.

"How's your pain?"

"I'm braw," Liam repeated, as if he didn't know any other words.

Sienna closed the distance between them, her two followers still right in step with her.

Trioblóid hopped up and down, trilling a greeting

and his hairy coat was pastel colors, blues and purples.

Liam couldn't help but smile at the wee creature. "Hello, Trioblóid."

The bogle chirruped.

Sienna smiled, and her sister giggled.

His Fae healer sat on the edge of his cot, her hip touching his thigh. That minimal touch snagged all of Liam's attention, even through the soft fabric of the blanket between them.

She didn't seem to be bothered by their closeness, and he cursed their witnesses, because he very much wanted to touch her in other places.

He couldn't talk himself out of the desire.

Didn't really want to, either.

"I need to check your wound." Sienna didn't wait for his answer, and moved the blanket down past his waist and then her hands were on him.

Liam wore a proper clean ivory bandage wrapped around his torso, and he was curious as to how they'd managed to treat him. He had no memory of it.

"You've been out for two days," she supplied, as if she'd caught his thought. "But you don't have a fever, which is very good."

"Two days?" Alarm washed over him.

He'd been gone from the Human Realm for two days?

His family would be panicking.

No doubt his former Fae princess aunt would know he'd opened the Stones. So, they would worry he was in the far future—as had happened with his cousin Lexi, or in their eyes, even worse—where he currently was, in the Fae Realm.

It wouldn't take them long to figure out where he'd ended up. They had magic enough for it, and somehow his aunt just always *knew.*

Liam needed to get well enough to go home, before his father and all the MacLeods put themselves in danger to find him.

He really *was* a foolish lad, after all.

Plus, he'd lost the beloved dirk his father had gifted him.

"Aye. *Móraí* cleaned you up and redressed your wound. I have a salve for your bruises, and we can apply that since you're awake. We would've done so, but we needed to wait for the swelling to come down some. The salve will also help with the pain. *Móraí* said you have bruised ribs, too. If you're still in too much pain, we can brew some Acana root tea, as I'd mentioned before, but it will put you back to sleep."

He tried to breathe through his concerns about his family and concentrate on Sienna's voice. He suspected he couldn't make it back to the Field of Light in his condition, not to mention how he could manage to get past more Fae Warriors and open the Faery Stones on this side to get home. His pride smarted.

Liam cursed himself.

His father was right.

He'd been irresponsible and had thought of nothing but soaring in the pink and gold sky, not caring who he'd put at risk or the consequences.

He'd been too cocksure.

Now, Liam was gravely injured, without a plan,

and unsure of how long it would take him to return to his realm of birth.

His father would never give up or mark him off as dead. Nor would his mother allow that, even if the former Fae Warrior conceded. The rest of his family would fall in line and agree to save his sorry arse. MacLeods protected their own, no matter what. The clan motto, *Hold Fast,* was bred into them.

Liam's actions had just endangered his whole family. His uncles and cousins might be human, but they were fierce warriors in their own right. Years before, his Uncle Duncan had already stormed the Fae Realm once, to rescue his Uncle Alex, the laird of their clan. He doubted anything would hold him back from trying it again, despite the dangers of humans in the Fae Realm.

"I can help, sister."

He glanced up, glad for the distraction from his self-deprecation and worries, no matter how accurate they were.

Sienna threw a glance over her shoulder. "Thank you, but I can do it." She gestured for the lass to come closer and put her palm out. "Liam, this is my sister, Amalie."

Liam smirked when the lass went pink again, without a word.

He inclined his head. "Good day, Amalie."

She squeaked again, and the pink in her cheeks melded to deep crimson.

Sienna shook her head, but a smile played at her lips. "May I please have the salve?"

Amalie scrambled to comply, placing a small brown clay jar in her sister's hand.

"Many thanks. Can you allow Liam and I a moment to talk? I think *Mórai* needs your help, anyway."

The fair-haired lass nodded, and retreated from the small room, the bogle on her heels.

They were alone.

Liam's heartrate kicked up a notch.

Sienna blew out an audible breath and averted her gaze, turning the lid on the small round container until it came off. "Don't fash over my sister. She's never seen a winged Warrior before."

"Ye look alike." The words fell from his dry mouth.

When she finally met his gaze, her delicate red eyebrow was arched. "We do? Her coloring is not mine."

"Nay, but 'tis the shape a' yer faces."

Sienna's cheeks tinged a light pink, which made her freckles more prominent, and Liam burned to kiss her.

She wouldn't look at him again, and she busied her fingers at his waist, checking the bandage.

Sienna put the clay jar on her thigh, and Liam made himself look away when he started to imagine bare, freckled flesh ripe for his touch.

"This looks good. We'll change the poultice later. No bleeding, and the cut has finally sealed. *Mórai* said, if it was still open today, she would have to sew you up, but it looks like the poultice did its duty."

"Amalie is bonnie, aye, but yer e'en more so."

What was even coming out of Liam's mouth?

She spoke of his wounds and treatment, and yet he'd been sucked into some fog of desire he couldn't escape, no matter his current perilous situation.

Hadn't he just decided he'd acted like a bairn, which was what had gotten him in such danger in the first place?

Getting tangled with the Fae healer would only complicate things.

Despite it all, he couldn't shake what he wanted.

Liam wanted Sienna.

Her fingers froze at the edge of his bandage, and her gaze collided with his.

Liam stared, giving in to the urge to get lost in the moment and slipping into her fiery burnished eyes. He swallowed. Sensations shot down his limbs, settling below his waist, making his cock twitch with interest.

"Liam…"

He liked his name on her lips.

Her Fae accent sounded Scottish of course, but not the rolling brogue of an Isle of Skye Highlander. She was refined, like his father or his aunt.

Sienna sounded highborn.

If she was highborn, how had her family ended up being outcast, as she'd claimed?

Liam hadn't asked before, and he certainly wouldn't now, not when she was looking at him as if she would invite his kiss.

He leaned forward, ignoring the burn in his torso from the movement.

Sienna planted a palm at the center of his chest, but it didn't cause discomfort. The haziness of would-be passion fell from her pretty countenance, and she glared. "You lied to me."

Liam sobered; reared back. "Lied ta ye?"

"You're no Fae Warrior."

Guilt chased away some of the burn in his libido, and he looked down.

She was right, he'd let her make assumptions and gone with them, especially after it'd been obvious she didn't realize he was half human.

"You're a halfling," Sienna accused.

"Aye," he whispered.

There was no use in denying the truth. At least she hadn't spat, *filthy half-blood,* as the Fae Warriors had.

He wanted to smooth away the anger on her pretty face, wanted the previous moment back. Wanted to kiss her so badly he seared from it, inside out.

Liam certainly didn't want to tell her how childish he'd been or admit how his actions had caused his injuries and put everyone he loved in danger.

Not to mention her and her people.

His father had told him Fae avoided Grànnda Falls but what if non-exiled Fae—or Fae Warriors— came to look for him?

Sienna might not be able to sense his human blood, but what if others here could?

Had he made things even worse by coming home with her?

Desperate people did desperate things, and Fae

lived by a caste system. What if someone among the outcasts thought they could earn a change of status by turning him in?

"How did you get here? To this realm, I mean." Sienna's voice went softer, holding less of the ire than before, and grabbed his attention again. "You can't have been here your whole life, they would've killed you years ago."

He winced; couldn't look at her.

The reminder was like a new wound to his battered body.

"My father was a Fae Warrior," Liam said finally, instead of giving answer to her query.

"Was?"

He finally looked at Sienna and nodded. "My mother is human, an' they are fated mates."

Her gorgeous eyes went wide. "Fated mates? I thought that was a myth."

"Nay."

"I don't understand," she whispered.

"I just wanted ta fly," he mused on an exhale, then grimaced. Liam hadn't intended to divulge that bit of honesty—it skirted too close to revealing what a fool he'd been, how thoughtless and selfish.

She cocked her head to one side, curiosity and confusion stamped all over her pretty face.

"In the Human Realm, home, I dinnae have my wings. My clan is MacLeod, from the Isle of Skye. Since Fae dinnae have surnames, I am known by my mother's."

Understanding softened Sienna's expression, and

she seemed so damn sad, he wanted to tug her to him and hold her, comfort her.

"I fully understand wishing for something you cannot have."

Liam took her hand because he couldn't bear not touching her right that second.

She didn't pull away.

"Tell me," he whispered.

She lifted her head and met his gaze again. "My family has no magic, which is why I couldn't sense your halfling blood. Lack of magic is the reason we were cast out; exiled."

Fae without magic?

He'd never heard of such a thing, in all the stories from his family.

All Fae were born with some level of magic, but generally, the less magic, the lower the caste — or place in society.

But nay magic?

No place in society, evidently.

His magic was lessened at home, but at least Liam had access to it.

"Are there others here tha' can sense my blood?"

Sienna nodded. "Aye, not all exiled Fae are void of magic."

Panic rammed into his chest, spreading until it chased all the physical pain away, leaving icy fright sitting on his lungs, making it hard to breathe. He sat up fully and lifted his wings to assist him, despite the discomfort. "I must go. I've put ye all in danger, I dinnae wish yer people harm."

"Liam, stop," Sienna ordered.

He shook his head. "I must go, fer all yer sakes." Liam would either have to lay low until he healed and pray he wouldn't be discovered, or make a run for the Field of Light, and the Fae Realm's Faery Stones.

He'd probably get killed, but he couldn't risk Sienna's life. Or her family's.

She jolted forward, grabbing both his shoulders and throwing her body forward, trying to force him back down on the cot. "Liam, calm. All is well."

"'Tis no'." He shook his head, startling when his much shorter hair tickled the back of his neck. He'd almost forgotten the Fae Warriors had cut it.

Sienna's closeness, especially her breasts against his chest and the heat coming off her body commanded him to take a breath and heed her words.

Somehow, despite his bruises and the wound in his side, with her this close, Liam wasn't hurting.

At all.

She smelled good, too, like a mix of wildflowers and the spice of healing herbs, and he just wanted her closer.

In his arms.

"I dinnae bear seein' ye harmed, lass. I dinnae bear it."

Her tempting mouth curved in a small smile. "I appreciate that. But I promise you, we're not in danger from your presence. A…friend…cast a spell to hide your human half."

"What?" Liam shook his head again. "Nay such magic exists."

"It does. But my *móraí* says it's not permanent."

He gaped, and words scattered.

His father and aunt—who had a great deal of magic, even on the human side of things—had never mentioned such a spell.

Perhaps Aunt Alana had not known of it?

How?

She'd been the crown princess, and he'd always considered her magical knowledge unmatched.

All of Liam's life he'd only been told it was dangerous to even consider going through the Faery Stones.

His family had been so emphatic, it couldn't have been a mere tale to dissuade him and Lexi from trying.

"Dinnae be true. 'Tis no' possible," he breathed.

Sienna was still tucked into his body, and her expression shouted concern. "Liam? What's wrong?"

He gripped her shoulders. Shook gently. "Tell me a' this magic," he demanded.

She tilted her head back, her eyes wide, confused. "I...I don't know. It was a spell. Round ball, purple light."

"Purple light?"

She nodded. "Aye. He hit you with it, and it surrounded you like an aura. Then it appeared to absorb inside you. He said to all others, you were Fae. Fully Fae. Why does it matter?" Her countenance was guileless.

Guilt bloomed low and cold, dominating his gut. Liam swallowed. "If I ken tha spell, this dinnae e'er have happened."

Sienna's brow furrowed. "I'm sorry, Liam." She leaned forward, wrapping her arms around him and hugging him tight.

He would never have had it within him to refuse her, so he tugged her against his sore chest, but didn't give a damn about any physical protest. Her intriguing scent, sweet and spicy, tickled his nose and he breathed deeply of her, reveling in his Fae healer.

"I'm sorry you were attacked, but I'm not sorry we met. I can't be." Her voice was low, as if she didn't want to say the words aloud, but he'd heard her clearly.

He rejoiced in every part of the confession.

Liam pulled back, and their gazes collided yet again.

Sienna's eyes were misty and the movement in her throat told him she'd swallowed, which just made him want to kiss her there.

He wanted to kiss her everywhere.

Liam was about to get a good head start with her lips.

He closed the short distance, covering her mouth with his and ignoring the negative twinge from his split lip. He pressed his tongue against the seal of her lips, begging entrance.

She didn't disappoint.

Sienna let him in on a mewling moan that just revved his blood even more.

Not to mention how she clung to him, and her palms burned his bare shoulders, but not in a bad way. It was a preview of what her touch would feel like all over his body.

His cock was more than interested, throbbing as he hardened, and he wished she'd straddle him.

Liam slid his hand into her flame locks, disheveling the gathered knot, but he wanted her hair down, dancing over her shoulders. It was softer than freshly churned butter, and he adjusted the angle of her head so he could deepen their kiss.

Sienna was right with him, kissing him just as hard, just as desperately as he tasted her, and it left him sweltering for more.

Liam wanted to lay her on the cot and take her, even if it meant his wound reopened and he bled out.

At least he'd die happy.

Another whimper against his mouth had him painfully, achingly hard. His plaid and the blanket were double constrictions he needed gone.

If he didn't get inside her, he might perish from want instead of as a result of being run through.

"Sienna, *Móraí* wants to know—" Amalie stood just inside the door, Trioblóid beside her, and her marigold eyes were twice the size they'd been before, when Liam had greeted her.

His wee Fae healer fled from his arms and scrambled to her feet so fast his head spun—not to mention how the room did, too.

He wasn't embarrassed or regretful, but his would-be lover seemed to be.

Sienna's face and neck were the same unnatural red hue of her hair, and she wouldn't look at him.

Amalie was speaking—probably explaining what

their grandmother needed, but Liam didn't track.

The bogle was making noises and changing colors.

He didn't try to interpret.

His would-be lover responded to her sister, and the two females left his room together, without another word or even a backward glance from Sienna.

Liam told himself the ache in his chest was from his bruising, and nothing more.

chapter seven

What Sienna wouldn't give for a disappearing spell at this moment. Or an invisibility spell. Or even a sinkhole opening up under her feet to swallow her this instant would do.

Right. Now.

"Sisi?" Her sister's whisper of her childhood nickname was wrapped in obvious hesitation Amalie usually reserved for strangers.

"I do not wish to discuss it," she snapped, but regret immediately bloomed in her tummy and rose to blister her throat.

Her sister was young, naïve, and sweet by nature. She didn't deserve any ire.

Instead of anger or hurt, Amalie's pretty countenance displayed an impish smile. One she didn't even try to hide with a hand.

Sienna's remorse evaporated. She glared. "Not. A. Word."

Her sister's smile widened until the lass was beaming.

How could Sienna have let Liam kiss her?

Who're you trying to fool?

She'd *wanted* to kiss him.

Since the moment he'd wrapped her in his wings on the banks of the burn, and then many, many times after, as she'd watched him sleep and worried he wouldn't wake.

Móraí had reassured her that his body needed the repose to assist in the healing process, but after he hadn't come around the first day, Sienna had panicked that she'd been too late, and he was going to die.

She'd clung to his hand, staying up all night to monitor him.

Her grandmother had gently ordered her to bed the next morning, further asserting Liam was just sleeping. He wasn't burning with fever, and he would ultimately be fine.

His mouth on hers had been…overwhelming.

The way her body had reacted was foreign and intriguing. Sienna had burned for more.

She'd caressed his bare shoulders and clung to him, but she hadn't been brave enough to send her hands on the journey of exploration she'd craved. His body might be battered but he was so full of muscles she'd wanted to touch each one, and not for healing purposes.

When Liam's tongue had touched hers, pushed into her mouth, her heart had gone into a canter that had made the roof over her head spin.

She'd been warm all over, and her most private places had throbbed with want. It was new, this desire. She wasn't naïve enough to not recognize it, despite never having been with a man.

Sienna wanted to go back to him, kiss him again and see where it led.

Her first kiss had been one she'd cherish for the

rest of her life.

"How's the stray?" Ealeric asked, as she and Amalie entered the kitchen and dining area of their tree home. He sat at the table eating a bowl of stew she'd made for midday meal.

Sienna suddenly wished she'd slipped some *freumh* root into it. The plant wasn't poisonous, and was even used as a spice sometimes, but was also known to cause indigestion if consumed in large quantities. That seemed like just the thing for Ealeric.

She turned her glare to her younger brother. "Both of you can sod off."

Her brother arched a dark eyebrow, cocked his head to one side and put his wooden spoon down. "'Sod off?' Methinks you've been near the halfling for far too long. Hasn't he been sleeping for two days?"

Sienna ignored him, barely restraining herself from smacking him as she passed by, as she'd done so many times when they were children.

At seven and thirty, she'd come into adulthood years ago, but there was nothing like a younger brother to bring out one's inner child — or murderous musings.

Her bogle lay on the chair next to her irritating sibling, and oddly quiet. His furry coat was a mix of colors of a contented blue and an orange of curiosity, and she didn't want to meet his eyes — which were the same mix of hues and emotions.

"How is Liam's pain? Did you use the bruise salve?" *Mórai* asked, snagging her from her thoughts.

The back of her neck burned, spreading to her cheeks and up to her ears, hot and fast, as if someone had cast a spell on her. She felt warm all over.

"N-n-ay," Sienna squeaked, reminiscent of her sister.

Her grandmother's leaf-green eyes narrowed, and she could feel her brother staring. Hard.

Amalie's expression shouted she was inordinately pleased that she held a secret, and if the lass opened her mouth, Sienna would turn her ideas of fratricide to her other sibling. The one who rarely incurred her wrath.

She cleared her throat and straightened her shoulders. "I…" Sienna blinked and tried again when the words failed. "I checked his wound, and the poultice looks good. The cut has sealed, as well. He says he is not in a great deal of pain."

"That is relieving news." *Móraí's* expression was expectant. "The salve, *mò ghràdh?*"

"I thought I'd get him some food before I applied the salve."

Her sister snorted.

Her brother arched an eyebrow.

Her grandmother's eyes narrowed even more, to slits. Studying her until Sienna wanted to squirm and flee the room.

Again, she wished for magic to open the ground under her shifting feet and swallow her whole.

"Go on, then," *Móraí* said, gesturing to the large pot of stew still hanging over the banked fire in their biggest cooking hearth. Her voice was normal, but her expression was too knowing.

Sienna groaned internally.

She shuffled to the cupboard, grabbed a wooden bowl, a trencher, and felt three sets of eyes boring a hole in her back, tracking her every movement.

It seemed to take one hundred years to accomplish the task of getting some stew for Liam, and every member of her family watched silently, ratcheting up her heartrate, which left her temples throbbing from her rapid pulse.

She didn't want to go back to the small room where the halfling was, but she didn't want to stay with her meddlesome family, either.

Sienna felt like an errant wee one, in trouble for the first time.

She cleared her throat again, but it didn't help. She ignored the slight quake in her fingers as they lifted the trencher.

Still, no one spoke, and she avoided looking at them, as she found some relief from scrutiny, and headed down the hallway back to Liam.

It didn't escape her notice that Trioblóid, who normally went anywhere she did, didn't even try to follow.

Perhaps the winged Warrior's company was preferred after all.

Sienna couldn't banish their kiss from her mind. She wanted *more*.

However, at the same time, it petrified her, because she was already attached to the half Fae man who should really remain firmly in the "stranger" category. Not to mention, he was a patient who needed her healing skills—and her *mórai's*.

Liam couldn't remain in the Fae Realm. When—not *if*—Feneal's magic wore off, all the exiles with magic would sense his blood; they would all know he was there. In their house. Putting everyone in danger, as her grandmother had feared.

Getting closer to him would only result in hurt.

They could never be.

When he was well, he would have to return to his realm—and the family he'd mentioned.

Surely, they were worried about him, too?

Did they know what had become of him?

Perhaps they'd already feared him dead.

Sienna's heart stuttered at the thought, and she inhaled a fortifying breath when she glanced at the doorway of her *mórai's* medicine room.

She'd declared to her sister she didn't want to discuss the kiss she'd shared with the handsome halfling. Should that apply to Liam, too?

Sienna entered the room, carrying a small trencher that held something that smelled good, but his Fae lass seemed unsteady on her feet.

"Fer me?" Liam asked. His stomach rumbled when the pleasant scent tickled his nose. He tried to remember when he'd eaten last.

The demand in his gut shouted that it'd been far too long.

She nodded and placed the carved wood tray on his lap but didn't touch him.

There was stew and bread.

He grabbed Sienna's wrist before she could retreat too far. "Why dinnae ye look a' me?" he whispered.

She still wouldn't meet his eyes.

Liam wanted to tug her down, making her sit next to him on the cot, like she had before, but his stomach had focused on the trencher, and he was torn. His body demanded fuel.

His Fae healer sighed and didn't speak.

He released her reluctantly, but caressed the soft skin of her inner wrist, as she backed from his grip.

Sienna shivered visibly, and he liked her reaction to his touch.

She dragged the chair from the worktable in the corner and moved it closer to his cot.

She was an arm's length away, much too far.

Liam's body again commanded him to eat. He closed his eyes at the first bite of thick flavorful stew, and breathed it in, as well as savored the meat and vegetables on his tongue.

Whether it was because he hadn't eaten in so long, or that it really was the best thing he'd ever consumed, he couldn't guess, but he shoveled it into his mouth.

"Slow down, before you choke. No one will take it from you," Sienna admonished. Amusement danced over her pretty face.

His gaze landed there, and he recalled her taste, which was much more appealing than the nourishing stew. Liam ordered himself not to reminisce. "'Tis good," he mumbled through a mouthful.

She smiled, and his stomach jumped, not because he was finally filling it. "I'm glad to hear it. I made it this morning from our share of the kill."

He cocked his head to one side; with a silent question she had no trouble understanding.

"Some of the men hunt and they share with us, since *Mórai* is the healer around here. We're not really a village, but not everyone who lives nearby are criminals. Like us, some were wrongly accused or cast out for frivolous reasons. The king is unforgiving."

Liam looked back at his tasty meal.

Sienna had spat "the king" so it would do no good admitting he shared the Fae ruler's blood. His father had said many times that it wasn't something to be fond of or brag about.

He finished his meal and thanked his savior.

She retrieved the trencher and put it on the worktable.

He tracked her graceful movements, dragging his gaze along the subtle, supple curves of her body. Indeed, the trews hugged a shapely arse he wanted to spend some time exploring.

"I need to apply the salve to your chest and ribs," Sienna said, drawing his eyes back to her face. She went red again, as if she'd read his mind.

She'd said she didn't have any magic, so it wasn't possible.

Maybe he was being too obvious. His cousin Lexi had always teased that his expressions spoke before his mouth did. Liam cursed himself.

Sienna pitched her perfect bottom on the edge of

the cot, and he shifted over to allow her more of a seat. Because he was big and the cot wasn't, his movement caused her body to slide even closer, her hip pressing into his. Right where he wanted her.

She opened the little clay jar, just as before. "Lie back for me," she said.

Liam obeyed, pushing into the pillows at his back and tucking his hands behind his head so he wouldn't snatch her to him like he wanted to.

Sienna's hands were gentle as she spread the thick yellow ointment across his pectoral muscles.

He shivered when she brushed his left nipple. His blood was already starting to warm, his ideas far from a simple healing as she touched him.

With every soft, but sure stroke, his ability to think coherently was diminishing, sliding lower, heating his groin.

Making him throb from want.

"We need ta talk abou' earlier," Liam blurted to keep himself from doing something stupid.

She paused her ministrations and let out a little breath. "What if I do not wish to?"

"Talkin' or kissin'?" He smirked.

Sienna pursed her lips, as if she was trying to hide a smile, and her fingers glided lower, inching closer to his waist.

Liam's abdominal muscles quivered in anticipation of her fingertips going over them, but his ribs screamed a protest as she massaged a tender spot on his right side. He hissed out a startled breath, his aching desire scattering to less of an intensity.

"Sorry, this must be where you're bruised the worst, despite the discoloring and swelling being better than yesterday. But *Mórai* was certain there're no broken bones, so that's good."

He cursed under his breath.

"Do you want me to stop? I promise the salve will help. You'll feel much better tomorrow, if not later today."

Liam caressed her forearm. "I dinnae wish fer ye ta stop touchin' me, nay."

Sienna didn't speak, but she swallowed, and it made him yearn to kiss her throat, drag his tongue across her soft skin and taste her again.

Her spicy scent swirled in the air around them, mixing with the remnants of the delicious stew. Somehow the idea that she'd cooked for him, fed his body, made him want her even more.

"I enjoyed kissin' ye," he whispered. "I intend ta do it again."

Her enticing freckles were stark against her crimson cheeks, and Sienna averted her gaze yet again. "My first kiss," she breathed. The small confession caused her face to brighten even more.

Liam's heart skipped and it was his turn to swallow. "Yer *first* kiss?"

She threw him a frown, her auburn brows drawn tight. "How could it not be? I was raised among only family, wary of other exiles and society's undesirables."

He could feel the embarrassment coming off her. He was no empath, like his aunt, nor could he read minds like his father, but he *felt* what Sienna was feeling.

Remorse hit, chasing away some of the pleasantness of having a full belly. "I dinnae mean ye any harm. My surprise is because ye dinnae seem…inexperienced."

Her burnished bronze eyes went wide, and Sienna still wore a deep blush, but at least she was looking at him. "Liam," she whispered.

Damn, what it did to his body when she said his name like that. Like he was the secret to all her fantasies she'd never dared share aloud.

Liam wanted to snatch her up, kiss her, and get inside her.

Caution screamed from somewhere in the back of his mind. He wanted to ignore it. If their kiss had been her first, then his wee Fae healer was innocent.

She hadn't claimed that, and he certainly wouldn't remark on it, but it couldn't be any other way. As she'd said, she'd only been raised around family.

He needed to avoid overwhelming her with his desire, but the idea of being the first man inside her didn't escape his psyche either.

It made his cock sear with want.

Liam grabbed her wrists because her hands were still covered in salve. "Thank ye."

Sienna yanked away and frowned harder. "Don't do that!"

He reared back into his pillows. "Do what?"

"Look at me like you're going to kiss me, then

give me mere thanks. I don't want you to kiss me because you're grateful. You did the same at the stream, too."

He smirked and reached for her.

Sienna shook her head and tried to move away, but Liam wasn't having it.

He slid his hands around her waist, urging her closer, until their torsos brushed, and their mouths were millimeters apart.

She whimpered and it made his cock twitch.

"Aye, I'm grateful fer ye savin' my life, an' 'tis true, I burned ta kiss ye on the banks where ye found me, but I dinnae kiss ye 'cause of tha'."

"Why didn't you kiss me on the burn?" she whispered.

"I dinnae think ye'd welcome it."

"I would have," Sienna admitted, and he wanted to map every bright freckle with his tongue.

Liam leaned forward, freeing his wings, extended them and wrapped them around his Fae lass.

He tucked her into his chest, ignoring the protest of his sore ribs and his sword wound. They hurt less than before, so the salve must already be working.

"Liam," she breathed, and her warm breath tickled his cheek.

"I'm goin' ta kiss ye now."

Without another word, Sienna slipped her arms around his neck and her mouth met his.

chapter eight

Sienna encouraged him like a bairn, which would've aggravated Liam coming from anyone else. However, he didn't want to admit he was still in a great deal of pain, and even though he was on his feet and his wings could lift him into the air, he was far from healed.

He'd managed a short hover a few feet off the ground, but the required muscle movements pulled on his sword wound, so full flight was probably a day or more away.

His ribs and chest were much better, thanks to the salve she'd applied every morning. Liam didn't mind that in the least, of course, because it meant her hands were on his bare skin for an extended time.

He'd also borrowed a leine from Ealeric, but Sienna had altered it in the shoulders and chest. Her brother was tall and muscular in his own right, but not close to Liam's height and breadth.

It was day five, and he tried to distract his worries of his family's possible advent by kissing his wee Fae healer whenever she permitted it.

Sienna allowed him to take her mouth a great deal, which was equally pleasing and frustrating, because he wanted to do so much more than kiss, and she was innocent, and they'd known each other less than a week.

Logic shouted no, and his drive to take her vehemently disagreed.

Not that she could be aware, but Sienna left him with aching bollocks, and the one time he'd taken himself into his hand hadn't given him any satisfaction.

Liam hadn't allowed himself to consider how frantic his parents probably were. His hot-tempered Uncle Duncan probably intended on storming the realm, or his more even-tempered uncle—the laird of the clan—likely had everyone organized for a thorough search party.

Would they know he'd made it to the Fae Realm and that Liam wasn't lost in the far future?

His father would want to protect him and flay him open in the same moment, too. He didn't want to imagine his mother's inevitable tears.

He winced.

"Liam, are you well? We can go back now if you want to."

"Nay, I need ta bathe."

Sienna's cheeks lit up, crimson to her ears.

Liam flashed a lopsided grin. "Ye can join me, ye ken."

She went even redder.

"Propositioning my sister, are you, stray?" Ealeric popped into view as if from nowhere and flashed an impish grin that made Sienna's freckled skin brighten even more, matching her hair.

Where did he come from?

He had no magic, so it wasn't like he could've

blinked — or teleported — as his Aunt Claire called it. Liam hadn't been born with such a talent, but his cousins, Angus and Lexi could. It didn't come easy to Angus, but it did to Lexi. She used to pop them all over Skye when they were wee.

At least the Fae man had been teasing and didn't sound angry, but Liam was less than fond of the moniker.

He growled low in his throat, wishing his claymore wasn't safely tucked into his trunk in his rooms at Dunvegan. He was also still mourning the loss of the dirk his father had gifted him.

However, it wasn't like he could kill the lad, anyway.

Although, Ealeric wasn't a lad, not really. He appeared to be about eight and ten, but he was older than Liam by seven summers.

He hadn't been shocked to learn that, or that he was Sienna's junior by twelve summers. Fae could live over two hundred years, so they held their age well.

"Go home, Ealeric," Sienna ordered, her hands perched on her shapely hips. The basket she'd been carrying with linens, soaps and bathing necessities rested at her feet. "You were *not* invited."

Trioblóid, who wasn't far from her, watched the interchange with moving colors of emotion. The bogle had picked up on Sienna's irritation, because he was tinged red, but he must've also understood her brother's amusement, because he swirled with greens and oranges, too.

Her younger brother flashed another grin, his

dark hair falling into his eyes. Like his sisters, Ealeric's hair and eyes seemed to match. Both were ebony. "Just protecting my sister's honor."

"I am in danger of no harm from Liam," she snapped. "Especially my honor." Sienna rolled her eyes.

Danger, nay.

However, Ealeric wasn't wrong.

Liam burned for her. Hardly considered her *honor*.

It wasn't unusual for Fae to have a few lovers before they married, so it wasn't as frowned upon, as it was in the Human Realm. Being innocent wasn't a requirement for being wed.

Imagining her with another man—Fae or not—made Liam want to stab something.

"I thought I would escort you to the Falls, so you get there with no trouble."

The lad was baiting him, but Liam couldn't help how he bristled. "I am hale enough ta protect yer sister," he barked. He towered over Ealeric, who just stood there grinning.

Her brother was taller than she was, but Liam still had a head on him, if not two.

Sienna sighed and slid between them, as if she worried he really would clobber her brother. "There's nothing to protect me from."

"Just see that you do, stray," Ealeric said. His tone was even, but his dark eyes flashed.

Her brother's concern was real, but he clearly covered it with humor.

Somehow, Liam's respect for the Fae man slid up a notch.

"Always," he said. He held out his hand for a shake.

Her brother cocked his head to one side, but accepted, gripping Liam's fingers with acceptable pressure to state he wasn't weak. Ealeric nodded curtly.

Liam had made a vow, but the look on Sienna's face—one of irritation—said she hadn't recognized it. Perhaps her brother had.

Soon, Ealeric retreated, without another word.

Trioblóid chirruped, but neither of them acknowledged him.

"What was that about?" Sienna demanded, but she retrieved her basket, slipping it onto her forearm and holding it in front of her body.

She wore skirts today, and Liam grieved how her perfect arse was hidden.

"He's just concerned abou' ye."

She laughed. "*My* brother? Concerned about me? Nay."

Liam smiled. "Aye, 'tis true. He dinnae ken how ta show ye, but he cares fer ye."

"Besides, what's to be worried about? I go out on my own almost daily. Even to bathe at the Falls. If *Mórai* needs me to find herbs, sometimes I'm gone for hours, if not all day."

He closed the distance between them and cupped her face. "But ne'er with a halfling."

"Feneal's magic—"

"'Tis temporary."

Sienna gnawed her full bottom lip and Liam wanted to kiss her, but he restrained himself—barely.

"How far are the Falls?" he asked, to distract himself.

"Not far." She smiled again, and it made his gut quiver. "There are some hot springs, too, so if you find the right spot, the water's warm."

Her speech had been innocent, but Liam had to swallow, because his head went all sorts of forbidden places. Sienna naked in all the visions, her red locks darker when wet and all her curves shiny with water droplets.

He had a fantastic imagination. Still wanted to know where else she had freckles, too.

"My da told me there's a natural warm water pool inside a cave behind the Falls," he said, pushing the words out and hoping they sounded even.

"There is?"

"Aye, he flew my mother in there years ago, before I was born."

Sienna's eyes studied his face, and her expression was open and curious.

She was so gorgeous it took his breath.

As they walked, Liam launched into the story he'd been told all his life, starting with the magic mate-finding ring his father had slipped on his mother's finger and her getting sucked into the Fae Realm. Xander had had to come find Janet, and they hid out in the cave behind Grànnda Falls because it was the only safe place they wouldn't be pursued by Fae Warriors, before they'd finally made their way back to the Human Realm, married and had him.

"All my life, I've been told fated mates aren't real," Sienna mused.

"I s'pose because they're so rare."

"It's like old lore."

Liam smiled again. "Aye, but 'tis true. I'm livin' proof."

"Do they… still love each other?"

Her whisper was so low he'd almost missed it because they were close to the Falls now, the roar of the waters was no longer distant.

Her cheeks were pink again, and Sienna wouldn't look at him.

Liam's heart stuttered. He stopped walking and stroked her arm, then caressed her cheek, until she finally turned her burnished bronze gaze on him.

Trioblóid made a noise, but it sounded far away, and Liam slid into his Fae healer's beautiful eyes.

"Aye, verra much. As if they were made fer each other, an' I've heard them both say so. My aunt says 'tis fate." He didn't say Alana's name, nor mention she was Fae.

Exiled or not, Sienna might recognize the former princess' name and do some figuring he didn't need. Xander and Alana were infamous in the Fae Realm.

Liam wasn't worried she'd turn him in, but he was concerned about how she'd respond to his undesirable blood ties.

Sienna swallowed but didn't speak right away. "I don't remember if my parents loved each other, but

Móraí says they did very much. I was so young when they…died."

Liam drew him to her, and she didn't protest. He wrapped her in his arms and wings, and it felt so natural, as if he'd done so hundreds of times, instead of just a few.

Why did he feel as if he'd known her for years?

His wee healer let him hold her for a few moments, before pulling back, and wrinkling her pert freckle-covered nose. "You know what?"

"What?"

"You really *do* need to bathe." She flashed a wicked grin, then slid from his grip and trotted a few feet from him.

Liam blinked, then chuckled, he couldn't help it. Even her insults were adorable.

"C'mon, I'll show you the best spot!"

Trioblóid trilled, as if agreeing. His coat, blues and purples of contentment, as he hopped after his mistress.

Sienna sucked her bottom lip into her mouth and chewed. She'd brought Liam to the warmest waters on the far side of the Falls where there were a series of smaller falls. She would often stand in them and let water cascade down over her to wash her hair and body with ease.

She usually bathed with Amalie, but she was grateful her sister had not come today.

Liam hadn't hesitated to undress as soon as they'd arrived, despite the openness of the area. There was no privacy or anything to shield the view.

That was good and bad—at least at the moment.

Sienna had turned around to give him modesty, of course, but Fae were not usually shy about nudity. He was a halfling, and she'd heard humans were shyer, but *her* halfling had dared her to watch, and repeated his earlier offer for her to join him.

She'd burned to peek, to see his whole powerful bare form, map every defined line with her eyes.

You're lying again.

She didn't just want to look, she wanted to touch, too. Wanted to take him up on his offer to bathe with him.

Sienna was familiar with how the muscles of his chest felt beneath her fingertips, and she liked the warm smooth planes of his torso.

Fae didn't have body hair, and Liam's chest was hairless. It made her want to know if the rest of his body was like hers—especially between his legs.

She'd felt his arousal against her tummy almost every time he held her close while they kissed.

His body wanted more than their mouths to touch, and so did hers.

So did *she*.

Sienna swallowed. Twice.

Her heart pattered against her ribcage, and her belly warmed with desire. Her thighs quivered until she squeezed them tight.

She wanted him.

Liam had been kissing her, holding her any time they shared a moment alone, but he'd been so polite and restrained, and when they parted, she was always left wanting, throbbing, yearning for more.

Sounds of him splashing in the water so close behind her made her moan and bite her lip even harder. She was likely to make herself bleed at this rate.

Sienna made her eyes scan the area in front of her, studying the greens and browns of the topography, so different than anywhere else in her realm.

The trees had dark, plain-looking bark, and the leaves were hued several shades of green. There were plenty of trees, large and small, dotting the area before her, surrounding the largest of the waterfalls and the pools around it.

Nowhere in sight were the maroon and pink Acana trees, or the Subh trees with their blue bark, bright yellow leaves, and the sweet round fruit they offered.

When they needed Acana root and leaves for healing potions, Sienna always had to go to the edges of the green and brown forests of Grànnda Falls, and she had to be careful because technically exiles weren't permitted.

She'd never been confronted by a patrolling Fae Warrior, and she was grateful they wouldn't enter the region where the outcasts lived.

Most Fae considered the Falls cursed, and no one seemed to know why the foliage resembled that of the Human Realm, or so she'd been told.

Thank the Goddess it did, or her people—the

exiles—would not have had a refuge to live.

Triobloíd snorted, his wee nose close to the ground at the base of a big tree, ten feet from Sienna. He was hunting for moss, small mammals, and a certain fungi he enjoyed.

Her bogle would entertain himself for hours because the mushrooms he loved only grew on this side of the Falls and were often hidden in the underbrush. He wouldn't be tempted by the warm waters, as he was afraid to be submersed. Bogles had short little legs and couldn't swim.

"Sienna," Liam called.

Shivers chased each other down her spine, but not because she was cold. Thanks to the king's mages, the day was warm, the sun high in the pink and gold sky—like most days, unless they needed rain for crops.

She ordered herself to remain where she was, facing the forest instead of the waters, where she really wanted to be. She fought for calm and inhaled before she tried to speak. "Aye?" Sienna projected her voice, without moving an inch.

"Ye were right," he called back.

She heard the smile in his voice and her body ached to face him.

"About?" she called, trying to sound nonchalant, but the shake in the word revealed she'd missed the mark.

"The water's warm."

Liam's voice was above the shell of her ear, not by the falls or the pools beneath them, where he'd been the last time she'd laid eyes on him.

A new round of tremors traversed her spine, heating her limbs even more. Her belly warmed slowly, like it was trying to boil.

Sienna gulped.

A large hand—dripping water—landed on her apron-covered tummy, wetting her. She hadn't heard him leave the water or his approach.

Liam had been making noises in the smallest of the falls just moments before, hadn't he?

How had he been so quiet?

Don't be a fool, he is a Warrior.

It made sense that he was capable of stealthy, silent movements.

Words fled Sienna's brain.

She jumped when his wings enclosed her. "Liam," she breathed. "You got me wet." This was supposed to be full of irritation, but instead, it sounded as breathless as when she'd uttered his name.

"No' tha way I want ta make ye wet." Liam kissed the back of her neck.

Sienna whimpered and didn't fight when he turned her around, gently into him, and pulled her closer to his massive damp chest. "Liam," she tried to protest. "I have all my clothes on."

"Aye, an' my mission is ta get them off ye."

"I...I..." For the second time, words and coherent thought fled, because he was burning a trail of kisses down the side of her neck.

Liam nibbled her earlobe, and she almost crawled out of her skin.

"Liam," Sienna moaned his name this time.

Quick fingers untied her apron, and it fell to the loamy ground at their feet.

Her gaze begged to follow the fallen fabric, because her halfling warrior was naked for the visual taking.

She wasn't embarrassed, but she was unexpectedly shy, so she didn't let her eyes drink their fill. After all, she'd never been this close to a naked man, unless he'd been a patient, and she hadn't really been tempted to study a male's sex when the man was only in need of healing.

"Touch me, lass," Liam begged.

Sienna's hands had been awkwardly hanging at her sides because she'd been lost in the sensations of his hot mouth dragging kisses across the sensitive skin of her neck. "Wh-wh-where?"

"Anywhere. Everawhere."

She glanced up, colliding with his gorgeous violet eyes. The deep purple seemed to be glowing or shining just for her.

Was it because he was aroused?

Sienna had never seen a sight so beautiful. Her heart stuttered before it stumbled to a rapid *tat-tat*, reverberating in her temples. "Liam," she whispered again, as if his name was the extent of her vocabulary.

He dipped down and took her mouth.

She opened for him before he could beg entrance, and she slid her arms around his neck so she could get even closer.

Her breasts pressed into his muscled chest, and Sienna pushed to her tiptoes to be completely flush to him, kiss him deeper.

Liam groaned into her lips, and the resulting vibration shot pulses of heat down her torso, pooling between her legs.

She throbbed there, an aching demand to be filled.

He twined his tongue around hers, enticing her to follow, dance, play, move against it with hers.

Unfortunately, he wrenched away far too soon.

"Do ye want me, lass?" Liam panted, his powerful chest heaving into hers, flattening her breasts even more.

The pressure made her want to go further. Her nipples tingled. "I don't *not* want you," fell out of Sienna's mouth.

What had she just said?

Her face burned for reasons other than desire.

chapter nine

Liam reared back, blinking. "Meanin'?"

His Fae healer hadn't left his embrace, or even pulled away, and her cheeks were adorably crimson, freckles standing out like stars in a night sky. Her mouth was swollen from his kisses and her red locks were mussed, half up and half down, loose strands playing over one shoulder.

Sienna looked deliciously ravished, and they hadn't even started.

However, with what she'd just said, perhaps he wouldn't get the chance.

She drew her brows tight and opened her mouth, but no words were born.

Alarm wrapped around his mind, and he told himself to release her, but Liam couldn't relax his arms or pull his wings away.

Sienna's body told him she wanted him, even if his lass couldn't say it aloud. It'd been telling him from the first time he'd kissed her in her grandmother's medicine room.

He couldn't be wrong.

Could he?

Something that felt suspiciously like hurt washed over him.

"Oh, Liam, I'm so sorry."

He cursed silently.

Sienna reached for his face, cupping his cheeks. She pushed to her toes, kissed him quick and hard, and when they parted, her burnished gaze was locked onto his. "I do want you, but…"

"Yer innocent?" Liam whispered.

She nodded and couldn't seem to look at him.

"I'd ne'er push ye, lass. I'd ne'er hurt ye."

Sienna swallowed and it made him want to kiss her throat again. "I know. Everything you've shown me of yourself tells me so. I trust you."

She trusted him?

His heart thumped and he smiled gently. "I'm glad. I trust ye, too."

When he'd explored the tender flesh of her neck and nibbled her earlobe, he'd almost come right then and there, as if he was the untried virgin. She tasted as sweet and spicy as she smelled, and he burned for her so badly.

It was disturbing, how drawn he felt to a lass he'd met less than a week ago. Liam had never experienced anything close to the like in the Human Realm with any of his human lovers.

He hadn't really wanted to fight the pull from the start—he was a man, after all—but it almost felt unnatural.

Magical, even though Sienna had none.

"The way you make my body feel…I never imagined it could be like that, and we've barely done more than kiss."

"Let me show ye more," Liam said.

Was this begging?

He wasn't begging a lass, was he?

She smiled but wouldn't look up at him. "I'd like that," Sienna whispered, the short phrase swirled in shyness.

Liam hadn't expected that from a Fae lass. He'd heard so many times they were brash, not bashful about what they wanted—including intimacies—and strong.

His Fae healer was strong, aye, but she had been raised away from society, as she'd pointed out. When she'd turned away from his undressing, it had been amusing and frustrating.

He'd wanted her to look at his body with the hunger she always hinted at when she applied salve to his bruises.

Sienna's touches were not all innocent anymore.

"Bathe with me?" he asked.

Her nod was almost imperceptible, but she reached for the ties on her leine.

Liam opened his wings and stepped back to allow her some room.

His palms already itched with a demand to assist her, but something told him Sienna needed to bare herself to him on her own.

She reached behind her and tugged on the back of her skirts. They soon pooled at her feet. She slipped from her leine next.

He had to gulp for air.

Sienna wore a simple diaphanous chemise that stopped at her knees, and hinted at the breasts, hips, thighs, and everything else he needed to see naked.

The undergarment's thin straps didn't cover much of her shoulders, revealing freckle-dotted skin that revved Liam's libido even more.

He needed to see all of her, *now.*

Right as he took a step toward her, intending to rip the offending fabric from her body, Sienna looked up, meeting his eyes.

Then, hers trailed downward, tracing his form with so much visual potency, it felt like a caress.

A shudder wracked his frame, making his limbs and wings shake, and his half-hard cock tingle.

When her eyes landed on his manhood, Liam had to swallow again. He felt himself plumping at her perusal, and she still had too many clothes on.

"Goddess, you're beautiful," Sienna breathed.

He startled, then smirked. "Men dinnae be beautiful, lass."

She grinned. "I disagree. You are beautiful, bonnie, gorgeous, whatever you want to call it, but you are, Liam."

He chuckled and closed the small distance; couldn't hold himself back anymore. Liam reached for the soft fabric hiding her from him. He couldn't help dipping down to kiss the skin of her shoulder.

Liam tugged on her chemise.

Sienna grabbed his wrist.

He froze.

"I may not have mind-reading magic, Liam MacLeod, but this is my favorite underdress, and it will come off just fine, without you ripping it." Her mouth was set in a hard line, and her bronze eyes flashed, daring him.

He grinned and snatched her against his chest, taking her mouth and kissing her until Sienna sagged in his grip, panting hard.

Liam could feel her peaked nipples through the barely-there chemise. Another zing of awareness traveled to his cock and landed in his bollocks, making them ache.

"I'll take it off," his Fae healer breathed.

Soon, the soft material joined her other clothing, tossed on the pile.

He didn't breathe for two, maybe three heartbeats, until his head spun, and he had to force air down again.

Bonnie wasn't strong enough, and neither was *gorgeous*.

Sienna was ethereal, angelic, stunning, and breathtaking — literally.

His heart rebounded off his sore ribs, and he didn't know where to look first. His guesses had been correct, most of her torso was covered in freckles, and her skin beneath was like polished alabaster. Perfect.

Her breasts were high and tight. Her inviting hips gently rounded up to her flat tummy, with a hint of abdominal definition, but she looked perfectly soft and flawlessly firm in all the right places. Supple.

Liam sucked back a curse when his gaze landed at the apex of her thighs. Fae didn't have body hair, and his lass was no exception. He burned to touch her there…to taste her, exploring her most secret spot.

Would Sienna be afraid to touch him?

She was a healer and surely had seen naked men before—Fae men—hairless in the groin where he was not. Would that make her change her mind about him?

He was not all Fae.

Knowing it and seeing proof of it were two different things.

"Liam?" Sienna gnawed her bottom lip and twirled a loose strand of her bright red hair around her index finger. "Is something wrong?"

"Nay, lass. Yer perfect."

She came back to him, and he tugged her into his arms, against his body, because he couldn't not touch her, couldn't not feel her against him.

Liam sucked back a gasp—maybe a curse. Sienna was tucked into him, her warm flesh against his, and nothing had ever felt so right.

She was completely fitted to him, as if she belonged, and should always be there. Like he should never let her go.

Her breasts brushed his ribs, and it was better than her healing salve.

She rested her cheek on one of his pectoral muscles, and he kissed the top of her head.

Sienna smiled up at him, but he didn't like the sad edge he read in her eyes. "I can make no promises," she whispered.

"I can," Liam retorted.

"Aye?" She arched an eyebrow.

"Ye an' I will enjoy each other. Nay matter what happens. I will promise ye tha'."

He didn't give her a chance to answer. Liam

pumped his wings twice, holding her tightly around the waist as he rose into the air.

Sienna squeaked and looped her arms around his neck. "What're you doing? You can't fly *you*, let alone *us*!"

"I'll pay fer it later, but I'm no' goin' far." He was pleased his voice had come out even, and not revealed the pain that was already daggering his sword wound.

He landed on a large boulder next to the warmest of the small falls—where he'd washed himself when she'd first showed him the place.

Sienna's eyes were huge and her hands all over him, but she wasn't trying to seduce him. "That was reckless," she scolded, her fingers exploring the large cut in his left side. "Thank the Goddess, it didn't open. Are you well?" She put her hands on her bare hips and glared up at him.

Liam chuckled and snatched her back to him. Needed her skin on his again. "I'm fond a' when ye fash o'er me," he whispered above her ear, then suckled her earlobe.

"W-w-w-orry for you? D-d-on't you realize how much effort I have put into healing you? Don't let it have been a waste of time."

He pulled back and smirked. "Ye wan' ta fuss now?" He cupped one breast, and swished his thumb over her nipple until it peaked in response.

"N-n-ay," Sienna whispered, then gasped when he dipped down and took the same nipple into his mouth.

"Scold me…later," Liam said, smiling against her

warm skin when she moaned and buried her hands in his hair. While he tasted her delicious clean skin, he backed them up slowly, into the path of the cascading water.

She threw her head back, eyes closed, and her hands made their way to his shoulders.

He almost came right then and there. His bollocks throbbed and a jolt of demand shot into the tip of his cock.

His Fae healer was all his fantasies come to life, her red hair wet and darker in hue, rivulets of warm water running down her breasts and flat stomach.

Liam moved closer, kissing his way upward, across her collarbone and neck. He took her mouth again, and Sienna was right with him, kissing him with a desperate edge that made his arousal pulse with a demand to get inside her.

She snaked her arms around his neck, and pushed into him, her glorious perfect globes to his chest, her torso touching his, trapping his erection pleasantly against her. Her fingers brushed the base of his wings, and he shuddered.

Sienna stilled and gently ended their kiss. "Did I hurt you?"

"Nay, lass. My wings are...sensitive, but nay pain."

Her cheeks pinked, and it wasn't from their shared passion. "I...I've always wanted to touch them."

Liam smiled and rested his forehead against hers. "Ye can touch me anawhere ye wish. Always."

She slipped from his arms, and he turned slightly, to allow her access to his iridescent appendages.

He shivered again when she gingerly rested her hands on either side of his right wing. The sensation was pleasant and made him want more.

He'd never associated touching his wings with sexual desire, but it certainly didn't hurt that she was naked as she explored him.

"They feel like skin, but they're so soft," Sienna mused, as if she was speaking more to herself than him.

"They are skin," Liam managed, but his ability to think and speak was already diminishing due to the passionate haze she was making even more intense with every stroke and caress of his wings.

"Will you fly me high into the sky? When you're completely healed."

"Aye, lass."

She flashed him a brilliant smile that made his control wane even more.

"C'mere," he demanded.

"I'm not done touching you."

Liam swallowed and tracked her movements like a hunting cat locked onto prey as she skittered around to face him.

Uncertainty darted across her pretty face, but she moved into his body again, and closed her hand around his erection.

He hissed her name, and his cock kicked in her palm.

"You have hair here…"

Liam couldn't muster even a one word affirmative, but he forced a nod.

She explored him, from root to tip, and even pumped a few times, then asked him if it felt good. She caressed his pubic curls, dragging two fingers through them, as if she needed to touch every hair.

He was about to come all over her hands. "I'm s'posed ta show *ye* pleasure," he gritted out, to distract himself. It didn't work.

Sienna squeezed him and moved her hand up and down again, then again. "You are. *This* feels good to me."

Liam groaned, tilted his head back and closed his eyes.

Wasn't this all wrong?

Not going according to his plan.

He was supposed to have had his way with her, but it seemed as if his wee Fae healer was having her way with him instead.

chapter ten

Sienna was lost in Liam's passion. It was impossible to tear her eyes away from him. His chin was tilted up, his head back, those gorgeous, vivid violet eyes half-closed.

His curly locks were black when wet, and dripping water over his shoulders, sending streams down his chest. If she was braver, or not busy with touching his manhood, she might've leaned forward to catch those droplets on her tongue. Yet making him feel good was more intoxicating—at least, at the moment.

She was offering this beautiful halfling Warrior pleasure.

Her—plain Sienna, who wasn't considered much to look at among the exile village—was the source of Liam's desire.

Liam had told her she was gorgeous many times, but it was hard to believe him.

Now, she did. As she touched him.

His huge body was taut, as if he was bunching all his muscles. The sounds he kept emitting were delectable, and Sienna moved closer, kissing his chest, and pulling one of his nipples into her mouth, as he'd done to her.

Between her legs throbbed, pulsed, demanded to be filled.

"Lass, lass, lass," Liam panted. "I…mm…goin' ta…"

She'd never seen a man climax, let alone been the cause of it, but she was eager to witness it.

Her grandmother had educated her in the ways of men and women, of course. Although, the elderly healer was the last person she wanted popping into her head right then.

"Show me, Liam," Sienna whispered, squeezing the base of his erection, and pumping him harder.

He called out, and his body went even tighter. Liam pushed his wings out straight, as if he needed help with balance to keep him on his feet.

Warm streams of his release covered her hands, and she couldn't look away, especially as her most intimate places ached even more.

She had the odd urge to put her mouth where her hand was, but she couldn't do that today. The courage required wasn't quite there, despite what she'd just done to make Liam orgasm.

He panted, his large chest heaving as he seemed to be struggling for normal breath.

The image was made even more tempting by the roar of the water and the rivulets still rolling off his beautifully defined muscles.

Their eyes met, and Sienna didn't even get a chance to comment before he was on her, tugging her to him and covering her mouth with his.

Liam kissed her breathless, but there was an urgent potency in this one that had only been hinted at in their earlier lip-locks.

Her halfling was finally done restraining himself, and that only heated her blood even more.

He grabbed her waist, lifting her off her feet and perching her bottom on a natural shelf in the smooth water-worn wall behind the warm falls.

The polished rock had been softened and shaped by the falling water, not painful on her bare skin.

"Liam, what're you—" Her question was cut off when he wrenched her thighs open and planted his mouth very close to her sex.

"I dinnae let ye fall, Sienna." He sounded so serious, but his eyes burned with desire, seeming to glow like they had before. "Let me show ye pleasure." As Liam spoke, he stroked the outside of her most intimate place with both thumbs.

Sensations shot deep inside her, answering with an immediate demanding throb. Sienna moaned and nodded.

"Ye smell so good, I dinnae think I shall hold back from tastin' ye."

Tasting?

Did he mean—

When Liam parted her center with his tongue, Sienna screamed his name and buried her hands in his wet curls.

He growled against her flesh, and the vibrations revved her higher.

She wiggled.

His large hands gripped her hips. "Be still, my lass." This was wrapped in humor, but Liam didn't look up. "I'll make ye feel good."

He licked her again, and Sienna tightened her hold on his hair.

She sucked in a breath when ecstasy washed over her, sending her heart into a canter. She wanted more; wanted to tell him so, but no words would be born.

"Yer so wet fer me," Liam slid a finger inside her, but he was so gentle, hesitant, she was able to concentrate on how it felt, rather than what he was doing.

Touching her in a way no one had before.

Her halfling licked and sucked her into his mouth, as well as gently thrust one finger in and out of her, then soon added another.

It felt so good, but his movements were shallow, stroking her inner walls as his mouth continued hot ministrations that made desire scatter all over her body.

He concentrated on the tight bundle of nerves at the top of her sex, and Sienna was lost in pleasure.

She threw her head back and forth, kept one hand in his hair, and grabbed the edge of the ledge with the other until her knuckles were white.

Sienna leaned into the cool wall behind her, the temperature contrasting the warm water that she could only currently feel on her feet. It made her head spin.

"Dinnae fight it, lass. Let go fer me. Come fer me."

Liam's voice sounded far away as passion made her mind foggy.

She could barely hear the sound of the falls anymore, the rushing between her ears drowning them out. Concentrating wasn't happening, as stars whirled behind her eyes.

When had she closed them?

Sienna couldn't open them now, either. They were pleasantly heavy.

Something was happening, building in her lower belly, only to land between her legs, a demanding pulse that was becoming more and more intense with every swipe of her warrior's tongue.

The sensation crested, and pleasure exploded.

Her muscles contracted and released of their own accord.

She had no control.

Sienna lifted her hips and screamed Liam's name.

She saw even more stars, and it took multiple attempts to breathe normally before she was successful, so she panted to assist in getting air down. "Oh, my Goddess," she blurted.

Liam chuckled, spreading gentle kisses and caresses all over her inner thighs as she came down from her first orgasm ever.

Of course, she'd done self-exploration, especially if alone while bathing. However, any pleasure she'd discovered paled in comparison to what her halfling had just given her.

Sienna darted off the ledge, grateful when Liam caught her, because she hadn't warned him.

She initiated a kiss, but he didn't hesitate to kiss her back, like always. Her muscles were warm and lax, and standing proved a challenge, so she was doubly appreciative of his large hands all over her, holding her steady, and caressing her back as their mouths moved together.

"Ah, lass, yer so perfect," he whispered when the kiss ended, resting his forehead against hers.

"So are you, Liam MacLeod." For some reason, tears pricked the back of her eyes and she had to blink them away, calling herself a fool.

What was wrong with her?

He'd shown her pleasure, as she'd asked him to, and it'd been wonderful. Something Sienna would remember for all time; despite the fact she hadn't taken him inside her.

A little voice whispered she would have to hold onto memories, because she would soon lose him.

There was no reason to get attached to her halfling warrior.

She ignored the voice that retorted how much she was already lost to him.

Had been from the start.

Why?

Liam flashed a smile that sent her heart into a scattered stutter.

"Let's cleanup, a'fore yer brother feels we were gone too long, an' comes lookin' fer us."

Sienna couldn't find her voice, so she forced a nod and let him pull her back under the warm spray of the small waterfall.

Liam's stomach was tied in knots. Sienna was quiet—too quiet—as they dressed. Did she regret what they'd shared?

He sure as hell didn't.

He'd wanted to take her, but he wouldn't do that in their current location, even if she'd wanted him to.

Their first time—when it happened—should be in a bed, where he could worship her fully. Taste every inch of her body, although he'd certainly appreciated what he'd tasted, and had every intention of doing so again.

"Sienna?" Liam ventured, belting on his plaid and climbing to his feet.

Her head whipped around, and her burnished eyes were wide, as if he'd startled her. "A-a-ye?"

He blinked and cleared his throat. "Are ye well, lass?"

Sienna smiled, but looked away, tying her apron back in place. She gave a tiny nod he might've missed had he not been staring so hard.

It was a shame her gorgeous body was fully covered by too much fabric again.

"I'm braw," she whispered.

He couldn't hold in his grin, and he breathed in a small relief. Maybe she didn't regret him, after all.

Liam closed the small distance to her side and grabbed her hand. "Yer what?"

Her cheeks were stained with the pink he loved so much when she finally looked his way.

"I'm braw." She flashed another smile. This one was shy, and it made his gut quiver.

Liam chuckled. "I like the sound a' my words on yer lips."

If possible, Sienna's face lit up more, and he wished he could read minds like his da—at least temporarily—because he suspected his lover had just recalled the feeling of his mouth on her intimate flesh at his words.

A shiver of delight and temptation slid down his spine, and he flexed his wings then blew out another breath, this one to cool his newly rising ardor.

Despite the pleasure they'd shared, Liam hadn't done everything he'd wanted to her, so there was a dull ache in his bollocks, no matter the release he'd had at her fingertips.

Sienna was brave and sweet and lovely.

Gorgeous.

She'd touched him and brought him to climax because *she'd* wanted to, without prompting.

It'd surprised the hell out of him and made him want her even more.

"Liam?" Sienna whispered, but she wasn't looking at him again. Her gaze was locked onto where their hands were still joined.

"Aye, lass?"

She finally looked at him, and her eyes were so sad, and a little misty. "Thank you for today."

He cocked his head. "Ye say tha', as if 'tis goodbye."

Sienna swallowed and didn't speak.

Liam tugged her into his arms. Couldn't help it. His heart cantered, and he cautioned himself to calm. He might not be an empath, but he felt the finality his Fae healer projected, and he wanted to shut it down.

Deny that what'd happened between them was a one-time thing, and he would never get the chance to fully make love to her.

She rested her cheek against his chest and slid her arms around his waist.

He closed her in his wings and held her tighter. Liam kissed the top of her head.

They didn't speak, but perhaps they didn't need to.

He wasn't ready to let her go.

Wasn't ready to go home—although it was past time Liam should've tried to make his way to the Faery Stones.

How could he walk away from Sienna now?

He ignored the voice in the back of his head declaring that perhaps soon he would be forced to do that very thing…and he wouldn't be able to at all.

chapter eleven

Liam slid out of the large tree home, shutting the thick door as quietly as he could and welcoming the warmth of the night.

One good thing about the Fae Realm was the mild weather, even late at night, as it was now. Insects chirped around him, singing to each other from the surrounding trees, and he smiled. Although the tones were different, it sounded like home.

He'd never laid his eyes on a Fae cricket, but they were no doubt wildly colorful, and different than the Human Realm's version.

Liam stretched his wings and it felt good, instead of pain shooting into his side. It was certainly a welcome change.

Sienna hadn't been wrong when she'd yelled at him for gliding them to the waterfall two days before, but he was much improved since then.

Perhaps that had a little bit to do with his new lover?

He smirked and headed for the trees to the left of the clearing. He wanted to fly, and without being caught by his Fae healer.

Liam was confident it would neither hurt too severely, nor open his now-sealed sword wound. However, he didn't want to endure a Sienna tongue lashing for trying.

He'd waited for her to retire for the night—much like he had the night he'd left home. The rest of her family had drifted off to bed, one-by-one. Ealeric had remained with him the longest. They'd sat by the fire and talked. He liked the Fae man and enjoyed getting to know him.

Sienna's brother reminded him of his cousin, Rory, who not many recognized had a sensitive side. Ealeric used humor to cover much, to protect himself.

Liam's wings ached to lift him into the air. He wanted to soar, close his eyes, and revel in the wind rushing over his body.

He'd come there to fly, after all.

The reminder made guilt stir low in his gut.

He was much better physically; no longer in mortal peril—in only a matter of days—and even if it would be a challenge, he should go home. His mother was probably beside herself with worry, and his father was no doubt already planning a siege, with his uncles and cousins at his side.

Liam tried to put the concern out of his head. He could see how far he was able to fly, and leave the next night, when it was more likely he could access the Faery Stones.

His heart slid to his stomach.

Going home meant leaving Sienna.

Besides a few stolen kisses, they hadn't had any privacy to finish what they'd started at the waterfall, and damn he wanted to.

Wanted her.

Burned for her. A mere thought of her gorgeous

bare form and freckled flesh made him hard and aching.

With her family around all the time, Liam didn't feel as if they *could* be together intimately, although Sienna also expressed the desire.

They could go back to the waterfall, but he didn't want to take her without a proper bed, and Sienna shared a bedroom with her sister, so it couldn't happen inside her home.

He shook the lust from his blood and concentrated on navigating through trees of all sizes.

Liam moved closer to the largest waterfall, loving the sound of the roaring waters. He avoided looking at the spot where he'd tasted Sienna's most private places — it would only rev his libido up again. His cock was already twitching under his plaid.

"Stop, ye sod," he ordered aloud.

He pumped his wings once, then twice. On the third sweep, Liam lifted into the Fae night sky, smiling as the sense of true freedom washed over him. He rotated in the air, wincing as his side protested, but he ignored it and rose higher, catching a thermal and gliding along the pocket of warm air until it ended.

Liam closed his eyes and went even higher, making the muscles of his wings work when necessary, and soaring free when he could.

His body was sore, but the long-overdue stretching of his sinew and bones felt good.

He hit another thermal, laying on top of the warm air on his back, as if floating in water. He studied the twinkling stars high above and sighed in contentment.

Liam had been born for this.

His gut clenched at the forbidden thought.

He'd been born a wingless member of the human Clan MacLeod, and flying was *wrong*, illicit stolen time.

The consequences of being left for dead on the side of the stream were *real*.

His father's worst fears.

Before Liam had sneaked to the realm years before, his parents had only suspected he had wings that were not visible in the Human Realm.

After he and Lexi had been caught trying to use the Stones when he'd been eight and ten, his cousin had slipped the truth to her brother, Angus—that Liam had successfully entered the Fae Realm and discovered he had indeed been born with wings.

He'd never seen his father so angry as that day.

Fury like *no one* had ever seen from the mostly stoic man.

Then *and* now—Liam was a selfish laddie, and no matter how right soaring through the air felt, it was tinged by the reality of his reckless actions, and the danger he'd encountered.

Not to mention the danger his half-blooded presence had brought to Sienna's family.

Then, his own family when—not if—they came after him.

Liam couldn't banish the sobering ideas or the swirling guilt.

He frowned and made his way back to the ground, gliding down until he landed in the loamy turf next to the waterfalls.

He'd been able to remain aloft without difficulty for the better part of an hour, at his best guess, which was a vast improvement on his previous flight attempts since being beaten and stabbed.

Liam glanced back at the roaring falling waters. Curiosity about the cave behind the largest of Grànnda Falls shot into his mind. He could fly up there, explore the place where his parents had sought shelter all those years ago, but he'd get wet, since the most direct route was through the waters. He knew a spell that might prevent a soaking but hadn't ever tried it.

Maybe he should steal Sienna away, take her there and make love to her in the hot springs his father had told him about.

His cock was fond of the idea.

Liam smirked.

He made his way back toward the exile's clearing. A nice long flight always made him sleepy, and his wings were tired, probably from disuse.

He'd sneak back into the tree and go back to the small medicine room and his borrowed cot.

Going home needed to remain at the forefront in his mind, but he didn't want to face it right then, and probably not in the morning, either.

For everyone's safety, Liam needed to return to the Human Realm, no matter how much he wanted to stay.

He didn't want to leave Sienna, but why?

For the sake of physical conquest?

His tongue soured on the question, and he quickly issued a mental denial.

Liam was grateful for her healing skills, of course, but that wasn't the reason he couldn't imagine leaving her side.

Sienna was sweet, funny, and easy on the eyes. He enjoyed being with her or even just talking to her. Couldn't imagine not seeing her every day.

The short time he'd been there felt much longer than the sennight it was.

Liam…cared about her.

Cared felt like too weak a word for his emotions regarding his Fae healer, but they'd just met, right?

It didn't make sense for him to feel more. To feel deeper than he should.

His heart skipped and he refused to answer himself.

Liam was close to the clearing now, and in just a few more steps, he'd see Sienna's home.

Voices lifted from behind him. He froze, then ducked behind a tree double the width of his body. He wished he had a weapon, and again mourned the loss of his father's dirk.

Who could be out here so late?

Then he recognized one of the voices.

"How dare you come here?" The demand was low and harsh, and he'd never heard Sienna's gentle *móraí* speak with such angry inflection. The elderly healer hardly seemed capable.

Liam moved closer, hiding behind another large tree.

Some source of artificial light—probably magical—caused a visible shadow of two figures in the tree-line.

The answer was a maniacal cackle. "My dear, Eilidh, do not be fool enough to take that tone with me. You shall *not* care for the consequences." The voice was nasally and harsh, with no indication to the person's gender. The figure's garment didn't help, either. From what Liam could make out in the shadows of the treeline, the individual wore a black mantel, topped by a huge hood, obscuring head, and face alike.

From his distance, he couldn't tell much more. Or risk more than a quick peek around the tree to obtain a better view.

That'd been the first time Liam had heard the older Fae healer referred to by her given name, although he had known it; she'd introduced herself to him.

A black smudge surrounded the tall wraith, almost like a smoke…an aura of evil.

He considered using an invisibility spell but quashed it. There was too much risk of being sensed by magic. There was no way to tell what magic the unknown Fae possessed.

The elderly woman didn't answer right away, but when she did, her words shook. "Wh-what d-do you want? We aren't supposed to meet for another fortnight."

Why would Sienna's *mórai* be meeting with this person?

So much darkness.

Her total opposite.

A shudder shot down Liam's spine, and he

wanted to flee, but who would protect the healer, if necessary?

Revulsion, danger, and warning bells went off in his head.

His magic tingled, a second encouragement to move far from the hooded figure.

Nay.

Liam wasn't fully well, but he would do whatever he could if *Mórai* was in true danger. He owed her for saving his life.

He wished he could inch closer undetected, but he didn't want to alert either party to his presence. He'd already risked being discovered with the shift from one tree to the other, even though he'd moved with the silence of a trained warrior.

"I heard an interesting rumor." The figure's voice was lower this time.

Male?

"You really should go, before you're seen. How would you explain to your beloved king that you associated with exiles?" Sienna's grandmother sounded so bitter.

So unlike the woman Liam had come to know since he'd been staying in her home.

"The Faery Stones were opened," the man said, speaking as if *Mórai* had not.

Ice slid down Liam's spine. His whole body stiffened, as if a natural defense mechanism to fight. He leaned into the tree, ignoring the bite of rough bark tasting his shoulder.

Wished again he could risk getting closer.

Sienna's grandmother didn't speak.

"A sennight ago, the Fae Warriors on duty were drunk, and lied in a poor attempt to cover up the arrival of a filthy abomination."

"I bet you enjoyed torturing the truth from them, Wardric."

Liam barely processed the Fae man's name or the disgust in *Mórai's* statement.

Arrival of a filthy abomination tromped across his head on a loop.

Sweat broke out on his upper lip.

"Torture *is* one of my best talents," Wardric retorted, his words wrapped in what sounded like genuine amusement.

Mórai spat a Fae insult that would've made Liam smile at any other time.

She'd sounded so afraid before, but she didn't now.

Why?

"Why are you telling me this? Fae Warriors kill anything that enters our realm uninvited, do they not?"

"You know *why* I'm telling you, my sweet Eilidh. I think you have secrets."

Mórai laughed, and it was as bitter as her earlier statement. "Everyone has secrets, Wardric."

"Aye, but this time, you're hiding something that has nothing to do with your family's history."

Family's history?

Liam hung on every word.

"I do not know to what you're referring." At least

she'd pulled it off; the lie had sounded convincing.

"The abomination got away. The king is on a mission to find it."

"To destroy it, no doubt," Sienna's grandmother snapped.

Wardric laughed again, but it was humorless. "All in good time. The king has ordered the abomination brought to him, of course."

"Well, I know of no such abomination, and as you're well aware, creatures as such are obvious to those with magic." This too, sounded bitter. "*It* should be easy enough to locate." This had come off nonchalantly.

Sienna's *mórai* was a decent actress.

Liam hoped, anyway.

"Ah, right you are."

A tense, pregnant silence fell.

"The king has dispatched several Wings of Warriors to locate the abomination. They will search the whole of the realm if they need, including Grànnda Falls and your precious exile camp."

Liam swallowed as panic crawled from his gut and settled in his throat, choking him. He tried to force air in and out quietly, so he wouldn't make a noise they might hear.

Aye, Feneal's magic covered him, and Sienna believed it would hide him, but what if it didn't?

What if it had already worn off?

"Again, why do you share this news with me?"

There was a gasp, and instinct told him that Wardric had grabbed *Mórai* in some fashion.

Liam growled low, helpless. He opened and closed his fists at his sides. Wished he could see better. Or move closer.

Despite Feneal's spell, he couldn't betray himself now. Unless her life was in true peril, he might as well be tied to the tree he crouched behind.

"If you're hiding this abomination, you'll wish for death when I'm done with you. Saving such a creature is just like you and your misplaced sense of justice."

Móraí made a strangled sound.

Did the bastard have her by the throat?

"I may not be able to read minds, but other mages can."

So, the sod was a mage.

Probably in the service of the king, who happened to be Liam's uncle once removed. He'd made a smart decision not to use his invisibility spell. Mage meant great magic, and he would've been caught for sure.

Móraí didn't retort or speak.

Liam's heart skipped, and he prayed she was well. He couldn't see them clearly from his position, only the back of Wardric's cape, the Fae man larger than Sienna's grandmother and obscured her body.

"If you have anything to do with the disappearance of the abomination, our agreement is off...no matter how much I desire your granddaughter's hand."

chapter twelve

"Who is Wardric?" Liam asked the elderly Fae woman when she stepped through the front door. He reclined in the chair closest to the hearth. The heat from the crackling fire warmed his back and neck. He didn't take his eyes off her as surprise crossed her troubled face.

He'd made it back into the home she shared with her grandchildren before her. Then he'd taken a seat where they'd already shared so many meals.

To wait for her and get answers.

There was no chance at sleep of any kind before he had them.

The idea that his Fae healer was promised to someone—someone who reeked pure evil—twisted his gut into knots.

It was more than his familiarity and affinity for the taste of her skin. He would've objected to *any* female being betrothed to someone like Wardric, and he hadn't even gotten a full look at the Fae mage.

Liam didn't question his instinct about that.

He also tried to squash the rage and jealousy over the idea that Sienna might belong to someone else.

His instinct shouted that she had no idea of her grandmother's…plans.

But why?

He wanted answers about the elderly healer's secrets.

He wasn't leaving this table without them.

Sienna's *mórai* froze, her hands visibly quaking. Then she shook her head, but came closer to the table, into the dim light of the kitchen and dining area. "How much did you hear?" Her words trembled as much as her petite form.

"Enough," Liam said, sitting forward in the chair and flexing his wings.

Her gaze landed there, and not on his face. "Why are you not resting?"

He arched an eyebrow at her attempted diversion and didn't answer. This wasn't about his first successful flight, or why he wasn't in bed.

It was about family secrets and evil mages.

"Ye need ta tell me what's goin' on," he prompted when she only stared.

After a few more tense heartbeats, Eilidh sighed, gripped the back of the chair opposite his, and swallowed audibly as she slid it out from the table.

She took a seat, but hesitated, as if she would rather stand — or was torn by what to do or say.

Liam considered her a strong woman, despite her advanced age and lack of size. She'd raised three children alone, in a camp of outcasts, and without the convenience of what most Fae took for granted.

Magic.

His instincts also told him her interactions with Wardric were about exactly that. He didn't question where the notion was coming from. Liam would've wagered all his favorite weapons on the fact.

Eilidh wouldn't meet his eyes as she spoke. "Wardric is one of the king's mages."

He'd assumed as much, but he didn't remark, because he wanted her to keep talking.

"Our family has been outcast for nearly twenty-five years. We were stripped of our magic after my son, Corsten, was executed." Her voice shook with emotion at the confession, and her gaze finally found Liam's.

Even in the dim light of the room, he could see the tears filling her eyes.

"Sienna said ye were exiled because ye have no magic."

Her grandmother nodded. "Aye, she was wee when it happened, as was Ealeric. They do not remember having magic, because the memories were removed. As a kindness. My son's wife was pregnant with Amalie—which was one reason our lives were spared, but our magic was not."

He swallowed, digesting her words.

Kindness?

Sienna wanted magic more than anything.

If—or *when*—she discovered these truths, she was going to be angry. She would never see her memories being removed as a *kindness*.

Liam didn't doubt that any more than he was sure Wardric was an evil bastard.

"My grandchildren do not know how their father died. Their mother, Kaydra, caught a birthing fever days after Amalie came into this world, and died. I could have saved her, had I my powers, but I could not *here*, with the nothing we were left with." Tears flowed down Eilidh's thin cheeks now, making her pale green eyes twinkle in the sparse light. She sounded bitter again, like when she'd been talking to Wardric.

"I'm sorry," Liam whispered, because he couldn't say anything else. He'd seen Sienna's fear of fevers, and now it made sense.

His healer cousin-by-marriage had lost patients to fevers before, too, in instances that not even the small amount of pooled healing magic his father and Aunt Alana could provide had been able to help. Lila would give in to her emotions over that, too, especially since such things were curable in the century she'd come from, or so she'd said.

"My son was the head healer for the king, for the realm, as I was before him. We held a place of prestige for generations. My father before me, and my grandmother before him. All healers were trained by our family."

Liam sat taller, focusing on Eilidh's words as she launched into the story before he could ask. Her voice was stronger now, less tearful and she made a fist, resting it on the table.

"Wardric was jealous of my Corsten and his position, as well as his closeness to the king, and King Fillan's fondness for my family."

"But Wardric is nay a healer." Liam may not know the man, but that much was obvious.

Healers did not enjoy torture.

"He is not but he *is* fueled by desire for power, and he has great magic." This was wrapped in anger and renewed bitterness.

"So why work wit' him?" he asked. "He spoke of an agreement." Liam narrowed his eyes and left unsaid the last of what the bastard had claimed—taking Sienna's hand.

"Sienna's birthright."

"Nay, 'tis no' worth it." The denial was quick and hot, and without much thought.

Eilidh sighed and gave what seemed to be a reluctant nod. "You're right, and I regret what I have agreed to."

"Which is what, exactly?"

Mixed emotions darted across her aged face, and her mouth set in a hard line. "Wardric promised to return our family's magic, our former rank, and place in the kingdom—among society. Sienna would take her rightful position as head healer for the king."

Liam's breath stuttered. "Surely, he has nay the power."

"Not alone, no. But he has…friends."

"In exchange a' what?" he demanded.

Liam needed her to say it.

"Sienna's hand in marriage, among other things."

"Other things?" His instant burning rage at what he already knew cooled just a touch, scattered by the curiosity of what else she'd have to sacrifice to that evil mage.

"Aye. To be named whenever he sees fit, as he is fond of reminding me." Sienna's *mórai* shrugged her slim shoulders, her expression stamped with helplessness.

Desperation emanated off her in thick waves.

A twinge of guilt at his ire reared up from his gut. She'd been acting in what she'd believed was her family's best interests.

If *he* knew how much Sienna craved her magic, her grandmother had to know, as well. Although Sienna had no memories of her healing magic or her family's place in the king's court—a much easier life than they had now—Eilidh did. She no doubt had a long memory of how they'd lived in luxury.

The elderly Fae healer wanted to give her granddaughter what she'd always wanted. What she'd been born with, only to have it stolen away, at no fault of Sienna's.

Ealeric and Amalie, too.

They were all victims.

Of Liam's great uncle, King Fillan.

Perhaps Sienna's *mórai* felt the time was right to restore what they'd lost. Too bad she'd picked such a dangerous route.

"He wishes ye ta serve him," Liam said, keeping his voice low.

"Without question."

It was his turn to sigh. "Fer how long?"

"The rest of my life. He doesn't intend for me to get *my* magic back. The agreement is only for my grandchildren. I am no danger to him without magic. He fears I would turn on him, had I my powers. He has bound my word to him with a spell."

Liam cursed long and hard—in Gaelic and Fae alike. "Nay," he ordered.

"Nay?"

"Sienna shall no' marry Wardric." He'd said the man's name as if he'd spat the word the Fae mage really was—a bastard. "I shall no' allow it."

"What?" The soft word shook, wrapped in confusion and alarm.

Liam's eyes landed on Sienna.

She stood just inside the arched doorway that led to the short corridor.

Her grandmother also stared in her direction, and the elderly Fae woman had paled so much her complexion matched her hair.

Sienna wore a long-sleeved white sleeping gown that skimmed the tops of her bare feet. Her hair had been braided for sleeping, and the long fiery plait hung over one shoulder.

She looked innocent and adorable—but her eyes were huge, her shock obvious.

Trioblóid scuttled close behind her, his coat flowing in reds, pinks and yellows of caution, anger, and alarm. The creature had clearly caught the tension in the room.

"Sienna, *mò ghràdh*—"

"Nay, *Mórai*. Do not "my love" me. What's going on here?" She padded over to the table, her bogle on her heels, but Sienna didn't sit. She perched her hands on her shapely hips, noticeable despite the fabric obscuring her body.

Liam exchanged a glance with Eilidh, but the elderly healer didn't try to speak again. Her slender shoulders were caved in, and she still had no color in her cheeks. She looked tiny in the chair, like a wee bairn trying to avoid punishment.

He cleared his throat. "Sienna—"

"Nay, Liam." She threw him a glare, then looked back at her grandmother. "Who in five hells am I *not* marrying?"

"But *Mórai*, I've lived my whole life without magic. Why would you do this? How…could…you?" Sienna had ranted, raved, and screamed like a child, and she should've been embarrassed it'd all been in front of Liam, but she couldn't have held back if she'd tried.

It was a wonder her siblings hadn't woken and joined them. Their home was not that large, after all.

Her face burned from rage and exertion. She'd long since shoved her sleeves up to her elbows.

Mórai had betrayed her in the worst way possible—and that didn't even include discovering the truth about her family's magic, and her father's death.

Marriage?

To an evil mage who'd been responsible for her family's plight? For the years she'd missed with wonderful parents who'd loved her and her siblings?

The whole idea smelled of the Subh fruit rotting in the underbrush at the base of the tree.

"*Mò ghràdh,* 'tis your birthright. It is past time for you to take your rightful place. You have trained all your life. Your healing skills are ready. All you need is the magic you were born with." Her grandmother's voice was an urgent, insistent plea.

Sienna shook her head, twice. Her head spun and her knees wobbled. She wavered on her feet.

Liam darted forward and drew her to him. At the same time, he kicked the base of an empty chair behind her, and it gave a screeching protest. "Sit, lass, a'fore ye fall o'er."

He kept her hand in his much larger one, caressing her skin with his thumb in what should've been soothing circles.

She didn't take comfort from his touch, as she would've normally. Her head was full of anguish and chaos.

Sienna sank into the familiar wooden seat without another word.

The truth had been too much at once.

Would she have preferred to remain in the dark?

Aye, she wanted her magic.

Sienna always had, but not at the expense of the woman who'd raised her. Certainly not in exchange for a marriage to a man responsible for her father's death.

A man who, by all accounts, was evil.

Being an exile, Sienna had never contemplated marriage much, assuming it would not likely happen. She'd trained under her grandmother's tutelage, ready, accepting of the fact she would take over healing duties for their small community when the time came.

She spared a glance at Liam.

Sienna had to swallow.

She'd declared she could make him no promises when they'd shared her first-ever intimacy by the waterfalls, and that was now truer than it had been in that moment.

Even still, she couldn't imagine being married to another man, even under different circumstances.

How could she help her *móraí* — and herself — out of this mess?

It wasn't possible, was it?

Fright flipped her stomach, shot up to her heart and squeezed, making it hurt to breathe. She suddenly wanted to cling to the large hand still holding hers.

Sienna wanted to be in his arms, ask him to hold her and make everything go away.

She couldn't do any of that, nor could he help.

Liam had his own issues, and dangers different than what she'd just learned were hers.

Sienna tugged free of her halfling's gentle grip and shot to her feet. She didn't wait for a reaction from either of her companions.

She darted to the front door, yanked it open, and fled the treed home she'd grown up in. She ignored her name when her grandmother called after her.

Sienna ran.

Through the clearing, then bursting into the forest.

Trio's chirruping was frantic, proving he'd given chase, but she didn't pause. The wee creature would not be able to keep up with her, or catch up, and right now that was fine.

She wanted to be alone.

Pretend the last thirty minutes that felt like a lifetime's worth of nightmares wasn't true.

That it'd never happened.

She kept going, pushing her legs until her thighs burned, with no conscious destination.

The roar of the falls was welcoming, drowning out the roaring between her ears from her racing heart. Evidently, her feet had carried her to Grànnda Falls.

Sienna skidded to a halt at the edge of the largest pool at the base of the falls, resting on a huge flat-topped boulder. She wanted to bend at the waist and perch her hands on her knees to catch her breath, but she didn't, so she had to pant to get air down.

She stared into the swirling waters at the point where they calmed, farthest from the heavy cascades, settling into a pool she and her siblings used to swim in when they were children.

Dark, still waters, glinting in the moonlight.
Calm.

The complete opposite of her chaotic emotions.

Warm air moving behind her ruffled the bottom of her sleeping gown, and Sienna whirled.

Liam back-winged gracefully, as he lowered himself to the ground, landing almost silently only a few feet from her.

He was so beautiful, his iridescent skin with points of colored light, dancing in the moonlight, and she was once again breathless, and she hadn't really even seen him in action, in the air.

Tears pricked her eyes. She was torn between running to him and fleeing.

"Sienna—"

The need for her halfling won out and Sienna darted to Liam, throwing her arms around him as the first sob rolled up.

"Oomph," he muttered as she slammed into his chest, and she buried her face against his pectoral muscles.

She'd knocked the air out of him, but she couldn't find her voice to apologize. She was crying too hard and shaking all over.

Liam hauled her even closer, wrapping her in his arms and his wings. He sighed against her forehead, making the tiny hairs that'd escaped her braid dance and tickle.

Sienna squeezed her eyes shut and willed some sense of control to return, but she couldn't stop the tears or the quaking in her body.

"'Tis okay ta let it ou'. I've got ye."

The odd word must be an affirmative, some sort of permission, and it was something she needed, because it made her breath come easier, and encouraged her heart to slow, despite the still-flowing tears.

She was safe with Liam, enclosed in his arms and his beautiful wings.

Sienna clung to him, hiding her face against his leine and cried until her eyes burned and her throat was raw.

He rubbed her back in long soothing strokes and it warmed her from the inside out.

She tightened her grip around his waist.

Liam chuckled, a rumble she felt against her body, as well as heard.

"Easy, lass, I need ta breathe."

Sienna lifted her head and met his violet eyes.

He wore an appealing smirk, and she needed to taste it.

She pushed to her toes and crushed her mouth into his.

Liam didn't hesitate to kiss her back, parting her lips with his tongue before she could open for him.

Sienna met it, twining hers around his and deepening their lip-lock. She rubbed her breasts into his chest and whimpered her desire.

They were only separated by the thin fabric of her sleeping gown. She wanted it gone, wanted his leine and plaid gone, too. Wanted her bare flesh against his, as she'd experienced days before at the waterfall.

Only this time, she wanted him inside her.

Sienna wanted to be with him fully.

Liam groaned against her mouth, kissing her with a heated desperation she echoed. His erection pressed into her belly, and her sex throbbed with the same urgency in response.

She broke the seal of their mouths, panting against him. "I want you, Liam. I need you. Now."

"Sienna—"

Her name in his brogue rolled over her like another caress.

"Please don't deny me. Not tonight," she begged, and couldn't even be embarrassed for it. "I know you want me. You've told me so."

Liam swallowed, and the apple of his throat bobbed. "Aye. I burn fer ye, lass."

Her breath stuttered in time with her tripping heart. "I burn for you, too."

He dipped down, kissing her hard and fast, but it still made Sienna's belly flip and her head spin.

"I ken where we can go, but we'll have ta get wet."

She smiled and slid her arms around his neck. "Take me there, then, and get me wet."

He growled as he caught her double meaning, then swept her off her feet, up into his arms, and shot into the air.

chapter thirteen

Liam pumped his wings with urgency that was only equaled by the pulsing in his cock. He held her close to his chest, and Sienna trailed wee hot kisses under his chin and down his neck.

That was damn distracting as he flew, and only made him want more, but they weren't going far.

Then he would have more.

Would have *her*.

He didn't bother trying his waterproof spell. His need for Sienna was too great.

They both gasped as the shock of cold water hit them when he soared through the largest of the waterfalls, but it didn't cool his ardor. The way Sienna still kissed and caressed him told him it hadn't affected her, either.

Liam landed on the natural stone floor of the cave behind the cascading waters.

They were both soaked from head to toe, but that didn't concern him much. They would be naked soon enough, and he would ensure his Fae healer was good and warm.

The cave was dark, but his eyes were already adjusting.

Sienna was still nestled against his chest. She pointed. "Look, I think those are magic lights. How—?"

He flashed a grin. "My parents. The magic lights have probably been here since they were here years ago."

"Do you think they still work? Feneal recharges the ones we have at home from time to time."

"There's only one way ta find ou'." He set her gently to her bare feet, and he brushed his lips against hers in a quick thing that had Sienna smiling.

Liam approached the nearest globe and cupped it. It was perched on the cave wall itself and didn't budge. "*Soillsich,*" he commanded.

The orb flickered a few times before it glowed dimly.

Sienna gasped behind him. "I can't believe it still works."

"Dinnae give much light."

"Nay, but there are more." She pointed to a spot farther down the natural wall, then another.

She was right.

He spotted eight magic lanterns total, equally spaced to offer light over the whole of the cave. It would take time to turn them all on.

Liam said the spellword loudly, and put force behind it, but the lights didn't obey.

"They're old, so you probably have to touch them, like you did the first one," Sienna said.

"'Tis takin' me away from ye," he grumbled.

Her smile was gentle. "Nay. I'm not going anywhere. Besides, how can I get out of here without you and your wings?"

Liam didn't answer because he intended to make

quick work of the globes that were no doubt a staple in Fae households.

Soon, the sizable cave had a nice ambient glow. Enough to navigate the place, like the last moments of twilight.

The Fae orbs probably wouldn't last long, maybe not even until the morning, but at least he'd be able to see the object of his desire when he made her come.

The cave had a wide mouth and naturally smooth walls and stone floor, as well as a few boulders strewn about, as if they'd been left on purpose for seating.

The roaring falls acted as a curtained arched doorway of cascading waters, but the interior wasn't wet.

Liam flexed his wings and whirled back toward the lass he intended to ravage. His breath and heart stuttered at the same time, and he almost tripped over his booted feet. He extended his right wing to keep him upright.

Sienna stood a few feet away, near the natural hot spring in the back of the cave.

She was naked.

His Fae healer had her hands tucked behind her back, and her supple body open and on intentional display.

She'd unbraided her hair, too. Despite its dampness, it surrounded her like a floating aura, flowing almost to her hips.

Her wet sleeping gown lay on a large rock, spread out to dry.

Sienna covered her mouth and giggled.

"Somethin' wrong?"

Liam swallowed. At any other time, he would've been amused at her attempt to sound like him. The beauty of her slender form, full of freckled flesh, gorgeous curves, and the perfection of her breasts with peaked nipples, and bare sex stole his words. No matter how many times he'd seen or tasted her before, she would always steal his breath.

He wasn't worthy of this Fae lass.

"I see something wrong," she said, as if he'd given an answer, closing the distance to him. Sienna grabbed his wet leine and walked backward toward the pool, tugging, and urging him to come with her.

"What's wrong?" he managed, his voice thick and foreign to his ears.

"You still wear clothes."

Liam blew out a breath, but his head still spun in anticipation and his drive to have her was taking him over.

Sienna loosened his belt without another word, then pulled it from his waist.

He caught his falling plaid but let her take it, and she put it on the largest boulder next to her chemise.

When she came back to him, he snatched her to his chest and covered her mouth with his, because he couldn't not kiss her again.

Sienna pressed her body close, mewling and whimpering, as she wound her tongue around his. Much too soon, she tugged away, meeting his gaze. Her beautiful bronze eyes went hazy with passion. She panted against him. "You're still not naked."

Liam's cock ached and throbbed with all kinds of demands. He struggled for words, but they weren't born. He swallowed.

Sienna pushed up his leine, and he assisted her in getting it the rest of the way off.

Unlike his plaid, she let the ivory fabric land in a heap at their feet.

Neither of them made a move to retrieve it.

She caressed his chest, sending little spears of awareness and desire across his pectoral muscles, and into his shoulders and collar bone, then down his stomach and even into his limbs.

His erection pounded even harder.

She explored him with the touch of a lover, not a healer.

Liam loved it and wanted more.

He shivered under the perusal of her hungry eyes, as much as her moving fingers. He scrambled for words and coherent thought. "I figured ye'd fash a' me fer flyin'."

Sienna frowned. "I should, but I can't. You came after me."

Liam cupped her face. "Always, lass." This was a vow, the same as he'd promised the first time she'd brought him to the falls to bathe.

Unlike that day, when she'd been irritated at her brother for his interference, and hadn't seemed to notice, this time Sienna's expression shouted that she'd understood his pledge.

"Liam, I—" She looked down and gripped his wrists, his palms still holding her cheeks.

"Hush, lass. Tha' talk is fer another time."

When she met his gaze again, her eyes were bright with tears. "Tonight…" Sienna's voice broke. "Tonight was too much. I…want to forget everything I just learned. Can you help me do that?"

Liam smirked. "So, ye only want me as a distraction?"

She gasped. "Nay!"

He chuckled.

Sienna narrowed her eyes when she'd finally spotted the tease for what it was. "I've wanted you from the first time you kissed me. Maybe before that. By the stream, the first time you wrapped me in your beautiful wings."

He smiled. "Good." He drew her into his arms and did just that—wrapped her in his wings. Liam shuddered when her warm bare skin encountered his.

"Touch me, Liam. Come into the pool with me. We'll get warm together. Then take me."

"Yer awful demandin'." Liam tried to keep the tease light and amused, but she reached for his cock. He gasped at her first caress.

"This says you want me." Sienna explored him, root to tip, skimming her fingers lightly until his bollocks throbbed so hard it was painful.

"I'd ne'er imagined an innocent could be such a vixen," he gritted out, closing his eyes, and fighting the lust threatening to swallow him whole.

She giggled.

He met her gaze, and his heart skipped at the appealing, mischievous smirk she wore.

"I've had a good teacher. However, I want more."

Liam growled and tugged her to him again, sealing his mouth over hers and lifting her into his chest.

Sienna met his kiss without delay, and wrapped her arms around his neck, and her legs around his waist.

He groaned into the movement of their lips and tongues from her sex hitting his erection. There wasn't nearly enough friction.

Liam walked them to the natural pool, without breaking the seal of their mouths. His hands were full of her delectable perfect arse and he kneaded her there, until she wiggled and moaned against him.

The warm water welcomed his ankles and then his calves, and he kept wading until it was to his thighs and above his hips.

Sienna stayed wrapped tight around him, kissing him with a fervency that made his blood boil.

He bent his knees, lowering them into the warm pool, and she gently leaned back.

"Hmm, this feels good," she whispered.

"Ye feel better," Liam murmured, nibbling her chin, then moving along her jawline.

Sienna tilted her head to allow him access, and he tasted every freckle covering her neck and collarbone, until she writhed on his lap.

He caressed her shoulders, her back, cupped her breasts and urged her to rest against the natural side of the pool. Like the walls of the cavern, it was smooth and almost soft from the long contact with warm water.

She mewled and moaned, encouraging his touches.

Liam licked her dusky nipples before sucking each into his mouth.

Sienna started to rock against his hard cock, but the warm waters gave too much resistance so he couldn't feel her like he wanted to.

"Liam, please…"

He dragged two fingers between her perfect breasts, down her stomach, and dipped his hand into the water, cupping her sex.

She cried out and lifted her hips, begging like she just had with words.

Liam parted her folds and felt the silky moisture of arousal, a wetness that had nothing to do with the hot spring around them. He circled his thumb on the tight bundle of nerves at the top of her sex, teasing, caressing, applying pressure and taking it away.

"Oh, Goddess," Sienna breathed.

He smirked but didn't stop his ministrations. He slid one finger gently inside her but didn't plunge too deep. Even so, Liam wanted to make her as ready as he could.

She whimpered, and he glanced up.

His breath stalled when he took her in.

Sienna had her head thrown back, her glorious red locks spread out, half floating in the water, and her pale flesh flushed pink from the humidity and passion.

She was the most gorgeous thing he'd ever seen.

"I..I...need you inside me, Liam, please. You're

making me beg."

Liam chuckled, and leaned forward to kiss her belly, and the inside of her bent knee protruding from the pool. "I want ye ta come first, my lass."

Sienna lifted her head and met his gaze. Her bronze eyes were intense. "Why?"

"'Cause, the first time hurts fer a lass."

"You'd never hurt me." She reached for him, caressing his cheek, his chest, and his arm.

"Nay, no' on purpose. 'Tis just tha nature of it."

She shook her head. "I'm not afraid. I want to come with you inside me."

Liam shivered from her words and the picture that formed in his mind. He imagined how she would feel, clutching his cock, and his body tremored again.

She was begging him to take her, so why should he imagine it, when he could feel it for real?

He shifted their positions in the pool, gripping Sienna's hips gently. He didn't have to tell her to open her legs for him, because she did that on her own, drawing him even closer into the cradle of her body.

Liam kissed her again and resumed caressing her sex beneath the surface of the water.

Sienna moaned against his mouth, rubbing her breasts into his chest. She dug her heels into his arse, bringing their pelvises together.

His tip parted her folds. He closed his eyes as a jolt of pleasure shot down his spine and into his bollocks. He cursed against her lips.

She broke their kiss and dragged one hand down his chest and stomach, ultimately gripping his erection and holding him against her sex.

Liam just about came, and he hadn't even entered her yet.

"I need you," Sienna whispered.

He nodded because words would never happen.

Liam gently dislodged her fingers and grabbed his cock. He was determined to go slow and lessen any pain for her.

He swallowed and pushed into her, inching forward gingerly, trying to ignore the sensations washing over him. The perfection of soft, pliant heat that welcomed him, pulsed against him.

His bollocks demanded he thrust hard, make her his, claim her, but he latched onto some sense of control he didn't know he held.

He slid through the resistance of her maidenhead.

Liam was seated fully inside her.

Sienna cried out and whimpered, but this time it wasn't because he was making her feel good.

Their gazes collided, and her eyes were wide and misty, no haze of passion in sight, and she clung to his forearms, nails digging in.

He cursed low and hard. "Sienna, I'm sorry…" Liam leaned back, intending to pull away, and out of her.

"Don't stop, Liam. Please. I just need a moment. Kiss me." As she spoke, his Fae healer urged him back to her, until his nipples brushed hers, and he couldn't help but do her bidding.

Liam cupped her face, wiped the tears from her eyes and took her mouth.

Sienna concentrated on the distraction of Liam's kiss, and not the ache that was more pain than pleasure between her legs. Of course, she'd been told first penetration would hurt, but she hadn't quite expected this sharp bite, especially since she'd been ready, physically, and mentally aroused.

Perhaps she'd been naïve. Liam was a big man, and his manhood was no exception. She should've allowed him to bring her to a climax, as he'd intended but she'd just wanted him — wanted *this* — so badly.

She was so full with him inside her. It didn't hurt anymore, but what would happen when he started to thrust?

Sienna kissed him harder, clinging to his neck and pressing her breasts into his chest. She wanted the haze of passion and desire back, the warmth in her belly and the burning demand for him again.

Liam broke the seal of their mouths and rested his forehead against hers. "We can stop," he panted.

"Nay, I want you."

He smirked. "Ye have me, lass. I'm inside ye."

Sienna shivered as his words shot a spark of something hot down her spine and into her sex. She rocked her bottom into his thighs.

He groaned and closed his eyes.

The movement didn't hurt, so she did it again, and her center pulsed.

That didn't hurt either.

Liam grunted and grabbed her hips.

She half-expected him to pull out of her and call it quits, but he rocked forward, gently, like she had moments ago.

Instead of discomfort, the small shifting made pleasure shoot all over her body.

Sienna gasped.

Liam's violet eyes were wide when their gazes met.

"Nay, I'm well. That…felt good."

"Are ye sure?"

She nodded. "Move, Liam, I need you to move."

He kissed her again and shifted his hips against hers. "I'll go slow," he said against her lips.

Liam thrust with obvious hesitation at first, but every movement forward and back made Sienna sear for more. Like he was igniting her fuse.

Pain was long gone, only ecstasy left in its place.

She rocked against him when he drove deeper into her, moving with him, under him, against him, until they found a rhythm.

The swirling warmth of the pool helped them move together and apart, heightening the heady humidity in the cave.

Liam kept kissing her, caressing her cheeks, her neck, and breasts, and held her close as he moved within her.

Sienna kissed and touched him back, running her fingers over the base of his wings until he quaked in her arms.

He grunted, groaned, and moaned, letting her

know without words she made him feel good.

Knowing she could make this gorgeous half-Fae Warrior melt with a mere touch stoked more than her ego. It made Sienna's blood warm and notched up her libido even more.

The newly familiar sense of something building in the heat in her lower belly signaled her brain that her climax approached.

This one was more intense than when Liam had used his mouth to do the same.

Her sex throbbed, and her muscles felt tight, as if on the edge of a cliff, destined for a freefall. Her inner walls contracted and loosened, and Sienna exploded, sensations slamming into her and making her head spin.

She cried out and clung to Liam's biceps, as stars blinked in and out behind her eyes.

He stilled above her, his whole body taut, including his wings. Liam panted, then grunted. With one last thrust forward, he called her name.

A warm rush inside her told her that he too had found release.

He dipped down and took her mouth again, but there was no urgency in this kiss. It was languorous and tender.

She whimpered and cuddled closer when he slipped from her body.

Sienna felt empty and needed her whole form against his again.

Liam settled her in his arms, shifting them so his back and wings were against the wall of the hot spring.

His eyes found hers. "Are ye well?" This was a half-demand, something a satiated man shouldn't have been capable of.

Her breath caught.

His handsome face was flushed with color up to his ears, and his mouth swollen from their kisses. His damp, dark curls were mussed, and he looked well-loved.

He'd declared that men could not be beautiful, but Liam MacLeod was the most beautiful thing she'd ever seen.

"Sienna?"

She gathered her composure, and smirked. "I'm braw."

He growled and tugged her closer, kissing Sienna breathless, all over again.

chapter fourteen

Sienna didn't want to go back home and face everything her *mórai* had confessed to. It was too much to contemplate or process. Perhaps to even understand.

She didn't want to accept the sense of betrayal or the pain that came with that, it was a physical wound in her chest that bled into her limbs. She wanted it to be how it had always been with her grandmother, nothing but love and trust.

That was gone.

A sense of helplessness filled her when she contemplated trying to heal it.

Not even magic would help.

Even thinking the word made everything feel worse. Her grandmother had been motivated by something Sienna had always wanted. Something she couldn't even remember ever having. Somehow it ruined her long-term desire to have magic.

She wanted nothing to do with it now.

Sienna wanted to stay in this cave, in her halfling's arms forever.

Where reality couldn't get to them.

Maybe they could live there?

He could hide from the Fae Warriors, and she could avoid her family. They could live off the land, like they did in the exile camp. Liam could hunt.

Surely, he was as skilled at hunting as he was a warrior. They could make this cave a home and seal the whole realm out.

The fantasy had merit.

The warm waters lapped at her languid body, and she sighed against Liam.

Her lover.

Sienna was no longer innocent of a man's touch—although she'd shed that the first time they'd come to the falls to bathe.

This was *more*.

She'd given herself to Liam, and she didn't regret it.

Sienna smiled and breathed him, them, and the humidity of the cave in, letting it wash over her senses. A musky smell from their lovemaking mixed with the scent of the moist and mossy rocks around them, and Liam's clean skin.

She could also hear the cold waters of the rushing falls at the mouth of the cave, and it was a pleasant contradiction, the warmth hanging in the air above the pool, and the chill from the nearby waterfall.

It just solidified her desire to stay right where she was. Even if her skin shriveled from remaining in the hot spring too long.

Sienna didn't care.

How long had they been in the cave?

Several hours, no doubt.

It'd been well after midnight when she'd fled her home.

"Sienna? We should go, a'fore the magic a' the

lights die."

Sienna roused at Liam's low voice. She must've drifted off. "I don't want to." She crushed her eyes shut, and snuggled into his warm chest, squeezing his torso.

The warm waters caressed her body as she shifted, moving more fully into Liam's side.

He didn't deny her, of course. He held her and kissed her forehead.

She smiled and sighed again, pressing ever closer.

His warm breath tickled her cheek and she leaned into him even more.

Liam was so tender. Gentle, and made her feel cherished. Sienna had chosen well when she'd picked this halfling to be her first lover.

Her only lover.

Ever.

The forbidden idea made her shiver.

She couldn't imagine wanting another man like she wanted Liam.

They both had dangers that would affect their lives.

They couldn't be together.

It was impossible to make it work, so her foolish thoughts and mixed emotions would only leave her with more hurt.

Sienna was far from stupid.

When—not *if*—Liam left, she'd be shattered.

It was too late for anything else.

One night in his arms had sealed her heart's fate.

He'd made her a vow that he would always come

after her, but how would that help her situation?

What a foolish lass.

"Sienna, love," Liam's voice was more urgent, and he gently cupped her shoulder.

She stilled and couldn't look at his face. The endearment rolled over her and made her heart stutter.

Love?

She refused to see meaning in it.

Sienna swallowed and eased away from Liam's large body. She needed to break their physical contact before she did or said something incredibly foolish. "I don't want to leave." Her voice was petulant to her own ears, like a whining bairn.

Liam framed her face, forcing her eyes up to meet his.

She didn't push him away.

Maybe she couldn't.

"If 'twas possible, I'd stay here wit' ye fore'er."

Sienna's heart cantered, making her pulse woosh in her temples. She reinforced the command that she could *not* read into his words, or the softness in his violet eyes. Worst still was the sincerity on his handsome face.

She couldn't read into anything. She had to protect herself, no matter how the voice in the back of her head declared that it was too late for that.

Sienna fought shivers that had nothing to do with the temperature in the humid cave.

Liam rubbed her upper arms. "Cold?"

She shook her head because unwanted emotions threatened to swallow her whole. She ordered herself to get away from him, when her body shuddered for more, demanding she move back into his embrace, beg him to hold her. Kiss her. Make love to her again.

You're a mess.

She told herself it was only the debris of wreckage her *mórai* had caused with her forbidden confessions, and not more to do with what this halfling Warrior had done to her heart. "I can't face her," Sienna whispered. "I just…can't."

"Ye dinnae need address ever'thin today, but we need ta go home." Again, his voice and expression were so earnest, so caring.

Sienna told herself to breathe. "You're right. I don't like that you are, but I can't argue."

Liam smirked.

She found herself smiling, if only a little. "What?"

He grinned. "My lass always argues."

The possessive words stole her breath all over again and her tummy dipped. She wanted to declare how much she wanted to be *his* lass.

"Let's dress, love," Liam whispered. He stood and flittered the water off his wings.

Sienna sat on her arse in the pool, trying not to stare at the play of his muscles, his pectorals, defined stomach, and even the way the dim lights danced colors over his iridescent skin.

He was so gorgeous; her mouth went dry.

His bruises had faded, and his sword wound looked better, but she didn't fool herself that she was observing him with a healer's eye. She hadn't considered his injuries at all that night.

She forbade herself from looking at his manhood—Sienna was already aching to have him again, and even if she didn't want to admit it, Liam *was* right.

They needed to get home.

Sienna took the hand he offered and found her way to her feet with his gentle encouragement.

When they exited the warm pool, she regretted that he went right to his clothing, without so much as a small kiss or another embrace.

She reluctantly padded over to the boulder where she'd left her garment.

"I ken a spell," Liam said, catching her attention as she donned her still-damp sleeping gown. He was dressed and fastening his belt to secure his plaid in place.

"A spell?"

"Aye, ta keep us dry fer the flight home."

"Aye?" Sienna cocked her head to one side.

He smirked like before, and it was just as appealing.

She closed the distance between them, barely ignoring the demanding tingle in her fingertips to touch him. "You knew this spell the whole time? So, it wasn't necessary for us to get wet, flying through the waterfall to come into this cave?"

"Nay."

"Nay?" Sienna arched an eyebrow.

"'Twas necessary." Liam's expression was so serious.

She stared him down until his mouth was

rippling, as if he was fighting a smile.

"Why was it necessary?" she prompted.

"I had ta get ye naked somehow."

Sienna tried to mock glare, but she broke into a fit of giggles, and let him sweep her up into his arms. "I should be so fashed with you!" she managed to accuse, but her body betrayed her, settling close into Liam's embrace.

"Nay," he repeated, amusement wrapping the word.

"Why not?"

"I gave ye what ye wanted, dinnae?" His violet eyes lost some of their mirth and were suddenly all heat and intensity.

Her cheeks burned, and a bolt of awareness shot all over her body, especially where they touched. Sienna wound her arms around his neck. "Aye, you did."

She met his kiss when Liam dipped down and took her mouth.

Sienna nestled closer as Liam lifted them into the paling night sky, and he wanted to close his eyes and breathe everything in. Fly off with her in his embrace, avoid everything closing in on them.

The problem was, there was no place safe for them.

Not in the Fae Realm anyway.

Sienna's arms were around his neck, and he held

her tight, as he stretched his wings to take them back to the clearing in the exile camp.

They'd only been gone a few hours and it was still dark, but daylight had already started to encroach on the horizon, swallowing the darkness inch by inch. Soon the blacks and grays would meld into the pinks and golds normal for the Fae Realm's day sky. Sooner still, the stars would wink out one by one, as if candles being extinguished.

He pumped his wings twice, sailing on a thermal and holding Sienna safely against his body. The warm winds caressed his face and legs, rustling his plaid and her chemise.

Her flying hair tickled his cheek, and he looked down, catching her burnished gaze.

His lover wore a soft smile on her delectable mouth. "I understand now," she said.

"What?" Liam asked.

"You're free when you fly. Truly free."

Emotion took him by surprise, and a lump of mixed notions settled in his throat. Liam blinked and nodded because words were impossible. He inhaled, taking in the fresh early morning scents.

Sienna's instant understanding of him and his desire to soar through the air was something he wasn't aware he'd needed until just now.

Validation.

Something he could never get from his father or rectify against his recklessness and the danger he'd put himself in, not to mention all the exiles.

Liam cleared his throat and fell into the

tenderness in her expression.

His Fae healer meant more to him than words. Or perhaps, he knew the words, but refused to utter them.

It wasn't like they could end up together.

Eventually, he'd have to walk away from her, no matter how much it would kill him to do so. As soon as she was safe from Wardric, he would have to go home.

Liam had no choice.

They neared the clearing, but instead of the normal peacefulness of the pre-dawn hours, a din of shouts caught his attention. Dread washed over him.

"Do you hear that?" Sienna asked. Her pretty face was stamped with alarm. She shifted higher in his grip, plastering her cheek to his as they both looked down.

"Aye." He nodded and dove lower, driving past the last few treetops before the clearing opened to see the cluster of treed homes encircling it.

Fellow exiles scrambled everywhere, rushing in and out of homes, shouting about something.

Someone had started a large bonfire at the center of the clearing, and at any other time, it might've been welcoming, or an indication of a celebration.

That was not the case with the scene Liam witnessed. Fear was in the air, and the people's movements were too frantic.

He landed harder than intended outside of Sienna's family's tree, jarring his sword wound, which protested with a throb.

Sienna struggled against his hold, accidentally tossing an elbow to his sore ribs as she scrambled to get free.

Funny, when they'd been in the cave not one of his injuries had bothered him at all.

He flapped his wings for balance, and his lover threw him an apologetic glance as her bare feet hit the grassy ground.

Liam glanced around. Exiles carried things out to the clearing. Broken tables, splintered chairs, and even a trunk that no longer had a bottom.

People still dashed past them, in and out of nearby treed homes, despite that the sun had not yet risen.

Some exiles were dressed, others still in sleeping clothing, and everyone seemed disheveled and scared. The air was ripe and thick with tension.

They tossed their broken things into the fire.

What the hell?

"What's going on?" Sienna asked, but no one stopped to answer.

Liam grabbed her hand, and they moved toward her tree's front door.

Her grandmother stood outside of it, her green eyes wide and her shoulders slumped as she too looked around the clearing. The elderly Fae woman didn't speak when she saw them.

Ealeric ran up to them, ripping his sister from Liam's grip. He embraced Sienna, hard. "Thank the Goddess you're well," he breathed.

"Of course, I'm well," Sienna retorted, irritation wrapping her words as she wiggled out of her brother's arms. "I was with Liam."

Had Liam not comprehended the panic in the air, he might have puffed out his chest at the confidence in his lover's voice.

"Well, I suppose it was better you and Liam were not here." The Fae man's dark eyes bore into Liam.

He fought the urge to fidget.

"What in five hells happened?" Sienna demanded.

"Fae Warriors came…looking for Liam."

chapter Fifteen

"**Y**ou! This is all *your* fault!" An angry shout went up, and a large man with long blond hair stalked toward Liam, Sienna and Ealeric. He was pointing a finger like he was thrusting a dagger, as he marched over.

Liam whirled around and threw his arm up when Sienna tried to rush around him. He would protect her from this unknown exile.

Ealeric flanked him, also in front of his sister. "Baret, stop. This will do no good. The Warriors have gone; the danger has passed."

A few other exiles, men, and women alike, trailed on Baret's heels, and they all wore anger and accusation like a cloak.

Liam sucked in a breath. Their fury aimed at him wasn't wrong.

He couldn't retort.

Did they know he was half human?

There were murmurs of "banished Warrior" and words of rancor, but none of the whispers included "abomination" or "half-blood."

He could only pray Feneal's spell held, and these people thought he was indeed an outcast Fae Warrior, and not a halfling.

As if Liam's thought of the man's name had conjured him, Feneal slid between those in the angry crowd.

"Baret! Hold! Banished Warrior is not at fault! Like us." The Fae man who'd hidden Liam's secret spread his arms and held his palms high, as if he would throw a spell.

It didn't seem to deter the oversized, fair-haired man and his companions.

"You side with a stranger, Feneal?" Baret demanded, as though a bitter taste filled his words.

"They sought a half-blooded abomination," someone else from the crowd said. She came forward, wearing a similar sleeping gown to Sienna's. "This man is not that.". Her dark hair barely skimmed her shawl-covered shoulders. "Do not be fools. Use your magic. He is no half-blood. Besides, each and every one of you was a stranger when you first arrived here."

Liam's heart rebounded against his sore ribs. He could barely hear the crowd of exiles through the blood thundering in his ears. Sweat broke out on his brow, despite the mildness of the early dawn hour's weather.

Would they see the Fae woman's reason?

"Let him speak for himself!" Baret's commanding shout quieted the crowd.

The man stepped closer to Liam and Ealeric, but Feneal didn't move, nor did he lower his raised palm, seemingly ready to throw magic if needed.

Eilidh joined them, parting the group of dissidents and clearing her throat. "He need not explain himself to any of you." The elderly Fae woman's voice was an order, and the crowd quieted from whispers to silence.

They may not respect Feneal, but it was obvious they all revered Sienna's *mórai*.

When they'd arrived back in the clearing and Liam had first laid eyes on her, she'd looked tiny and defeated, not far from the entrance to her home.

The elderly woman now stood tall and her thin shoulders firm, tight. She was imperious.

"As Lainya said, we were all strangers when we first arrived here. Exiled, but not alone."

Still, no one spoke, and Eilidh's green gaze landed on Liam.

For some reason, he wanted to stand taller, or shift on his booted feet.

"Like the rest of you, Liam has lost everything. He was broken and left for dead by those who paid us an unwanted visit tonight, tearing us from our beds. Warriors, who are his former brothers. He was banished, and not expected to survive. My granddaughter brought him to me for healing, as I have done for most, if not *all* of you over the years. Now that he is on his feet, he will no doubt contribute to our community. He's a credit to us exiles, not a danger."

Liam watched the acceptance settle over the expressions of the clearing's residents, as awe for Eilidh seeped into his pores.

Sienna's grandmother issued edicts that were lies, and the group of banished Fae believed every word.

Thank Jesu, as his Uncle Duncan would say.

He swallowed, and exchanged a glance with Ealeric, then Sienna.

His lover took his hand and squeezed.

Of course, he couldn't refuse her. Liam sucked in a breath and entwined his fingers with hers.

"It is early. The spectacle has passed. Clean your homes, as we must do to ours." Eilidh gestured to her tree, her grandchildren, and to the clearing as a whole. "I am sorry for all the things they destroyed, but we proved we are not harboring any abomination, so the Fae Warriors should leave us be. Goddess knows they do not like exploring Grànnda Falls. No one was harmed, and for that I am grateful, as I know the rest of you are. Things, we can, and will, replace. Working together, as we always do."

There were a few murmurs through the crowd, then nods, and finally, the exiles dispersed.

Feneal exchanged a long look with Sienna's *mórai*, but neither spoke aloud.

"That was brilliant, *Mórai*!" Ealeric pumped his fist.

"You will nay think so when your empty belly aches. Baret will not be eager to share his next kill with us." Eilidh's tight brow matched her frown.

"I can hunt," Sienna's brother retorted, undeterred.

"As can I," Liam said, his voice thick and rusty to his ears.

"Where's Amalie?" Sienna asked, pointedly looking at Ealeric, and not their grandmother.

"Inside, where we all should be," Eilidh said, her voice suddenly urgent. She didn't seem to be bothered that Sienna refused to acknowledge her. "Quickly, before they change their minds about Liam." She gestured for them to enter the treed home. "Unfortunately, we've got a mess to tidy."

"I'm not ready to speak with you," Sienna declared when her grandmother sat at the table. His lover didn't sound harsh, but she was resolute.

Liam quietly shut the door, but he was in no danger of waking anyone.

Amalie, who had not been outside, was up and dressed, despite the early hour, in the pale-yellow gown he'd seen her in most often.

She tended something cooking over the hearth and didn't speak when the rest of her family and Liam joined her in the dining area.

Had the elderly healer bore any of the truths revealed before he and Sienna had gone to the Falls, or had she kept Sienna's siblings from it?

Perhaps Amalie could've been spared, but Ealeric was man enough to handle it—and would want to act to protect his family. The Fae man had a right to demand every detail.

The arrival of Fae Warriors searching for Liam had certainly given Eilidh an excuse to postpone any further confessions, and it seemed their home had been inflicted with the same damage as others evidenced outside by the bonfire.

One of the chairs from their table lay on its back, a spindly leg broken and barely hanging on. Shattered pottery littered the floor, since gathered in a pile. Obviously, Amalie had already started cleaning up.

Liam scanned the room for any other damage,

and only noticed minor things, like drapes not hanging straight and a pile of wood for burning no longer stacked neatly by the hearth.

Perhaps the lass had tidied a great deal while they conversed outside.

Sienna's brother asked her something at a whisper, so Liam didn't catch it, but his lover only shook her head, her mouth a hard line.

When Ealeric's dark eyes landed on him, Liam gave a half-shrug. Nothing of what had transpired was his secret to share.

Sienna and her *mórai* would have to reveal what they wished when they chose.

Liam would just do what he could to keep them all safe from Wardric and get Sienna and her grandmother out of the agreement, somehow.

He had to.

Even though the *how* eluded him.

Eilidh looked at her oldest grandchild and gave a nod saturated with sadness. She was again the morose being that Liam had first seen outside of the tree home when they'd arrived back in the clearing. "That is no longer my primary concern." Her green eyes landed on Liam, sharp and worried, yet determined. "You must get them out of here. For your safety and theirs." She squared her shoulders, as if bracing for an argument.

"What?" he sputtered.

"Take my grandchildren to the Human Realm."

"Nay, *Mórai*, 'tis mad." Ealeric made a cutting gesture with his hand to punctuate his refusal. He paced by the table in the dining area, shaking his head as he went and kicking the broken chair out of his way.

"Aye, lad. 'Tis the only assurance you and your sisters will be safe." Their grandmother's voice was just as hard.

It was a battle of wills.

Sienna didn't often see her brother so serious, none of his jovial personality evident. She would've been impressed at Ealeric's rare show of being an adult if it were any other time.

Instinct told her their grandmother hadn't confessed to her siblings what she'd walked into earlier, the dark family secrets, and Sienna's unwanted betrothal.

The fight was not fair because her brother did not know why they were in so much danger. There was no way he would believe it had something to do with Liam, not after their grandmother's request.

She was tempted to shout everything *Mórai* had done and said, including the agreement with Wardric. Had Amalie been asleep, she might've, but she couldn't shatter her sister's heart like that. The lass already felt responsible for their mother's death, irrational as that was. Sienna wouldn't burden her with the way their father had died or why their family truly didn't have any magic.

Ealeric could handle it.

It wasn't fair to put that on sweet, innocent Amalie.

"Nay. I won't go. I will not leave you," her brother declared.

"Neither will I." Her sister's voice was low; but it was about as firm as Sienna had ever heard her. She stood by the hearth, her hands in tight fists at her sides, and her jaw set. Her countenance turned more serious than Sienna would've thought Amalie capable of.

It was almost as if they had switched personalities. Her sister vocal and Sienna sitting silent, observant. That had little to do with the fact she wasn't speaking to the woman who'd raised her.

Liam too, looked entirely stunned at her grandmother's declaration. He'd paled out and his pretty violet eyes widened. He hadn't moved far from the front door. His arms were crossed over his broad chest, and he leaned against the wall, his wings at rest behind him. His pensive expression meant perhaps he was considering her grandmother's desperate order.

Her tummy quivered at the idea.

The Human Realm?

It would delay dealing with Wardric, aye, but for how long?

The mage couldn't get to her, her sister, or her brother if they weren't in the realm, right?

She could see Liam's world.

Maybe stay with him?

Forever?

Her heart tripped at the forbidden notion.

Móraí had no intention of going with them. Even though Sienna was devastated by what the elderly woman had done, she loved her. Wouldn't leave her to the evil mage's wrath. Couldn't.

Nay. We cannot go.

Disappearing would thwart the mage's plans, and would no doubt place her grandmother in grave danger.

From what Liam had told her, the man who intended to marry her embodied evil like no other, and whose power was unparalleled. Without magic, her grandmother would have no protection. She was no match for him.

No matter the magic of their closest neighbors and the outcasts' respect for *Móraí*, they were no defense against a king's mage. Nor would any exile dare go up against one. They'd all prefer banishment over torture and death. Wardric could kill any of them without much resistance or likely punishment. Why would the king care about the fate of the people he'd exiled?

"I'll do it." Liam's whisper was as effective as a shout in the tense silence.

All eyes, including Sienna's, landed on her lover.

He pushed off the wall and flexed his wings. Planted his feet and held his broad shoulders stiff. Her halfling sucked in an audible breath. "I dinnae how we'll get ta the Stones, but I'm in."

Her brother and sister's protests followed instantly, identical, and loud.

Ealeric's dark gaze pinned Sienna to the chair she sat in. "Why aren't you saying anything?"

She opened her mouth, but no words were born. She couldn't tell him he lacked all the facts to make an informed decision and their grandmother was right.

She couldn't tell him why the elderly healer was so anxious for them to leave the realm. "W-w-e—" Sienna cleared her throat and tried again. "We should go with Liam."

Her brother slid into a chair; his shoulders slumped and his disappointment heavy in the air. Probably more about Sienna not backing his side as much as the thought of leaving.

As much as they disagreed, they were usually allies when it counted most, so guilt gnawed at Sienna—for more than one reason.

Ealeric leaned forward, planting his elbows on his knees, and stared at her so hard she squirmed. He blew out a breath, narrowed his eyes, then appraised their grandmother with the same scrutiny Sienna had barely survived a few heartbeats before.

She swallowed and glanced at Liam; a small thing that ended in something intense. She couldn't look away from the halfling she'd grown to care about so much in the small time they'd shared.

Her lover nodded slightly, reinforcing his agreement with her *móraí*.

"Something is not right here," her brother announced. He resumed pacing and shook his head. "Sienna knows something you're not saying, *Móraí*. I think the stray knows, too. Why else would he agree to this madness?"

Sienna didn't say a word.

Ealeric was sharp; she'd never fault him for that.

"I'm not going as far as the edge of the clearing until someone tells me exactly what in five hells is going on here."

Liam cursed, but it was too low to make out the words.

She glanced at her grandmother.

Móraí closed her eyes.

chapter sixteen

"**N**ay, I don't want to go. I will not go!"

Sienna held her sister while she cried. Amalie had refused to leave the room for the truth-telling, and— as predicted—it wasn't something her youngest sibling could handle.

She shouldn't have *had* to handle it.

Her own rage at her *móraí* was reignited.

A little voice whispered in the back of her head— *hypocrite*.

She was upset at her grandmother for keeping truths from Sienna for her own protection—the betrothal notwithstanding—and Sienna had wanted to do the same for her sister, for the same reason.

In both cases, the information was something Sienna and Amalie had the right to know.

She sighed and her ire cooled, slightly.

Sienna didn't have the answers now. They had to figure out the next steps. She needed to deal with one thing at a time, starting with questions, or tasks, for which she did know the solutions.

Her brother continued to be staunch in his refusal to leave *Móraí*.

Did that make things better or worse?

"*Móraí*," Sienna said.

It was her turn for all eyes to land on her.

She took a deep breath and set aside her earlier

thoughts of refusing to speak to her grandmother.

How else was she going to get the answers she needed?

Sienna stared at her hands, and then turned them over on her lap.

Trioblóid — who'd finally come out from hiding — chirruped his concern from the hearth. No doubt he could feel the tension in the room. He was pastel blues and pinks, but still tinged with the yellows of alarm.

Her brother had told her no one had seen him for a few hours.

Her bogle had probably hidden because he was upset at her for running away, as much as he'd feared the Fae Warriors.

After a small cuddle, her beloved pet had kept his distance. A sign that Trio had not forgiven Sienna for leaving him yet.

"*Mò ghràdh*?" her grandmother prompted as a few more heartbeats passed before she could say what was on her mind.

"If the Human Realm means safety, then we'll *all* go." Sienna made eye contact with her lover, and Liam cocked his head to one side.

Did he disagree with her idea?

"Nay, lass." *Mórai* shook her head to punctuate the denial.

"Why not?" Ealeric demanded before Sienna could retort. "'Tis a perfect solution. 'Twill get you away from Wardric, too. Away from the oath spell."

"Nay, it dinnae work as such," Liam said, his expression stamped with regret.

"Why not?" her brother repeated, this time, harder. He was perched on the edge of the chair, as if he would spring back to his feet at any moment.

"The magic," *Mórai* said. "If I leave, it is a violation of my oath, and it will make me sick in the least, and kill me at the most."

Sienna exchanged a glance with Liam.

How had he known that?

"Then I will stay. The lasses can go with the stray." Ealeric narrowed his eyes, daring an argument from anyone.

Her grandmother sighed. "Nay, love. You cannot stay here."

"Wardric will kill ye when he realizes Sienna has gone," Liam said. His expression was serious, but concern radiated from his violet eyes.

"Perhaps." *Mórai* nodded. Her thin shoulders were loose, and her countenance calm. As if she'd already accepted that particular consequence.

"Nay, *Mórai!*" Amalie wailed, voicing what Sienna was feeling. She was crying again, and clinging to Sienna, leaning into her and half-strewn across her lap.

She slid her arm around her sister's shoulders, then rubbed her back.

The slight elderly woman sat taller in the chair. "The choices I made are my own, my loves. I made them to better your lives and return what should have always been yours in the first place. You were not born of my son to live your lives magicless as an exile." Her grandmother's mouth shook before she calmed, and her green eyes flashed.

The inner strength Sienna had always admired about her *móraí* shined through her misty eyes and the stubborn set of her lips.

Her grandmother rarely wavered once she'd made a decision. The fact that she cared little about her own fate made Sienna's gut ache with helplessness.

"I care not for what I've never known," her brother said, and for the first time, his voice shook from emotion.

Sienna's eyes burned with tears, but she refused to cry.

Liam met her gaze, and he looked as if he wanted to comfort her, but she was still holding her sniffling sister.

"Oh, lad," *Móraí* said, the words thick with regret. "It should have been so different. Healing is your birthright, as much as it is Sienna's and Amalie's. Can you not feel it within you, even with what you're missing?"

Ealeric closed his eyes and gave a small nod. Like his sisters, he had been trained by their grandmother in natural healing.

Her brother often scoffed and acted as if he wasn't interested, but he could name more herbs and plants and list their uses from memory than Sienna ever could.

When they were wee, and memorizing had been a part of daily lessons, her brother hadn't had to look at the tomes even once.

She'd always been jealous of that. She'd had to

work hard. Things had always come easier to him, yet Ealeric often distanced himself from using what they'd learned, even now.

"If I am dead—"

Amalie screeched a protest at the same time Ealeric started to speak one, but *Móraí* raised a palm, and both her siblings quieted.

"If I am dead," their grandmother repeated, "before you have your magic returned, none of you is a threat to Wardric. If you go to the Human Realm, it will buy me some time to come up with another plan."

Her brother scoffed. "A plan? How, with no magic?"

Liam cleared his throat and stepped closer to the table. "I believe yer *Móraí* is a lady of resources."

Her grandmother's expression changed to one of approval at Liam's compliment.

Sienna frowned.

"I'll take the lasses," he said. "Keep 'em safe. Then I will return—with help."

"Help?" Amalie asked before Sienna, or their brother could remark. For the first time since they'd started this conversation, her sister's voice didn't shake.

Liam closed his eyes and took a breath, as if fortifying himself before he spoke. "My da. He was a Fae Warrior and has more magic than I do. He kens a thing or two abou' oath spells. My aunt, weel, she used ta be the princess a' this realm."

Ealeric was the first to break the very pregnant silence that fell and lasted a few heartbeats. He was on his feet, his expression a mix of anger and wonder. "You are kin to the banished princess, Alana?"

Sienna gaped.

Liam winced. "Aye. Although, she dinnae be *banished*, as ye say. She fled, ta be with my Uncle Alex. My da was her bodyguard, an' went, too."

"The human laird." *Móraí* said, looking thoughtful.

Sienna and her siblings were too young to remember but she'd heard the stories of the runaway princess and her personal bodyguard, who'd disappeared years ago. "They fled to the Human Realm?" she whispered.

Her lover nodded; his brows drawn tight.

"The rumors were always there, but steadfastly denied by anyone of position," her grandmother said. "It's more commonly believed that they are lost. Their whereabouts are a highly speculated mystery. The king did not want it known they used the Faery Stones to escape, and live on, of course."

"Your father is Xander," Ealeric breathed.

"Aye." Liam nodded.

"Do you have *any* idea who your father's father is?"

Again, Liam nodded. "The captain of the king's guard, and leader of all the Fae Warriors."

Her brother's rear end hit the chair hard, and air whooshed from his mouth. "I agree with *Móraí*. Take my sisters and go. It is not safe for you to be here anymore. It was *never* safe, despite Feneal's spell." Ealeric blanched, and the apple of his throat bobbed.

Liam closed his eyes and nodded. "I ken it. I'm sorry fer any danger I put ye in, including yer neighbors. 'Twas ne'er my aim."

"Why did you come here?" her brother demanded, his composure back and fury shining from his dark eyes.

Sienna's heart dipped to her tummy, and she gently urged her sister to sit up. She moved to Liam's side. "Liam is half Fae and has as much right to come here as you do. He is not an abomination."

He was beautiful, funny, and sweet. He was a good man, strong and loving, and she had no regrets that he'd entered her realm. If he hadn't, they would never have met.

Instead of yelling at her as Ealeric was prone to do, he pinned her lover with a stare. "Your…family…will help us?"

Liam nodded. "I'm sure of it."

"Let us get some rest," *Móraí* said. "Then we must seek some help from one of our own."

Sleep had failed Sienna, so she'd dressed quietly in the small room she shared with her sister. She didn't want to disturb Amalie, who'd fallen asleep after some more tears and still rested peacefully. Sienna surveyed the damage in her home, determined to right it before dealing with what her family had decided during the strained conversation that morning.

She and Amalie would go with Liam to the

Human Realm, and Ealeric would stay behind with their grandmother. Her task was to ask her lover's family to return to the Fae Realm and break the oath spell. Free *Móraí* from her magical contract.

Her grandmother was still determined to restore their family's magic, but it was an impossible feat Sienna didn't have the energy to contemplate.

Hopelessness filled her chest and made the seemingly constant lump in her throat burn.

Móraí had said they would need Feneal's help and magic to get to the Field of Light, and Liam had assured them he could open the Faery Stones.

It was all much too overwhelming, despite that her heart leapt a little at the prospect of remaining at Liam's side — at least for now.

However, there was no hope in ignoring all this was in motion because of her grandmother's secrets. She wouldn't fool herself into thinking they stood a real chance of succeeding. Happy ever after was as unlikely as their magic returning.

Her heart took a further dive, sliding all the way to her toes, when she entered the small room she was hoping to find her lover in, but Liam wasn't there.

Her grandmother's medicine room was destroyed.

The worktable still stood undisturbed, but all the drawers of dried herbs, plants and healing medicines had been pulled out and dumped, leaving a mix of piles of leaves and colorful powders all over the table and floor.

Bottles meant for liquids and jars for salves were

everywhere, instead of neatly stacked or lined up. Some were broken, adding *wet* to the mess of it all.

Why?

If the Fae Warriors had truly only been looking for Liam, there was no purpose to all this debris and mess.

Why ruin things meant to heal wounds and the infirm?

"Bastards," Sienna spat. She whirled in the small room, further surveying the destruction.

The cot she'd come to think of as Liam's was overturned, pillows and blankets strewn about, proving that he'd not tried to rest, either. The two chairs both lay on their sides, but at least they weren't broken.

"Why would they do this?" she demanded.

Sienna had worked so hard to build up the stores of medicines. The labors of years had been demolished in moments.

She barely held in her anguish behind a hand-covered whimper.

Liam's large palm slid onto her forearm, and his welcoming heat sank into her skin.

She hadn't heard him come into the room, but it didn't matter. Sienna wanted to lean into him, or ask him to hold her, but her mixed emotions about what her *mórai* had done, who Liam really was, and what she saw before her, churned low in her gut. She wanted to scream.

Fae Warriors had ripped to pieces something she held dear. They'd been looking for this gorgeous halfling who'd stolen her heart in a matter of days.

Her grandmother had betrayed her.

All of it together was too much.

"Hey," her lover whispered, squeezing her wrist gently.

One look into his concerned violet eyes had her own pricking with tears, and she was so tired of it.

All of it.

Sienna bit her bottom lip to stave off the threatening sob and threw herself at Liam's chest. She called herself a fool for not being able to do anything else.

He caught her up, as he had since the day she'd met him.

"'Tis all gonna be okay."

"O-okay?" she whispered, maintaining his gaze instead of burying her face against him like she'd wanted.

Liam nodded.

"I'd never heard that word before you said it, last night by the Falls. What does it mean?" She understood that it was an affirmative, but it was…odd.

Chagrin settled over his handsome face. "'Tis just somethin' my aunt says. It means all will be weel, which it will."

Sienna sniffled and nodded, snuggling into his body. It didn't feel true, but she couldn't say that, either.

"Yer *mórai* was in the wrong, 'tis true."

She stilled. "And?" she whispered, not looking up from his neck.

"Ye love her still, dinnae?"

Sienna nodded. Still didn't move out of his embrace. Maybe she couldn't, even if she wasn't fond of where he was probably going.

"My da...he was right about e'erthin' he ever warned me about comin' ta this realm."

"What's your point?" she demanded, even though it wasn't exactly a mystery.

Liam's expression was soft, and she hated that it sucked her right back in. "Jus' that parents—grandparents—make choices fer us sometimes they feel are in our best interests. E'en if we dinnae agree."

Sienna glared. "So, it was in my *best interests* to giving my hand in marriage to a monster?"

Instead of arguing or yelling, he shook his head and cupped her cheeks, so she would be forced to look into his beautiful eyes. "Nay, love. Eilidh only wanted ta grant yer greatest wish. Somethin' ye should've already had. Yer magic, yer birthright."

"Means matter much more than the ends," she ground out.

"Aye, I dinnae disagree. 'Specially in this case."

Sienna sighed and bumped both fists against his chest. "What're we going to do?"

"I'm gonna take ye an' Amalie home with me." Liam grabbed her wrists and pressed a warm kiss to her knuckles.

Her heart sped off, making her head spin with the rush of blood in her ears.

It'd already been decided, had it not?

Then why was hearing him say it like that so exciting and yet, so petrifying?

"Your father, and Princess Alana…they'll really help save *Móraí*?" She swallowed and her eyes burned with a new round of tears.

"Aye, love. They will help."

"I can't marry Wardric."

Liam growled. "I ferbid it." He tugged her closer and wrapped his wings around her.

Sienna might've smiled at his vehemence if it was another time, but her lower belly quivered and warmed anyways. "I wasn't finished, Liam." No accusation was in her voice, as intended. She just heard the defeat and exhaustion that dominated her body and soul.

He rested his forehead against hers.

She sucked in a breath and closed her eyes to stave off tears. "I haven't forgiven her. But I can't lose her, either."

chapter seventeen

"*This* is the man ta help us?" Liam tried and failed to keep the incredulity from his voice. Aye, the man had seemed lucid in the pre-dawn hours of the day before, when he'd intervened by the bonfire, but that man was nowhere in sight compared to the large figure before them now.

"Liam."

His name was all admonishment from Sienna, but he couldn't help his impression of the pitiful creature.

The Fae man had size, aye, but that seemed to be Feneal's only redeeming quality. Black dirt coated his clothes, and his trews were deteriorating rags, rough and uneven, stopping about mid-calf. Brown stains and holes covered his leine, and was probably white once, perhaps years ago.

His long hair was caked with mud and grime. The dark strands stuck out in multiple directions.

Feneal sat in the dirt, like a wee child, and laughed to himself, as if filled with glee.

Sienna grabbed Liam's arm and urged him to follow as she approached, but he didn't really want to close the small distance between them.

The warm early evening breeze shifted, and in seconds, it was even more obvious Feneal did not traverse to the Falls to bathe.

Liam detested the smell.

"The spell he put on you to hide your human side helped save your life, Liam MacLeod, so be kind. Not to mention he saved you again yesterday, with Baret. We owe him many thanks."

She didn't spare him a glance as she spoke, just continued dragging him toward the exiled Fae man, so Liam didn't answer.

All too soon, they were standing adjacent to Feneal.

Liam shifted their position downwind from him.

"Feneal, can we speak with you?" Sienna asked, her voice gentle, as if addressing a wee bairn.

He laughed again and didn't acknowledge their presence. He picked up a flat rock about the size of his palm. A brightly colored bird was painted on it, a fair rendition of a josta.

Feneal chuckled, passed his other hand over the stone's surface, and muttered a spellword under his breath.

The bright red bird hopped out of the rock, shaking its yellow comb as though woken from a deep sleep. It called a raucous tweet, flapped its wings, and fluttered off.

Feneal clapped his hands in delight like a child. He was very pleased with himself.

The spell was close to the conjuring word Liam had used when he'd arrived in the Fae Realm and made his own josta bird. He'd have to remember the variation for later.

At least the man held magic, but bringing a bird to life wasn't what they needed.

They needed real power and protection, serious magical knowledge to escape the stealth spells surrounding the Faery Stones and the Field of Light.

Hopefully, Feneal could actually help.

"And I do not have any magic at all," Sienna whispered on a sigh.

Liam smirked. "Be kind, Sienna."

She threw him a dark look, narrowed eyes and all.

He grinned.

Sienna lifted her skirts and squatted down next to the Fae man. "Feneal, we really need your help."

"Help?" Feneal whispered.

"Aye, help." She smiled slightly.

The man looked up at Liam abruptly, as if he'd just realized Sienna was not alone. His crystal blue eyes speared through him.

Liam had to stop himself from stepping back. He flexed his wings and planted his feet.

Those eyes were bright and lucid, not what he'd expected after they'd witnessed the little magic display.

Maybe the exile wasn't as mad as people thought he was.

Sienna had explained that his awareness seemed to come and go.

His long, tangled beard was as messy as his hair. It somehow made his gaze even more intense.

"Xander," Feneal said.

Liam blinked. "What?" Shock rolled over him.

Sienna looked between him and the Fae man. Surprise crossed her pretty face, showing she was just as stunned as he.

"Xander child."

Liam nodded. "Aye, I am Xander's son. Ye ken my father?"

Feneal looked away from them again. He whispered, "Xander child," a few more times, then seemed to tune them out, caressing the four or five other painted rocks on the ground in front of him.

Liam exchanged a look with Sienna, and his lover shrugged then released a breath before she scrambled to her feet.

"Stew," Feneal said, breaking a small silence.

"You're hungry?" Sienna asked.

He nodded.

"I will bring you supper, Feneal." Her voice was that same gentle, even tone she'd used when they'd joined the large, exiled man.

"Now?"

Sienna threw Liam a look, her eyes wide and her expression apprehensive.

"Go, love," he said, pressing a kiss to the back of her hand. "I'll stay here wit' Feneal."

She nodded, and it took all he was made of not to watch her go, and instead focus on this man who was somehow supposed to help them in this altered state.

How would it even be possible?

Liam cleared his throat. "Thank ye."

The man met his gaze again. "Why?" This was clear, and hard; a demand, as if Liam had just insulted him.

"Fer casting the spell so 'tis safe fer me here.

Thank ye fer yesterday mornin', as weel."

Feneal nodded and looked back at his painted rocks.

"I see yer a man a' little words," Liam said, more to break an awkward silence. He laughed, too, but it didn't get the desired response, nor did it make him feel at ease.

"Xander child," the man repeated.

Something clicked in his head. "Ye helped 'cause ye knew my father? Ken who I was?"

A simple curt nod was all the answer he received.

"Weel, I thank ye nonetheless."

Feneal didn't answer, nor did he speak again. He juggled two of his painted rocks, as if Liam had left his side. He seemed to sink back into his head, but then he pinned Liam with that clear, contradictory gaze again. "You care for the young healer."

"Aye, I do." He nodded. His heart skipped a beat. Those words weren't nearly enough to describe how he felt, but he wasn't about to explain that to this huge, filthy brute.

The man had spoken an actual full sentence.

Liam didn't want to insult him again, so he hoped his face wasn't betraying his surprise.

Shuffling noises behind them caught his attention, and he glanced over his shoulder.

Sienna headed back toward them. With a trencher and a steaming bowl of stew.

There was no bread or drink with it, but he didn't question her hospitality. She knew the man much better than he. Maybe Feneal didn't like bread.

The Fae man took the food and didn't even thank her before he tucked into it, shoving stew into his mouth messily and loudly. Specks flew onto his shirt and beard.

Liam was half-surprised the man used the wooden spoon she'd brought.

Sienna slid a warm delicate palm onto Liam's forearm and squeezed. "Let's give him peace to eat. We can ask again, later."

He sighed and nodded.

She was right; they hadn't gotten anywhere anyway.

"Will help," Feneal grunted. "Tomorrow. At dark."

His lover's gorgeous face lit up. "You will? Oh, thank you, Feneal."

The Fae man ignored them and continued eating, mumbling to himself between slurps.

Sienna tugged on Liam again, this time more insistent. "C'mon."

"We dinnae tell him what we need."

She smiled and cocked her head to one side. "He'll know. He always just kind of knows."

Liam frowned.

Maybe the large man wasn't mad?

"Let's go, I'm hungry, too. Amalie already set the table."

He nodded, and followed her into her home, but nerves made his appetite evaporate. There was too much riding on Feneal's magic.

Failure meant death, and Liam wouldn't put his

lover and her sister's lives at risk.

"Aye, lad, I assure you, Feneal can help," Sienna's grandmother insisted, gesturing from the dining table.

"Talkin' ta him dinnae convince me," Liam muttered. Although, he hadn't admitted to anyone that the large man had spoken a full sentence.

"I know he doesn't seem like much—" Sienna said.

"Much?" he cut off a scoffing laugh, lest he offend the two females he already cared a great deal about. "He's closer ta nothin'."

"He has powerful magic," Eilidh argued.

Sienna's siblings also sat at the table, unusually silent as they watched the tense exchange. Most of the plates were barely touched.

"Are ye willin' ta stake our lives on it?" Liam retorted.

The elderly Fae healer's mouth was set in a thin, annoyed line.

It wasn't a mystery where Sienna got her stubbornness. Not that he'd ever voice the notion.

Sienna was far from over her anger with her grandmother, and Liam understood. However, she seemed to put it all to the side so they could tackle the task at hand—gathering enough magic to get back to the Human Realm.

What would happen after that, he couldn't guess.

After they flayed him open for sneaking away, his father would help, and so would his aunt, despite the danger in entering the Fae Realm. They were exiles, too, in a way—traitors to the king and probably ordered to be killed on sight.

Liam didn't want to contemplate the *what-if's* — the oath might not be breakable; they might not be able to save Eilidh.

Not to mention, what about Sienna?

He would still have to walk away from her.

His gut clenched.

How could he walk away from her?

The previous evening, she'd sneaked into the medicine room and slept in his arms on the tiny cot. Liam hadn't been able to make love to her again, but he'd been content holding her, if only for a few hours.

"He said tomorrow eve?" Eilidh asked, tugging him from his head.

Sienna nodded as she bit into a piece of bread. "Aye, at dark."

Ealeric shook his head and grunted. "I still do not like this."

Eilidh put up a palm. "There is no choice, lad. Tomorrow eve must be the ideal time, if Feneal chose it. Good." She nodded.

Sienna's brother frowned but didn't retort.

Liam didn't like the idea of leaving the lad and the elderly Fae healer either. They had no magic, and it would likely not take Wardric long to learn his "betrothed" was no longer in the realm. "Perhaps we shall return a'fore he is alerted," he said, to comfort himself, as much as Sienna's family. There was no reason to say the mage's name. There were no doubts as to whom he referred.

"I'm counting on that," Ealeric said, meeting his

gaze.

There was so much unsaid emotion in the Fae man's midnight eyes, Liam's respect for him shot up a few more notches.

He didn't like feeling helpless, either.

"I'll keep the lasses safe," he said.

Ealeric swallowed audibly and gave a curt nod.

Sienna slid a palm onto Liam's thigh under the table and squeezed.

He patted the back of her hand, but couldn't seem to pull away, so Liam held her there, caressing her knuckles with his thumb and wishing they could sneak away.

Wretch.

There was so much going on, and he was thinking about *that*?

Aye.

Liam couldn't help it. He'd had her once and it wasn't nearly enough.

"Sienna and Amalie need not return to this realm," his lover's grandmother announced.

Liam's stomach jumped. Aye, his family would take them in. Without question.

Could he keep his Fae healer?

Wed her?

He didn't even have a moment to think about it before her brother shouted.

"Nay, *Móraí*." Ealeric slammed his fist down onto the table, stopping each of his sisters from speaking. "Enough of this madness."

Amalie shook her head, and Sienna's cheeks

reddened, a frown marring her face.

"We shall return," Sienna said, her voice hard. "With Liam's family. They will help us." Her mouth was set in a determined line.

"*I* matter not, only you do, *mò ghràdh*, and sweet Amalie, *mò bhilis*." Eilidh's expression was just as sober, but her green eyes shone with emotion.

Sienna shook her head. "Nay. You said my birthright was my magic, and returning to the place we lost, as healers of the realm. How can I do that from the Human Realm?"

"Unless you do not truly believe your oath is breakable," Amalie said, her voice wobbling around the words and big fat tears rolling down her cheeks.

Liam frowned.

What was the elderly Fae healer playing at?

Was Amalie's accusation true?

Did Eilidh really believe all hope was lost, and the only thing to do was for Sienna to flee, so Wardric could not force the marriage?

Eilidh would surely die.

They certainly wouldn't get their magic back, either.

"I want you lasses to be safe, and there are no guarantees." The regret their grandmother felt radiated out from her thin frame.

It rolled over Liam and made him sit taller. "I assure ye all, my da an' my aunt have powerful magic, an' they can help. My cousin, Angus, too. He's a halfling, like me, but he has gifts stronger than my own."

"Angus? Is the princess his mother?" Eilidh asked.

He nodded.

"Xander was legendary," Ealeric said.

Liam was torn between rolling his eyes and pride that his father was still known, after being gone from his people for more than twenty years. The former Fae Warrior was not a boastful man, but he had heard stories, especially from his Uncle Duncan, about when they'd rescued Aunt Alana and Uncle Alex from the dungeons of King Fillan's castle. Even he had to admit that his father was a fierce warrior, and the man had always protected his own, even in the Human Realm.

Eilidh didn't relax, but her throat worked as if she'd swallowed. Her countenance was stoic, giving nothing away, but her green eyes filled with a dark and stormy color.

"Trust me," Liam said. He was compelled to do so and didn't question it.

The elderly Fae woman nodded.

"Like we have a choice," Ealeric muttered.

chapter eighteen

The warm night air kissed his cheeks, and ruffled his hair, cooling him and contradicting the patter of his heart. Liam couldn't stop obsessing over what they were about to do. He wished he would've asked Sienna where Feneal lived, but he hadn't wanted her to know he was going to seek the Fae man out and try to get more information from him. Or at least test the theory that he wasn't as mad as he wanted people to believe.

However, after circling the clearing twice on foot, and flying overhead, he'd failed to find the large, exiled man, and he was about to give up and go back to Sienna's family's tree, hopefully before anyone discovered he wasn't in the medicine room.

He landed in the clearing a few feet from where he and his lover had spoken to Feneal. Several of the rocks with the painted josta bird still lay on the ground.

"Looking for me?"

Liam whirled toward the nearby trees. Cursed the startle and flexed his wings. He still didn't have a weapon, and although the exile meant him no harm, he felt naked without a blade.

Feneal leaned against a tree that didn't seem as if it was large enough to hold his weight.

Sienna's words, *"He always just kind of knows,"* teased his mind.

Liam cleared his throat and closed the distance to the Fae man. "Aye, I was."

Feneal eyed him up and down with that unsettling icy blue gaze. He didn't speak nor straighten from the tree.

When the man didn't speak, Liam continued. "I wanted ta discuss tomorrow night."

The man's eyes still appraised him.

"You look like him. Despite the coloring difference."

Liam cocked his head and tried not to stare at Feneal just as intently. Another full sentence. Not broken or missing any words. "My mother has dark hair, like mine," he said absently, still trying to figure out this exile.

Feneal's gaze shifted to Liam's wings. "Don't have them over there, do you?"

He shook his head. "Nay."

"It was why you came? To fly?"

"Aye," Liam said, crossing his arms over his chest. There was no use denying what the man seemed to instinctively know. Somehow his lover was right about him.

"I well know what it is like to live without them." For the first time, emotion darted across Feneal's dirty, bearded face.

"What do ye mean?"

The Fae exile pushed off the tree and ripped off his filthy leine. He presented his back.

Liam gasped and stepped closer, letting his arms fall to his sides.

The man's back was broad and muscular, his wide frame displaying incredible physical strength despite his advanced age. However, two large scars marred the skin between his jutting shoulder blades. Two pits of skin that appeared to be burn marks, healed over, and thickly pocked, craggy, and lined.

Wings should've protruded from those spots.

Liam swallowed hard. "Ye...ye were a Fae Warrior?"

Feneal donned his filthy leine. His face was implacable, but his blue eyes still burned. He nodded.

His gut told Liam the man would say no more about his former status.

He wanted to ask so many questions, the words piling against his lips, begging to be voiced. "I'm so sorry," he whispered, ramming a hand through his hair. "When I am home, 'tis bad when they feel missin' but I ken here, I have them. I dinnae imagine—"

"I will help you tomorrow eve." The former Fae Warrior's voice was gruff. "Go now, she waits for you."

Liam reared back, but before he could even blink, Feneal had disappeared from view, despite the bright moonlight alighting the clearing and the edge of the woods.

He grieved for the man.

What had Feneal done to have his wings removed?

Exiled without wings was likely worse than death for a powerful Fae Warrior. Perhaps the madness was less of a show, after all.

Had they burned them off?

Liam fought a shudder. The edges of his wings curled in slightly around his body, as if assuring himself they were still present.

He stared into the woods for a few more heartbeats, but the Fae man did not return.

When Liam made it back into the small room in Sienna's home, he found his lover sitting on his cot, dressed in the same sleeping gown she'd worn the night they'd gone to the Falls. Her long, fiery locks were twisted into a thick plait, lying over one shoulder.

How had Feneal known she was waiting for him in his room?

"Where were you?" No accusation in her voice, just curiosity.

Liam quietly closed the door and crossed the small quarters. He took a seat next to Sienna, and she grabbed both of his hands.

"You smell good, like the night sky."

He smiled.

"You needed to fly?"

Liam nodded. Although he didn't want to keep things from her, he also didn't want to relay the unusual conversation he'd had with Feneal or reveal any of the man's secrets.

Despite that he hadn't talked to the man regarding the reason he'd sought him in the first place, he felt better about what they had to do. Now, he knew he could rely on the exile. Trust him.

His head spun at the idea of Feneal as a Fae Warrior.

Did Sienna's grandmother know?

Did any of the exiles?

"Why are you so quiet?" Sienna asked, an amused smirk on her delicious mouth.

He smiled again. "Jus' thinkin'."

Silence fell but it was companionable.

Until her grip on his hands tightened. "This…this is our last night together."

Liam's breath stuttered. "Nay, love."

"It is, though, isn't it?" Her voice wobbled, and she averted her pretty bronze eyes.

He cupped her cheeks and forced her chin up, so she would have to look at him. "Nay, 'tis no'. Ye'll come home wit' me, an' no matter how long we'll be there, ye will still be a' my side."

"Will I?" Sienna sounded so small, so hurt.

His heartrate kicked up.

Liam covered her mouth with his, intending for the kiss to be something soft and sweet, but his lover had other plans.

Sienna clung to him, then slid onto his lap, kissing him hard and desperately. She shoved her tongue into his mouth and grabbed his face, then wound her arms around his neck and squeezed him, as she pressed her torso into his.

He was hard and aching in less than two seconds. His erection was pleasantly trapped beneath her delectable bottom, throbbing. There were too many layers of clothing separating them.

The creak of the cot when she started rocking her pelvis against his made Liam pull away for a breath.

"Love, stop. Ye'll wake the whole house." His amusement stalled when he looked into her beautiful countenance.

Sienna's face was flushed, her lips swollen, her gaze intense with want Liam didn't have the willpower to deny.

"I don't care," she panted. Her fingertips were on his belt, tugging. "I need you."

Liam grabbed her wrists. "Love—"

"I…I can't lose you, Liam." Emotion threaded the confession.

He had to swallow before he could speak. "Who said ye will?" he asked, intending to reassure her, but the query had come out so full of obvious regret it made her freeze on his lap.

She swallowed too, and he wanted to kiss her throat, but he needed her to feel better first.

"We come from two different worlds. It's impossible."

His lover's voice was even thicker with hurt Liam didn't want to face; despite the fact she was only saying aloud many of the same things he'd told himself over and over, since they'd met.

All of it was true.

Liam reached for the ties at the neck of her sleeping gown and tugged.

The garment slipped low, exposing one shoulder and some of the speckled skin he loved so much.

He laid a trail of kisses across her collarbone, pushing the soft fabric out of his way, until her perfect breasts peeked out. He needed the offending thing gone.

Sienna whimpered and buried her hands in his hair.

Liam kissed and nipped his way to her nipples and sucked on one through the chemise.

She gasped and pulled his hair.

Their gazes met, and he smirked.

"Want me to take it off?" she whispered.

"Aye, love."

"You, too, Liam MacLeod," Sienna ordered as she slid off his lap.

He didn't look away as she finished loosening the ties on her sleeping gown, and it pooled at her feet. The dimness of the room didn't obscure her supple curves and his bollocks ached.

She grabbed his belt and pulled it open and off, then tossed it over her shoulder, and the buckle clanked on the floor, as if protesting.

Liam chuckled at her impatience and let her help him gather his plaid and move it to the worktable.

Sienna tugged on his leine. "Off."

He stroked her arm. "Why?" he teased.

"I need your skin fully against mine," she admitted, her cheeks an adorable shade of pink.

Liam smiled softly, trying to ignore how that particular look on her gorgeous face made his insides quiver. He didn't want to lose her, either, but somehow, he couldn't find the words to voice what Sienna had expressed earlier. "C'mere," he said instead, opening his arms. He sat on the cot like he had before, hoping if they stayed on the edge, it wouldn't make too much noise.

Sienna straddled him, much like she had moments ago, but this time they were both naked.

He closed his eyes for a heartbeat at the feel of her breasts against his chest, and her bottom on his thighs.

She was right. He craved her skin against his, too.

The feel of her in his arms was unmatched.

Sienna was perfect.

She rubbed her sex against him, and a jolt of desire rocked his cock, making his tip throb.

"I want you, Liam," Sienna breathed, her mouth hovering millimeters over his.

He caressed her cheek, then cupped the side of her face. "I want ye, too, love." *Always.* He didn't say that aloud.

Maybe he couldn't.

Liam kissed her.

She deepened things, and at the same time, dragged her fingertips down his chest.

He shivered and settled his hands at her hips. She was undulating and it wasn't enough friction, nor was he centered in the right place.

Sienna gripped his erection and guided it to her sex.

Liam sucked in a breath against her mouth and his bollocks tingled, as if he would orgasm, and he wasn't even inside her.

Without his assistance, she positioned him at her entrance, and then slowly started to lower her body, letting him fill her inch by inch.

Sienna gasped into their kiss when he was fully

inside her.

Liam leaned back. "Are ye hurtin'?"

She shook her head and wove her arms around his neck. She skimmed her fingertips on the base of his wings and touched him as far as she could reach.

He groaned, it felt so good. He caressed her sides and her breasts, cupping her and thumbing her nipples until Sienna moaned and writhed against him. "Ride me, love," he whispered, kissing a hot wet trail on her neck, and nipping her earlobe.

She was tight and hot, and he was fitted inside her completely, but it wasn't enough.

Liam needed more. He grabbed her hips and encouraged her to rock, then thrust.

They moved together, and he helped her work up and down his shaft when Sienna seemed to tire.

Sensation shot down his spine and tightened his bollocks. He was close, but he wanted her to come first.

He found her mouth again, and propelled her against the length of his cock, driving into her harder and faster.

Sienna moaned and threw her head back, her inner muscles quivering.

Good, his love was close, too.

Liam encouraged her to lift her bottom, and when she did so, he raised his hips off the cot to meet her downward thrust.

They came together again in one last hard jolt.

He grunted and ground his teeth, as his release shot into her.

Sienna's climax hit at the same time, her sex

contracting and releasing against his cock, milking him.

He sealed his lips over hers to cut off her scream of pleasure. She didn't hesitate to kiss him back.

They panted chest to breast, still in an upright position with their arms around each other, for minutes that stretched out like hours.

Liam caressed her sweat-dampened back and Sienna snuggled into his torso.

Neither of them spoke, and he closed his eyes and buried his face against her hair, smiling as he felt her heartbeat echoing his, working its way back to a steady rhythm.

"Will ye stay wit' me?" he whispered into her overheated flesh.

Sienna nodded and kissed him again.

It was a soft, tender thing that made Liam's heart skip.

He looked into her face.

Clarity hit him, as if it was a spell, cast to restrict his respiration and diminish his life-force. His head spun, and it had nothing to do with desire or the haze of passion.

I love her.

Liam didn't want to walk away from her because he'd fallen in love with her.

Completely.

In such a short time it shouldn't have been possible.

He startled and tried not to let the shock of the realization show in his body. They were still connected, and he didn't want her to notice.

Liam couldn't tell her how he felt.

It wasn't fair.

It changed nothing.

He might not have addressed her earlier sentiments verbally, but Sienna had been right.

They *did* come from two different worlds, and it *was* impossible.

Especially if her grandmother managed to restore the family's magic.

Sienna would take her place in Fae society and be the head healer for the king, returning her family's legacy. She would truly be lost to him.

He couldn't stay in the Fae Realm, and she couldn't be who she was meant to be in the Human Realm. Liam couldn't ask her to give that up.

"Liam?" she whispered. "Is something wrong?"

"Nay, love." He forced out the lie and caressed her face. "That was perfect. Yer perfect."

The ghost of a smile curved her lips. "Let's sleep." She pressed another quick kiss to his mouth.

"Aye. I need ta hold ye."

When they were lying prone on the cot, Sienna cuddled into Liam's body, resting her cheek on his pectoral muscle, and sliding her arm across his waist.

Her legs mingled with his, as if they slept together all the time. It was natural and felt so right it made his body ache and soar at the same time.

He gathered her close and kissed her forehead.

Soon, her breathing slowed to a deep, even pattern.

Liam stared at the rough-hewn ceiling of the medicine room, his heart burning with every beat. He wasn't likely to sleep a wink.

Everything about Sienna was perfect...and yet nothing between them could ever be so.

chapter nineteen

Whether she was inside the treed home, or outside in the clearing, he'd been staring at her all day, as if she'd disappear, and Liam hadn't said much.

Normally, he was talkative and witty, making Sienna laugh, but *this* Liam was silent and broody, and she didn't like it.

Her lover also hadn't strayed far from her side, even when she'd gone outside to use the privy. He was following her more closely than Triobló id did on a daily basis.

Liam kept touching her, too. Although Sienna didn't mind *that,* she wished he would just talk to her. Share with her what was on his mind, tell her what was wrong.

Of course, she knew the answer to those questions.

They were going to embark on a dangerous mission soon—going to the Field of Light, where Liam would open the Faery Stones and take her and Amalie to the Human Realm.

Every time Sienna met his much-too-somber violet eyes, she wanted to blurt what she hadn't had the courage to say last night.

I love you, Liam MacLeod.

She gulped.

By the Goddess, she did love him.

She shouldn't love him.

It was only tearing her to shreds, and they hadn't even parted ways yet, but they would.

Her heart probably wouldn't survive it.

Sienna hadn't been able to hold back that she didn't want to lose him, but she hadn't been able to answer his *"Who said ye will?"* either.

She hadn't told him she loved him because it wouldn't change their fates.

Nor had Liam declared love for her, despite his chosen endearment.

Her heart skipped.

It was all for naught.

She'd kissed him and basically begged him to make love to her in the medicine room.

He had. That memory she would always cherish, as well as her gorgeous halfling saying he needed to hold her. The feel of his arms around her all night long lived in her soul.

Sienna hadn't even cared that they were on a cot too small for him, let alone the two of them. It'd been fine for their purposes.

She'd felt embarrassingly desperate and had needed to say a proper goodbye to Liam, but it'd backfired. Because she loved him and couldn't tell him.

Which was foolish and stupid.

He didn't love her.

Right?

"Sienna?"

She jumped and met her brother's dark eyes.

"What?" she snapped.

Ealeric frowned.

Immediate remorse hit her chest and spread down her limbs. Sienna launched herself at her brother and threw her arms around him.

He enclosed her in a tight embrace. "What's wrong?" Ealeric demanded above her ear.

"Nothing. Everything," she whispered, squeezing her eyes shut against his shoulder. His familiar scent—so different from Liam's—mixed with the scent of the sweet woods they burned in the hearth.

Her brother smelled like fresh grass and the earthy forest. He must've been cutting wood for their *mórai*.

Ealeric's smile was wry when their gazes met.

He cupped her cheeks, and his midnight eyes were so earnest and grown up, Sienna didn't pull away. The touch was unusual but meant so much to her.

They didn't often exchange serious words, let alone those of love, but she did love her brother. His expression said he loved her, too.

"I trust Liam. My gut is in knots, but I believe the stray cares about you, and of course I trust Feneal."

She nodded because she couldn't speak. Emotion clogged her throat. She sucked in a breath. "'Twill be okay."

Her brother cocked his head. "Okay?"

Sienna grinned. "Just something Liam says. It means, all will be well. I believe it will."

It has to be.

Ealeric arched an eyebrow. "When I thought the stray couldn't be more odd… Okay?"

Sienna popped his chest with a fist. "Be kind, brother."

He batted her hand away. "Ow. That was unnecessary."

"Do ye two need ta be separated?" One of Liam's dark eyebrows was arched to match Ealeric's, but his delectable mouth rippled with the smile he tried to suppress.

Her heart skipped and slid to her tummy.

He was so beautiful.

Colored shadows from the retiring sunlight danced over his wings, and he crossed his arms over his impossibly broad chest.

The movement made the leine he wore—one of her brother's—tighten to his form, hinting at defined muscles she'd mapped with her fingers, lips, and tongue. Sienna was as familiar with them as she was her own body.

A shiver shot down her spine, and she cleared her throat. "Nay, I've control of the situation."

Ealeric chuckled, instead of yelling or retorting like she expected.

Maybe her brother was grown up, after all.

She took a step closer to her lover, and Liam wrapped his arm around her shoulders, drawing her into his side.

Like most of the day, he still didn't seem to be able to keep his hands off her.

Sienna let his heat seep into her. She needed his

strength. Didn't even care that her brother was there to witness the affectionate display.

"Just take care of my sisters, Liam." Ealeric stared at her lover.

Her brother hadn't called Liam *the stray*.

"Always."

Silence fell, but it wasn't unpleasant, and the two men sized each other up.

She looked from one to the other, these two males she cared about most in the world. Sienna didn't know whether to holler at them or respect their appraisal of each other.

They seemed to be communicating without words, and it bothered her somehow.

"I believe you," her brother whispered finally.

Liam threw his hand out for a shake, and Ealeric complied. "They're my own now."

Sienna bit her lip to stave off a gasp and ordered herself not to move. If she gave into the fidget or showed her shock, her lover would feel it in her body tight up against his.

His?

She wanted that.

More than anything.

Foolish lass.

She wanted to look him in the eyes and tell him so. Demand to know what he meant by what he'd just said.

Tell him she loved him.

It would do no good, except leave them both with heartache. Sienna and her sister might be journeying with him to the Human Realm, but it was only temporary.

"You take care of *Móraí*, brother. Feneal will help protect you with his magic," Sienna said, because she needed something to focus on other than her torrid Liam-related emotions.

"Aye, sister. I will."

Amalie called from the doorway of their treed home, waving her arms to gain their attention.

Sienna glanced at her sister instead of answering Ealeric.

"*Móraí* says it's time," Amalie shouted.

Trioblóid chirruped from behind her, worried colors traversing his hairy coat.

Just as the last peeks of light disappeared and gave way to the night's full darkness, they met Feneal in the woods by the clearing, not far from where he'd shown Liam the scars on his back, proof of his missing wings. Even the stars seemed dim, as if approving of their quest and aiding in this small way.

Sienna's grandmother and brother accompanied them, but they would soon part ways. The next portion of their journey—to the Field of Light—wasn't safe for them. They had no magic.

Feneal couldn't protect them all at once.

The former Fae Warrior would provide cover and a distraction, so Liam could climb onto the dais and open the Faery Stones.

He prayed the plan would work, and no one got hurt—or worse.

Feneal hadn't explained what his distraction would be, and it made Liam twitchy, despite Sienna's reassurances that he could—and should—trust the Fae man.

While he did trust him, he couldn't lessen his apprehension. The training with the sword and the ways of war from his father and uncles circled in his brain, specifically the most important rule. *"Never go into battle without a plan."*

"Come, come." Feneal beckoned with a hand, moving into the trees without another word.

"*Mórai*," Amalie wailed, reaching for her grandmother, as Sienna tugged on her sister to follow the former Fae Warrior.

"Go, *mò bhilis*." Eilidh motioned for them to obey Feneal and blew a kiss to both her granddaughters. "I will see you again, my lasses."

Ealeric stood next to the elderly healer, his expression stoic. He threw a nod to Liam.

Liam returned the gesture, and sucked in a breath when Ealeric slid his arm around his grandmother to hold her up.

"I love you both!" Sienna called, pulling her sister with her in front of him, as they'd planned.

His heart stuttered, and he had to remind himself what he was about to do. Because, damn, he wished she was telling him she loved *him*.

Feneal led the way, and the lasses were behind him.

Liam brought up the rear until they had to get closer together. They weren't afraid of running into Fae Warriors until they exited the area of Grànnda Falls, where the foliage turned colorful, the greens and earth tones fading into blue and orange grasses at the edge of the Field of Light.

"Shouldn't we fly there?" Amalie asked, her voice a strained whisper.

"I would have ta take ye one at a time, an' 'tis too dangerous," Liam said. "The journey is no' so long on foot."

Sienna caught his eye and he smiled, but she was pale, with trepidation stamped all over her face.

He darted forward and squeezed her hand.

Amalie was clutching her other one, looking even more frightened than her older sister.

Feneal grunted, proving he'd followed their conversation, but he didn't offer a retort.

Liam's heartrate notched up the closer they neared to the Field of Light, and when he saw the maroon bark of the largest Acana tree at the edge of the dais that held the Faery Stones, his pulse thundered in his ears.

When—*if*—they pulled this off he would lose his wings again.

It was a selfish thing to worry about, but he already mourned their loss, especially since he'd not had the chance to fly once more before they'd started this expedition.

Feneal stopped beside the tree, holding up his hand to silence and halt them, as if leading a military exercise.

Liam might've been amused at any other time. He met the man's pale blue gaze, and Feneal looked away quickly, scanning the area before them.

Not for the first time, he wished for his da's mind reading so he could know what the exile had planned. Not knowing made him feel so exposed…vulnerable to an ambush.

"There are six," the former Fae Warrior said, low and serious. The clarity of his full sentences gave Liam a smidgeon of relief. However, the challenge of six winged soldiers ahead of them tamped that small notion.

Liam had expected six. Every time he'd come to the realm, there had always been six.

Sienna squeezed his hand, and he spared her a glance.

"'Twill be okay, love," he whispered. He didn't want to release her, but he needed to spot the lay of the land with his own eyes, and not only rely on what Feneal said—especially since they hadn't discussed what they would do. He inched closer to the exile, and they both observed the winged soldiers guarding the Faery Stones.

Two Warriors patrolled the Field. Two stood on the far side of the dais but talking to each other in low murmurs.

The last two weren't visible from where their group was huddled by the Acana tree's great roots, but if Feneal said there were six, Liam didn't doubt it.

The Fae Warriors were at rest, but it didn't mean

they weren't alert.

"We stay together," the exile grunted, gesturing to the lasses. "Liam, open the Stones. Then you all go."

Amalie's golden eyes were wide, but she didn't speak.

Sienna pushed to her tiptoes and pressed a hard, fast kiss to Liam's mouth.

He smiled and wanted to say something to her—so much—but it was far from the time.

"Let us go," Feneal announced. He shouted a fast spellword, and a bubble appeared around the four of them.

It wouldn't last long, because the Faery Stones were warded against stealth magic, but Liam would take all the help they could get.

"Stay low," Liam whispered to the lasses, because Feneal was already at a crouch at the front of the bubble spell.

If they crept along the trees and the far side of the dais, they could stay out of sight—hopefully.

Shouts and a few bright flashes of magic snagged his attention.

The Fae Warriors had been alerted to their presence, much sooner than Liam had anticipated.

Dammit.

Amalie squeaked from fright, and Sienna hushed her, but their leader stilled, and threw a command over his shoulder.

"Move fast, together," Feneal barked.

Liam flexed his wings and grabbed Sienna's upper arm with one hand, and Amalie's with the other.

He urged them forward, closer to the former Fae Warrior as they snaked around the dais, trying to stay low as a unit, on the far side. The bubble spell was still in place around them all.

Perhaps the Stones' wards didn't consider protection spells a threat, and for that he was grateful.

Shouts in Fae and more flashing lights winked in and out, but nothing hit them or bounced off the magic bubble.

Feneal threw a few blast spells over the orb that contained them.

It must be working enough to keep the Warriors back, because so far, no one had rushed them.

Luck seemed to be on their side, but how long would it last?

Liam could help with the magical assault, but he wanted to ensure Sienna and Amalie were as calm as possible, for as long as possible.

They both sported wide eyes and blanched complexions.

The idea of leaving them felt wrong, even if it was for their protection.

Feneal conjured a bright yellow ball, gathering it in the center of his hands and working his palms in a circular motion, until it was about the size of his head.

When he released it, the glowing lighted globe rose high in the air, and started to shoot daggers of radiance out, targeting the Fae Warrior guards.

Liam stilled, fascinated. He'd never seen anything like it.

A few of the winged soldiers darted up into the

air, and back, and the daggers of light followed them.

"Go, Liam! That will not busy them for long, it is not lethal," Feneal said, throwing a few more blue blast spells that made the two closest Warriors scatter.

Liam jolted in his boots. He'd been transfixed and it was foolish.

Sienna clutched his forearm. "Liam...."

"I ken it, love." He kissed her like she'd kissed him before they'd moved behind the dais. Liam wanted to tell her he loved her, but he wouldn't do that as a goodbye. "I dinnae be long. When ye see the portal open, go through it, no matter what's happenin'."

He didn't wait for an answer. Liam left the protection of the bubble spell and dashed along the side of the dais, counting Fae Warriors he could see.

As soon as he touched the first crystal, alarms would sound at the king's castle, dispatching reinforcements, probably two full Wings of twelve, if not more. King Fillan's fortress wasn't far.

Feneal could not hold them off alone.

Liam couldn't fight and open the Stones at the same time.

They hadn't much time.

A redheaded Warrior screamed when he noticed Liam sneaking up the dais steps. He lifted into the air; sword drawn.

Liam straightened and threw a blast spell, hitting the gliding figure square in the chest.

The Fae Warrior crumpled to the blue and orange grass. The spell was only to stun, and he'd be back up and fighting in only a moment.

He ran to the Faery Stones, the welcoming magic melody washing over him. There was no time to breathe it in and savor it like he normally did.

Opening the portal wasn't a quick thing. Liam had to concentrate for it to work correctly, even in the Fae Realm where his powers were stronger. The pattern of touching each crystal had to be completed in the right order, too.

He tried to block out the chaos around him, bright flashes of magic and shouts of the Fae Warriors Feneal fought all on his own.

His heart thundered in his ears and his whole body was taut. He needed to calm, or he would fail.

The Faery Stones thrummed, responding to his touch. Warm air swirled around him. The tune of the magic reverberated in his ears, and Liam finally breathed a sigh of relief at the familiar *pop-pop-pop,* each louder than the one before, following the sound of tearing parchment.

Wind blew even harder, a gale ruffling his hair into his face, obscuring the small round opaque doorway, in front of the perfect half-circle of the five crystals that made up the Stones on this side.

Thank Jesu, the portal to the Human Realm was already opening.

It would get larger, second by second.

Then they could go through it.

The feminine scream made his heart stutter and threaten to stop.

Liam whirled.

Feneal and the lasses were trying to cross the

small distance to the dais stairs, but the protection spell was no longer in place.

The former Fae Warrior threw brightly colored magic hand over hand, but two Fae Warriors had cornered them.

Liam shot into the air, pumping his wings harder and faster than he ever had in his life. His muscles stung from the force. He landed on the Warrior on the left, grabbing the man's wings and yanking him backwards.

The soldier screamed and tried to buck him off, like an unbroken horse, but Liam clung to him, digging his hands into the Warrior's iridescent flesh when he tried to flap his wings.

At the same time, Feneal landed a blast spell center-mass on the Warrior on the right, and the man gave a grunt before he toppled over.

Dead or unconscious, Liam couldn't guess.

"Go," Liam yelled. "Sienna, Amalie, run. Go through the portal."

The Fae Warrior still in his grip tried to flex his wings again and use the ground as leverage to rise into the air, but Liam held him too tight, restraining him.

He used his own wings for balance and pumped them, dragging the Warrior back even more, away from the lasses and Feneal.

His arms and legs burned with the effort to hold on, but Liam couldn't release his captive. If the soldier got free, he could draw his sword or throw magic.

The sounds above them—of many sets of flapping wings, the clanking of armor, and the swish of swords clearing scabbards—told him more Fae Warriors had arrived.

A bad situation was about to get worse.

Had he been a fool to think one Fae man with magic would help them get safely away?

Liam had gone back and forth on his own several times, so had that made him overconfident?

He cursed in Fae and Gaelic, then lifted a few feet off the air still holding onto the struggling soldier. Liam braced his feet on the back of the Fae Warrior's green armor covering his torso, and pulled with all his might, until the man screamed and bowed his back.

Sienna and her sister dashed toward the dais. Feneal continued to throw magic, trying to offer the lasses some cover.

He grabbed the Fae Warrior's long dark plait and yanked it back, wrenching his head to one side. There was a sickening snap, and the man hit the ground.

Liam winced, but bounced up and off the dead winged man, just as another Fae Warrior landed in front of him, sword drawn.

"Abomination!" the man yelled.

Liam paused. He was familiar; one of the Fae Warriors who'd *greeted* him the day he'd arrived in the realm. He screamed the MacLeod battle cry and rushed the Warrior, equal him in size.

He punched the winged soldier in the nose, and snatched his sword, taking him completely by surprise. Instead of running him through, which was no less than the bastard deserved, Liam smashed the Fae Warrior in the face with his own weapon's hilt, and down he went.

Another feminine scream made him freeze.

Sienna was on the dais, almost to the glistening portal, but another winged soldier had seized Amalie by the stairs.

He flew to his love's sister, brandishing the stolen sword.

Feneal rushed toward them.

"Sienna, go!" Liam yelled as he attacked the fair-haired Fae Warrior.

The portal wouldn't remain open much longer.

His love was frozen on the dais, her body jittering with obvious panic. Her mouth was half-agape, and she reached toward them, but didn't move.

"Sienna, love, go!" Liam repeated.

The large Fae man shoved Amalie away, and the lass landed on all fours in the blue and orange grass. She was sobbing, but otherwise appeared unhurt.

Liam fought the Warrior, as Feneal grabbed Sienna's sister and urged her back, toward the woods.

His opponent was ready for him, meeting the stolen blade with his own.

Liam parried and darted out of the way of several slashes, making a few good strikes of his own, but he hadn't cut the man. He'd also managed to remain unmarred.

Which was a feat because the winged man was well-trained.

More and more Fae Warriors landed in the Field of Light.

Too many to count.

He fought the sudden sense of despair and stabbed the sword at the huge soldier again.

Liam had made it to the Fae Realm and back several times, and he would today, too, with the lasses he'd promised to protect.

He had to save Sienna and Amalie. Couldn't give into any encroaching fear.

Be strong for the lasses.

A blast spell came out of nowhere — not from the Fae Warrior he fought.

Pain exploded in his chest, radiating down his limbs, and making them vibrate.

Liam dropped the weapon and hit a knee. A white-hot jolt shot into his thigh, but it didn't rival the hurt in his torso or the stolen breath from the blue magic ball.

Another bright flash of magic followed, this one red. He was knocked to his back, against his will.

They must've used a paralyzing spell because he couldn't move anything.

Liam heard the portal shut with a loud *pop*. He sent a silent prayer to God and the Fae Goddess alike that Sienna and her sister had made it to the Human Realm.

A heavy boot came down on his face. Agony bloomed, and everything went dark.

chapter twenty

Sienna hit all fours. Some invisible energy yanked her off her feet and propelled her body forward. She had no control, and the breath fled from her mouth, forcing her to pant for air. Pebbles bit into her palms and knees, making her wince.

It was dark, and she had no idea where she was.

The rush of moving water caught her attention. She glanced to her left.

She must be on a beach.

Sienna flexed her fingers in the gritty sand surrounding them and pushed to sit back on her knees.

Her thigh muscles ached, as if she'd been running for hours, and she didn't trust her legs to hold her up.

Going through the portal had worked.

She was in the Human Realm.

Alone.

A shiver darted down her spine.

Feneal had dragged her sister into the forest, and she'd obeyed Liam's urging as soon as they'd disappeared from sight.

The man would no doubt take Amalie home, and she would be safe with her family — for now.

Sienna refused to contemplate otherwise.

Liam had gone down with that spell, and she'd had to flee through the portal. She couldn't have waited any longer. Two huge, winged Fae Warriors headed toward her, and another had landed on the dais, intent on stopping her.

Why they hadn't thrown magic at her when she'd stood there fully exposed, she couldn't guess, but she was away now.

Safe?

Sienna scanned the area, but the moonlight wasn't strong enough to do more than glint off the distant waves crashing to the shore. The fresh sea air made her inhale deeply. Her first one since before they started their journey to the Field of Light. Or further back than that…before her grandmother revealed the truth.

No, don't go there. Focus. Breathe.

The salty air was pleasant and for some reason, had a soothing effect on her fears.

What was she supposed to do now?

Liam had told her they would seek his home, the castle of his human clan, called Dunvegan.

How could she ever find it on her own?

How could she tell his family what'd happened?

Fears that he'd already been killed by the Fae Warriors gnarled inside in her gut, igniting embers of her worry. Tears burned the corners of her eyes.

Nay.

She refused to believe he was dead.

He couldn't be.

She would just know, wouldn't she?

She'd feel it, after all they'd shared?

Sienna loved him, and she'd shout it to him the next time she saw him. Not confessing her feelings might become her biggest regret, but she refused to believe it was too late.

She *would* see him again.

His family had magic, too, and they would help. Just as Liam had promised.

They had to.

Deep male voices came from a ridge high above her. One she could not see atop.

Renewed panic, for a different reason, shot down her spine and flipped her belly. Sienna tried to scramble to her feet, but as feared, her legs refused to support her. She landed in a heap on her bottom, all her muscles screaming a protest.

"Liam?" someone called from above.

At the sound of his name, more tears pricked her eyes, and she swallowed. No words were born when she tried to speak.

Other low voices followed, like the men murmured to each other, but she still didn't see anyone.

There was a scrambling of booted feet, and cascading rocks and dirt down the cliff-face, as someone—or someones—made their way to the beach.

Sienna's panic cooled. They'd called Liam's name, so they were likely his family, and she wasn't in immediate danger.

"'Tis a lass," a male breathed. He sounded young, but she couldn't make out the figures coming toward her.

"Where's Liam?" someone else demanded.

A large palm filled her line of vision. "Can you stand, lass?" He didn't have the rolling brogue Liam used, but the other two males did.

Sienna blew out a breath and nodded. Her mouth wobbled, and the tears filling her eyes spilled over. She sniffled and looked away from the helping hand.

"Is she clothed?" another voice called from the ridge. It too, was in an accent reminiscent of her halfling warrior. Although this one sounded older.

"Lass?" The man put his hand lower, offering more insistently.

"I—"

"Let's get you to your feet, first." His voice was impossibly gentle, as if she was a wee bairn who required tender care.

A few of the men came closer, two carrying lanterns. There seemed to be three men behind the one in front of her.

"Aye, she's clothed," the one who seemed young called.

Why wouldn't she have clothes on?

Sienna glanced down at herself just to be certain.

Why did they care?

"Lass, take my hand," the man in front of her urged.

Sienna obeyed, sliding her palm into his huge one, and he pulled her to her feet in less than a heartbeat, as if she weighed nothing.

Her knees wobbled and he grabbed her shoulders.

"Are you hurt?"

She shook her head because words of thanks she'd intended wouldn't come out. She was compelled to look up at the man, and Sienna gasped when she met violet eyes.

Just like Liam.

He was huge, also like Liam, but his hair was pale blond and short. His face was beardless, and he was handsome beyond words.

The man had to be Fae.

Was he Liam's father?

"Aye, Liam is my son."

Had he read her mind?

"Aye, lass, I did."

"Fae Warrior," Sienna blurted, and more hot tears rolled down her cheeks.

"Why's she cryin'?" a younger man asked.

"Hush, Iain MacLeod," another of the nearby men ordered. He too, sounded young.

Maybe they were the cousins Liam had mentioned.

"Aye, I was at one time." Liam's father nodded. He still addressed her in that same gentle tone.

Sienna's cheeks heated from the embarrassment swirling in her stomach. The man probably thought her daft.

"Nay, lass, but I cannot make sense of the chaotic jumble of your thoughts. I'm sorry for invading your mind, but I need you to tell me what happened." His grip on her upper arms firmed. "Where is my son?"

She bit her lip to hold back a sob bubbling up in her chest. "He-he…tried to protect me and my sister."

"What happened?" this was just short of a demand, and he shook her gently.

"Feneal was fighting them with magic. Liam was, too, with a sword. He screamed at me to go through the portal."

The man paused briefly. "Feneal? A name I have not heard in many years."

Sienna's gaze found his purple eyes again. "You know Feneal?"

"Aye, one of my brothers. A mighty Fae Warrior."

"A Fae Warrior? Feneal has no wings."

"The king's mages removed them. But that is a story for another time. Lass, what happened to Liam?" This was even more urgent, and he forced her to maintain his lock on her eyes.

"The Fae Warriors captured him."

Agony defined Liam's new reality. His wings were bent at odd angles beneath his body, and he couldn't shift them to a more comfortable position. His chest burned, his arms and legs ached. He still couldn't move, but it wasn't because of the paralyzing spell—that had worn off.

He'd woken from the stomping mid-air, but instead of being held by limbs and dangling as when he'd been dumped by the stream, he was contained in some sort of netting, and two Fae Warriors flew him high in the air.

When he struggled against it, the net came alive, constricting him until he couldn't breathe. Liam stopped fighting. At least until they were on solid ground.

No doubt he was being taken to the king, as Wardric had told Eilidh days ago. Days that somehow felt like years had passed.

"The abomination is awake," one of his captors called.

Liam couldn't tell if it was one of his transporters or one of their Wingmates. He was surrounded by the Fae Warriors flying in formation.

"Good. We have to prepare him for King Fillan." This voice was closer, deeper, laced with a maniacal edge.

"Captain Daegus has his orders, first," another answered.

Liam shuddered against the roping. He didn't need an imagination to figure out what *preparing* him for the king meant. He would be lucky to survive.

However, the first mention of his father's father was more concerning.

Would he actually see the man?

Did he want to?

It wasn't like his grandfather would save him.

Liam wasn't fool enough to hope the captain of all the king's Fae Warriors would give a bogle's shite about his half-blooded grandson.

Most of what he'd heard of Captain Daegus hadn't been good, although his father had settled his own heart and ill feelings about the past with the man.

It didn't mean his grandfather would help him.

Liam was curious about the leader; he couldn't help it. His healthy fear of the ruthlessness he'd heard about currently overrode that.

He needed to survive this and get back home.

Back to Sienna, to help her cause.

He had to believe his love would find his father and aunt and tell them what'd happened to him. That was his only chance. He'd wager on that more than a man he'd never met assisting him, even if they had blood-ties.

Suddenly he wanted all the MacLeods to storm the Fae Realm and rescue him. He still feared for their safety and lack of magic, but if they didn't come for him, he would die.

Liam should've told Sienna he loved her.

The bastards dropped him, and he landed hard on the ground. What little air was left in his lungs whooshed from his mouth and he grunted in pain.

It must've been more than a few feet above the ground.

Laughter surrounded him.

Liam told himself to calm and breathe, instead of showing them any kind of reaction—including verbally.

He could quietly plan their demise, but it would do him no good. He didn't have a weapon. Stealing another sword wasn't likely.

The Fae Warriors had also slapped magic-inhibiting manacles on him, so he was bound magically and physically.

His powers wouldn't respond to any call.

Worse than when he was home in the Human Realm.

One of the Fae Warriors snapped his fingers and the netting around Liam's body loosened and fell.

"Clever trick," he murmured.

Two others stepped forward and yanked him to his feet. They gripped his biceps, one on either side.

Liam didn't bother struggling. His wrists burned from the Fae metal bracelets, and the short chain hanging between them glowed blue. If he resisted, the magic would react, and it would hurt.

The dark-haired Fae Warrior he'd stolen the sword from at the Field of Light appeared in front of him, wearing a wicked sneer.

"Nice ta see ye again," Liam drawled. He took some silent satisfaction that the man's nose and mouth still oozed blood, but he could seek a healer, no doubt when they were done with him.

Liam wouldn't have the same option.

The winged soldier smirked and punched him in the face.

His head flew back, and stars exploded behind his eyes. He tasted blood but didn't utter a sound. He wouldn't allow them more pleasure from his reaction.

Liam should've run him through, after all.

The two holding him weren't bothered by the force behind the hit; they just perched him upright, and the dark-haired Fae man hit him in the gut.

A few others took turns, and Liam's vision was blurry, and his head spun. His body was on fire, but oddly numb at the same time. He wished the numbness would swallow him whole and he could slip into peace.

He tried to shake the idea. Had to survive.

For Sienna.

"Enough!" a tall, redheaded Warrior yelled. "The captain has ordered the abomination be brought to the dungeon. Besides, I cannot abide the stench of his blood."

Another of the Fae Warriors uttered a spellword, and an iridescent rope appeared, wrapping itself around Liam's battered body.

The two soldiers holding him stepped away quickly, as if they didn't want any contact with the bindings.

Liam hissed. Not only did the magic rope constrict his movements and pin his wings to his back, it burned his bare skin.

He was in and out of consciousness as they moved him through some sort of bailey, and then down a winding stairwell.

No one was touching him, so they must've had some spell propelling him forward, and he had to admit that would be handy to learn.

The odor of dank moist air made his nose twitch, along with other smells, blood, piss, shite, and rot.

"What a welcomin' place," Liam said, but no one acknowledged him.

Three Fae Warriors took him down two corridors that were poorly lit, but the sparse torches on the walls contained purple and blue fire instead of reds and yellows. Somehow, they still offered dim light that didn't reflect the colored flames.

"Get in there," one of the winged soldiers spat,

shoving Liam forward into a small room, and not a cell.

They placed him at the center of the room, still on his aching feet, but they did not remove the magic bindings.

The redheaded one that had been the voice of reason in the bailey darted forward and punched him.

What little air was left in Liam's lungs abandoned him, cutting off his ability to retort. He'd wanted to snipe, *"So much fer hatin' the smell of my blood."*

With calls of encouragement, the other two took turns, until they presented a triple assault, hitting and kicking him.

They jarred his body against his will, and every time Liam shifted with a hit, the rope took a bite of his skin, holding him upright and on his feet, when all he craved was to lay down and curl in a ball. Protect himself in some way.

Maybe he was going to die here after all.

Hopefully, his family would defend Sienna and help her grandmother rid herself of the agreement with Wardric without Liam.

"Leave me with the prisoner."

The barked order made his ears ring.

The three Fae Warriors who'd been inflicting abuse scattered like wee ones caught stealing bannocks in the kitchen.

A huge man cleared the room and shut the door in seconds. He was larger than most of the other Fae Warriors, as were his wings, which towered over him. He was probably a few inches taller than Liam's half-past six feet.

Liam swallowed. He instantly recognized the man before him.

His grandfather.

Captain Daegus' long ebony hair was not gathered in a thick plait like his men, but loose around him, floating like a foreboding aura.

There was a huge sword sheathed at his thick waist, but Liam could feel the magic pulsing from the weapon. A glow surrounded it, despite the fact he couldn't see the weapon itself.

"Where did you get this blade?" The captain of the Fae Warriors held the dirk high on open palms, presenting it in a harsh demand.

The same dirk that'd been taken from Liam the day he'd come to the Fae Realm.

"My father gave it ta me fer my nameday, when I turned eight an' ten." He lifted his chin, despite the new pain in his body. There was no need for subterfuge. Liam wanted his grandfather to know who he was and see what the man would do with the knowledge.

The Fae Warriors hadn't beaten him as badly as the night he'd arrived, but his less-than-fully-healed sword wound was seeping blood and aching. His ribs had taken on new bruises, destroying the work Sienna's salve had done.

Liam was in agony, his wings tied tight and bound to his back, but he wouldn't show an iota of discomfort to this man.

This Fae Warrior Captain and father who'd rejected his own son.

Xander had explained the public renouncement was *for* his sake, and the sake of Liam's paternal grandmother, the Lady Aileana, but the way the captain glared at him through slitted yellow-gold eyes surely didn't shout that the man was merely acting for the sake of his men and his command.

The gold chest-plate he wore glinted in the light from the blue and purple fired torches mounted on the walls.

Like the corridors Liam had traversed, the lighting was magical and not like normal fire, but this place was brighter than the hallways.

He was in the dungeon, as the redheaded Warrior had said, but not a tiny, barred cell. He'd been told his father and uncle had been kept in cells years before, with magic crystal bars that burned or shocked if touched.

Instead, Liam had been brought to a plain, gray stone-walled room with a cot in the corner and a small window high on the outer wall, to his right. It had the crystal bars on it, but it wasn't like he could move from his current spot, let alone explore the sting of putting his fingers on it.

Why hadn't he been thrown in the cells, where he assumed all other prisoners were usually taken?

The shiny magical rope was now suspended from the ceiling, but his booted feet were flat to the dirt floor. Since the bindings had kept him upright, Liam hadn't been aware when they'd put it high above his head. If they'd intended to hike him up and leave him hanging, perhaps the arrival of his grandfather had interrupted their plans.

The leader of all the Fae Warriors took a step back, as if he couldn't remain so close to Liam. The apple of his throat bobbed. Twice.

Then his gaze was on Liam, studying him from head to foot, but he didn't speak. His striking yellow eyes were wide, but Liam couldn't read any emotions in them.

Liam tried not to pull against his constraints because he'd already been burned enough but standing still under that scrutiny tested his resolve.

"What is his name?" Captain Daegus demanded. "Your sire?"

"Ye know his name." His heart kicked up a notch. Despite his earlier internal declaration that he wanted the Fae Warrior Captain to know his identity, he really shouldn't dare the man.

He'd been told many times that his father's father was the perfect winged soldier to stand at the king's side. King Fillan's weapon many times over.

At the merest command.

Emotions darted across the huge man's countenance, but for only about a half-heartbeat before his expression became as hard and dark as obsidian, matching the hue of his hair.

Anger shot up from Liam's gut.

The captain was obviously readying himself to reject him, renounce him. As he had his da.

Not that he'd expected the man would release or rescue him, but perhaps he'd had a tiny hope in the back of his mind.

His father had mentioned that the Fae captain had reconciled with his wife before Liam had been born, and Xander had stated he'd seen his father differently than he had in years past. His grandparents were in a supposed happy marriage.

Guess ye were wrong, Da.

"Should I call you *Daideó* or would you prefer *Sheanair*?" He managed a smirk, despite his damaged face's protest.

The words had been human Gaelic, the informal and formal titles for one's grandfather, but there was no doubt the oversized man had understood him.

Captain Daegus blinked. Cleared his throat. The huge man's wings vibrated. He whirled and left the room.

Liam winced with the shouted slam of the wooden door.

chapter twenty-one

Sienna couldn't stop trembling as Xander sat her on the back of a huge gray horse and mounted in the saddle behind her.

He wrapped her in his arms with her back against his broad chest.

After ceding to his demands and retelling all she'd witnessed, she couldn't get the image of Liam crumpled on the ground out of her head.

Her halfling had sacrificed himself for her. So, she could go through the portal and Feneal could get her sister to safety. The plan to bring her sister with her into the Human Realm was already dashed in only a few moments.

She had to believe that Feneal would protect her family. Against the Fae Warriors, even against Wardric if necessary.

They had places they could hide. Hollows in the forest of the Falls, or even in the caves.

They would be fine.

They had to be.

Besides, all of Fae society avoided Grànnda Falls and the land around them, so it was an extra layer of protection. Right?

Liam…

He was probably in the king's dungeon, being tortured.

Or worse.

Nay.

She shuddered against Xander, belatedly recalling the former Fae Warrior could read minds, and he'd probably caught all of her torment, including very private things, like her love for his son.

"Not everything, you're thinking too fast. All over the place, and it is difficult to follow."

Sienna's cheeks burned. She might not know the man, but she'd heard the amusement in his words, and there was nothing to laugh about.

She didn't answer him but built strong walls in her mind to keep him out. Hopefully.

"Sorry, lass, it's not something I relish, I assure you."

"Liam told me you call it your curse."

Xander made a noise that could've been more amusement, chagrin or even agreement. Maybe it was all three.

"Thank you for saving my lad's life."

Tears burned the corners of her eyes. Sienna couldn't find her voice. The man was a stranger but had treated her so kindly since pulling her to her feet on the beach.

Liam was right. His family hadn't—and wouldn't—turn her away.

Never had she imagined she would meet them without him at her side.

Her heart ached.

Despite the darkness of the night, around the bend in the path, a structure came into view, large and looming. It had to be the MacLeod stronghold, Dunvegan.

Sienna swallowed.

Torches lined a tall, thick-walled embattlement. Shadows moved in the light provided by the small flickering fires. Patrolling men.

The walls seemed to grow higher the closer they came, the expansive castle as intimidating as it was impressive.

She shivered again.

"Are you cold? I know it's milder in the Fae Realm."

"Nay," Sienna whispered. She scanned the wall as they rode through the first set of huge gates into a small bailey, then into a larger courtyard. "Dunvegan," she breathed.

Xander jumped down from the horse and offered his arms to help her dismount.

He wore a smirk, the same one Liam had…it stole her breath all over again.

"I see my lad has told you all about us."

Sienna gave an absent nod and let Xander pull her off the horse.

There was a ruckus at what had to be the front entrance. The area was well-lit enough to make out three slender figures spilling into the courtyard.

The other men dismounted and talked amongst themselves.

A dark-haired woman lifted her skirts and dashed to the pair of them.

She glanced at Sienna, and back at Liam's father.

"Where's Liam?" she demanded of the large former Fae Warrior.

"*Mò aingeal*, 'twill be all right."

This had to be Liam's mother.

The woman shook her head and put a hand over her mouth. "Nay, Xander." Her voice wobbled, and emotion wrapped her words. "Where's our lad?"

Xander gathered her into his arms. "We'll get Liam back. All will be well."

Sienna bit her bottom lip, sucking back her own sob. She wanted to believe what his father had said, with all her heart.

"Who's this, then?" another woman stepped closer. She had long blonde hair in a thick plait, and her inflection was off somehow. She sounded Scottish, but not.

"Let us go inside, an' we'll get the whole story," one of the men replied. He wasn't one of the young ones from the beach. He had a short, neatly trimmed beard, and long dark hair, free of restraint. Hints of silver teased at his temples, threaded through his beard and a few streaks in his long locks. His attire was like Liam's when she'd first met him; a plaid and long-sleeved ivory leine tucked into it.

The man standing next to him dressed similarly, and looked *just* like him, except for the beard—he was clean-shaven—with a saffron tunic.

The fair-haired woman who'd spoken moved close to the second man, and he slid his arm around her shoulders, which drew attention to how big the men were.

Instinct told her they weren't Fae, regardless of their bulk. Not to mention her current location. They had to be Liam's twin uncles, and they were the same height as Xander. Despite being older—by human standards anyway—they were still full of muscle, with broad shoulders and trim waists. As handsome as Liam was, too.

One of them had to be the laird, the leader of Liam's human clan, the MacLeods.

Four other large men crowded them. They had to be the cousins.

They also resembled Liam's uncles, and were dark headed, except one. He appeared to be the youngest, and his locks were lighter, sandy-colored. The oldest one looked so much like the twins he was like a younger version of them.

An ebony-haired lass joined him, and they whispered to each other, stepping away from the other three.

Liam's family was so numerous, and the crowd of people overwhelming. Sienna couldn't imagine having a family as large as this. What must that have been like for her love during childhood?

To have this many people supporting you, to trust with your life…

Xander still held the brunette woman in his arms. "Alex is right. 'Tis no use lingering here. We must make a plan and get our lad back. Sienna is also in need of our assistance."

Her cheeks burned, as all eyes landed on her.

"Sienna, is it?" the blonde woman with the long

braid asked, smiling. "Nice to meetcha." She didn't leave the beardless twin's side, but the welcome in her expression was comforting.

However, Sienna didn't get a chance to answer.

"Let us inside," the bearded twin repeated, gesturing, but it was more order than suggestion.

Sienna followed her love's parents.

There were MacLeods in front of her and behind, and she tried not to skitter closer to Xander, or flee from the large male forms behind her.

It wasn't like any of Liam's family would mean her any harm, but she *was* among strangers. Strangers who loved the man she loved and might blame her for his capture. She didn't relish the idea of repeating her tale.

The great hall was huge, and had a welcoming fire in the hearth, despite the late hour. Three massive, candled chandeliers hung from the ceiling, lighting the space with a soothing ambient glow.

Tables were positioned in horizontal rows, and another at the head of the room on a raised dais. The rough-hewn dark wood reminded her of the table in the dining area of her treed home.

The hall felt surprisingly welcoming and warm, even though it was vast. Plenty of chairs and long benches provided enough space to feed a small army.

How large was Liam's clan?

Sienna wanted to look around, and study the place, but she didn't get the chance. They shuffled to a bench seat at the table closest to the fireplace.

Then Liam's family surrounded her.

The couples among the group were obvious and stood together, Liam's parents, his oldest cousin, Angus and his dark-haired wife, the blonde woman with the long braid and the clean-shaven twin.

The twin with the beard had to be the laird, because Liam's father had called him *Alex* by name. The man, Alex, who'd married the former princess of her realm, Alana.

Sienna scanned the crowd trying to recognize the woman with Fae features, but she wasn't present.

The other three cousins stood together near their parents. They were brothers if she remembered correctly.

The men, older and younger alike, started asking questions all at once. Some of the information they sought she'd already told Xander.

Her love's father wasn't having much success when he'd tried to intervene.

They fired off demands faster than Sienna could process.

Her heart thundered, her face warmed and she wanted to flee. She squirmed on the wooden seat, her hands becoming clammy.

"Stop, everyone. You're overwhelming the lass."

The crowd of MacLeods parted with the statement that sounded more like a gentle royal decree, laced with amusement.

A diminutive figure moved toward her, covered from head to toe in a simple, but elegant purple gown. Her pale locks gathered in a knot at the back of her neck were the same color as Liam's father's. She was beyond beautiful, ethereal.

She was Fae.

Sienna gasped. "Princess Alana."

Liam's aunt smiled, kind and gentle.

Fresh tears pricked the corners of Sienna's eyes.

"You know of me, lass? You do not look old enough to remember when I was still the princess I am no longer." Amusement danced in her violet gaze.

"Everyone knows of you and your human laird," Sienna blurted, instead of voicing her age of three and seven. "They merely speculate what became of you." Her words were rushed, and embarrassment threatened to swallow her whole.

Her love's aunt gave a rich peel of laughter and glanced at her husband. "Do they? I am not surprised that my father does not want it widely known that Alex and I still draw breath."

Sienna swallowed, and her words evaporated.

Her beauty was truly beyond words, even more so than other Fae. Her love had told her the former princess was cousin by blood to Xander, but the two standing in front of her looked more like siblings.

A few heartbeats passed before she could speak. "I was raised an exile, so you are a hero in many of our village's eyes, Your Highness." She averted her gaze.

The beautiful Fae woman closed the distance and grabbed both her hands. "I meant no offense, lass." Her voice was the same gentle tone, and her expression impossibly soft.

Staring into the former princess' eyes that were so much like Liam's made Sienna's heart crack. She had to fight off a new wave of emotion.

She needed Liam to be alive. So she could tell him she loved him. She wished he was at her side.

"I am glad my nephew found you, Sienna."

"Th-thank you, Your Highness." Calmness floated over her, and she sat taller on the bench. She'd forgotten that she'd heard the princess was an empath, but whether it was just the woman's presence, or actual magic, Sienna suddenly felt a little better. No matter the cause, she was grateful.

Alana shook her head. "Just Alana. *Your Highness* is years behind me."

Again, Sienna looked down to mask her embarrassment. She bit her bottom lip.

"Sienna, will you tell us what happened to Liam?" The Fae woman's question maintained the same calm gentleness as earlier, but the order was unmistakable.

She nodded and let the former princess break their physical contact.

Alana joined her husband, but some of the MacLeods took nearby seats.

Despite all their eyes still glued to Sienna, them being seated felt like less of a demand, and she managed to inhale another fortifying breath.

Before she began, she sent a silent prayer to the Goddess...

Hear my words. Be alive. I love you.

Then she launched into the story.

A shuffling sound jarred Liam awake, and he teetered against the magic ropes. Liam hissed as the bindings sizzled his skin and he ordered himself to still. He hadn't planned on sleeping, but it wasn't like he was going anywhere. He must've drifted off.

His wings ached and he couldn't so much as twitch them. He planted his boots more firmly into the dirt floor, to be ready for the next onslaught.

No one had entered the room after his grandfather had left.

Perhaps the large man had ordered the reprieve from abuse, but how long could it last?

A slight figure approached, and Liam's gaze landed on what had to be a female, due to the slender build and a light floral scent that swirled around her as she neared.

She wore a dark purple mantel reminiscent of his Aunt Alana, and the hood obscured her face. The long garment flowed down to her feet.

Maids wore brown, so she couldn't be a servant, nor did Liam believe they would deign to feed him.

She stopped within arms' length and slowly lowered her hood.

Large, misty violet eyes collided with his. Her hair was stark white, and the material covering her body hid its entire length, but his gut told him it had once been the same platinum hue of his father's.

Liam blinked as unexpected emotion rose from his gut and clogged in his throat. "Lady Aileana?" he whispered.

"You're my lad's lad," she breathed, covering her

hand with her mouth as the tears spilled down her alabaster cheeks.

"Aye, I am," he croaked.

She darted to him, closing the distance, and cupping his damaged face with no hesitation. "Oh, my lad. What have they done to you?" Her voice was thick with concern, and maybe pain, as if this was not their first meeting.

Unnatural—magical—warmth spread from her palms, brushing into and then engulfing Liam's skin.

It felt so good, he closed his eyes.

Then it hit him, as the gentle heat kept going down his shoulders, across his chest, inching into his torso.

His grandmother was healing him.

His father had told him that before her Acana root addiction, she'd been a renown healer in the Fae Realm, as much as she'd been a princess—as sister to King Fillan.

As the story went, she'd met Captain Daegus in the course of her duties, and they'd fallen in love, married in secret, and bound themselves together with a permanent spell the king could not tear asunder. It sealed them to each other, so if one perished, the other would as well.

The magic was intended to ensure that no matter how angry the king became, he could not put Daegus to death without killing his sister, too.

It'd worked, but the marriage had not been happy. Liam's father's childhood had been difficult, without the love he'd been raised with.

After meeting his grandfather, he couldn't imagine the man *in love.* No matter how beautiful Lady Aileana was—and she was. His grandmother held the stunning ethereal beauty of the Fae, she very much looked like his Aunt Alana, her niece. She had to be well over one hundred years old but looked no older than sixty human years. Her face wasn't lined like Sienna's grandmother's. It was hard to tell how old the Fae were by looking at them, and Lady Aileana was no exception.

Xander had mentioned that his mother had overcome her dependency and returned to her former station. Obviously, that was true.

Had his grandfather sent her to him down in this dungeon on the orders of the king, or because of their blood-ties?

Perhaps she'd sneaked down here to see him when her husband had revealed Liam's presence?

His heart skipped.

She was the opposite of the huge Fae Warrior. Where he exuded darkness and aggression, she was all warmth, love, and light. Where her husband towered over Liam, she was petite, barely reaching Liam's shoulder.

How in any realm could they be together—or in love?

Liam winced as the heat in his left side intensified.

His grandmother was fixing where he'd been run through.

"This is not a new wound," she whispered as she worked.

"Nay," he gritted out. "A *gift* from tha Warriors tha night I arrived."

"You are *not* an abomination, my lad."

Liam arched an eyebrow. "Ye can read minds, like my da."

She glanced up from her task, a soft amused smile curving her mouth. "Aye."

He frowned. "I'll guard my thoughts."

"Aye, 'tis for the best."

"What're ye doin' here?" he ground out, because her ministrations had taken a painful turn, despite the warmth of her touch and the healing magic.

"My Daegus told me you were here, hurt. I cannot abide that. Besides, I wanted to meet my only grandson." She met his gaze again, flashing a smirk.

It was so reminiscent of his father, he had to blink the emotion away. He'd never imagined his da resembled his mother—not that Liam had contemplated it much. He'd never considered that he would ever meet his Fae grandparents, let alone both in the same day.

"You look like him, too. Although I see your mother in you, as well."

Liam startled. He hadn't built up the shields in his mind, and she'd plucked the thoughts from his head. He hadn't been around a mind-reader in almost a fortnight, so perhaps his skills had waned.

"Ye…ye remember my mother?"

The smile his grandmother wore was gentle, loving. "Aye, she was a pretty lass."

"She still is," Liam said. "How…how did ye ken

I'm yer only grandchild?"

Lady Aileana's smile widened. "When I heal, I see fully into my patient's head and heart. I see it all, at a deeper level than just reading minds. I also saw that you've been with Eilidh's family. I'm glad she was able to help and keep you safe." His grandmother's expression turned knowing. "I can see how you feel for her oldest granddaughter."

Liam blinked. Should be embarrassed, but his wonder was greater and won out. "Ye…ken Sienna's family?"

"Oh, aye. Her son used to be the head healer, the best in all the realm. We trained together." Sadness settled over her pretty face. "My brother is a ruthless bastard sometimes." This was spat with a bitter edge, and at any other time, he might have smiled at such a lady speaking a curse word. "Wardric convinced my brother that Corsten had betrayed him, with whatever evidence was needed. My brother is implacable when a decision is made. He put the healer to death and banished the rest of the family, but that isn't all."

Liam nodded. "Their magic. Eilidh tol' me."

His grandmother echoed his nod. "He had it stripped from them. Eilidh was the head healer before her son. They had the most powerful healing magic the realm has ever seen."

"I ken him, this Wardric. 'Tis a mage. What threat was a healer ta him?" Maybe she would tell him something more than what Sienna's grandmother had revealed. He reinforced his mind's walls, so she wouldn't think he was being deceptive.

"That I do not know. How do you know him?" This was a demand, and her violet gaze landed on his.

"He came to the exile village and met with Sienna's grandmother."

A mix of emotion—and perhaps fear—darted across Lady Aileana's beautiful countenance. "Do you know why, my lad?"

Liam nodded, then hissed as he shifted, and the magic ropes took another bite from his arms.

His grandmother looked at the fresh burn on his bound forearms and shook her head. "I'm sorry I neglected to free you before I healed you."

He didn't get a chance to answer, because she said a firm spellword and the tension in the bindings snapped away from his body with a sizzling sound, as if they protested releasing him.

They hung limply and innocent-looking from the hook above his head, the color fading until they were gray, as if the magic dissipating had left them dead.

She did the same to the manacles, which fell away, *thunking* to the dirt floor. Then her hands were back on him, healing the rope burns and the bruises on his wrists.

Liam's magic rolled over him and returned to the surface of his skin, as if it too, was grateful for being free. He flexed his wings, letting each of his cramped muscles stretch. "Thank ye," rolled from his lips on a relieved sigh.

"You are as bonnie as my lad, Liam." Lady Aileana's smile was soft and loving, and her eyes misty again.

It should've startled him that she knew his name, but she'd no doubt gleaned it from his thoughts. There was no need to introduce himself.

His grandmother grabbed both of his hands; her grip urgent as she tugged. "Tell me, my lad, what Wardric wants with Eilidh and her family."

chapter twenty-two

With so many large male bodies surrounding her, Sienna should've felt safer, but she didn't. She couldn't contain her fear—or *not* think about Liam crumpled at the foot of the dais in the Field of Light or the bright flashes of magic winking in and out. Not to mention the oversized winged soldiers in green armor brandishing large swords and dangerous spells alike.

Getting to the Human Realm had been a battle, and now they were returning to the fray, to the realm of her birth.

To rescue the man she loved.

To help her *mórai* break the oath spell and the agreement made with the evil mage.

Despite the magic and all the male bulk and swords around her, fear froze her heart and filled her limbs with ice.

"Breathe, lass." A large hand landed on her forearm.

Sienna looked up into the violet gaze that was so like Liam's. She nodded, because she couldn't find words, and her belly quivered at Xander's reassuring smile. It was gentle and soft and made her want to cry and run away from her problems.

"Stay close to me, and I'll protect you. We'll find Liam and then help your grandmother; I promise you that." Her love's father kept his voice low and steady, obviously intending to calm her.

She smiled and nodded again, accepting the vow. Sienna sucked in a breath and glanced down at the stark white sand in the cave that held the Faery Stones in the Human Realm.

Liam's uncles and three of his cousins were with her, Xander, and Alana.

The laird had insisted his wife would not venture to the Fae Realm without him, and they'd shared low heated words. Evidently Alex had triumphed, because he brooded by his wife, his hand on the hilt of a huge sword.

Their son, Angus, was also present, appraising his father with a smirk and a shake of his head. He carried a matching claymore, as all of the MacLeods wielded.

Duncan, the laird's twin, stood with his two oldest sons, Lachlan, and Rory.

Iain, the youngest MacLeod, had not been permitted to accompany them, despite his loud protests. His father had bid him to protect their womenfolk—his own mother, Claire, and Liam's, as well as Angus' wife, Lila, but that duty had not appeased the lad.

At only seven and ten, he was too young, although Iain also sported a huge sword and had declared that he was man enough. Sienna had hid her smile then—as not to offend Liam's cousin.

"The portal will not remain open long, so we must go quickly, together." Alana's voice snagged her attention. "I will open the Stones."

Alex growled something unintelligible, but his wife did not acknowledge him.

Sienna sucked in another breath, holding it in until her lungs burned.

The former princess stepped up to the five magic crystals and tapped each one in a pattern.

Sienna couldn't tear her eyes away as Alana worked.

The Faery Stones consisted of five naturally grouped Fae-made formations that emerged from the bottom of the small cave, arranged in a semi-circle with perfect spacing between each crystal. Four other stones flanked around the central Stone.

The crystals glinted, as though reflecting light from an external source, but the glow originated from within them. They gave off enough radiance, so the cave was not too dark, yet they were concealed effectively to deter unanticipated visitors.

Humming filled the air from the main crystal. The illumination brightened with each pass of the former princess' fingers.

A warm air filled the cave, kicking up scents of their group. The clean sweat, leather and sandalwood, as well as something sweet, mixed with healing herbs Sienna always associated with her *mórai*.

A popping noise filled the space, and then a sound like something tearing. Three more *pops*, and the warm air increased in pressure, whipping her hair in her face. Everyone's garments flapped and whirled around their ankles.

Alana stepped back from the glowing crystals,

and her husband grabbed her arm.

Sienna's focus darted to an opaque globe hovering above the stark white sand. It grew before her eyes, the same as when she'd been on the dais.

The portal was opening.

Alana moved away from Alex, reaching for her son and Liam's father, her arms outstretched. "Stay behind us," she instructed Sienna and the other males of their group. Xander grabbed one hand, and Angus the other, with her between them.

Alex grumbled, but obeyed, falling behind the only three of Clan MacLeod present with Fae blood. "Sienna, with me. Duncan an' tha lads will bring up tha rear."

She nodded and swallowed as she moved closer to the laird.

He drew the huge sword from its scabbard, the same sound echoing around them as the rest of the MacLeods did the same.

"They will be ready for us," Xander threw over his shoulder. "Especially since it's been less than twenty-four hours since Liam opened the Stones and Sienna escaped. There will be extra Warriors. Stay close until Alana, Angus and I perform the stunning spell. It will take all three of us, but hopefully we will eliminate the threat in one go."

More trepidation slid down Sienna's spine, making her quiver from head to toe.

Breathe.

The portal grew larger, and the blue and orange grasses of the Field of Light wavered in the early dawn hours through it, as if a reflection on a pond's surface.

She met the laird's blue eyes, and he offered a curt nod in return. His gaze turned fierce, but protective, and Sienna instantly trusted the leader of Liam's human clan. The same way she'd instantly trusted his father.

After two more heartbeats and a scattered prayer to the Goddess, they stepped through the magical doorway to the Fae Realm.

An impossibly thick arm shot across Liam's chest, and he froze behind his grandfather's huge form.

"The Faery Stones," his grandmother breathed from her position on his other side.

Magic tingled beneath the surface of his skin. "I feel it," Liam whispered. "Someone opened them." He met violet eyes, then a yellow pair.

Daegus grunted.

It could only be one thing.

His family had come for him, but Liam didn't voice the conclusion.

The twin worried expressions on his grandparents' faces confirmed they'd done the same figuring.

"This just got complicated," the captain barked.

"Nay," his grandmother retorted. "'Tis perhaps turning to our advantage."

They'd just landed in the forest behind the Field of Light, but on the opposite side from the previous night, where Liam had approached with Feneal and the lasses.

He'd flown with the Lady Aileana in his arms at her insistence, and with his Fae Warrior grandfather's grudging acknowledgment. He couldn't go as far as approval—because she didn't have it.

His slip of a grandmother had shut down, "You're not going," from the imposing figure she'd married.

Liam might've soiled himself if the man had turned a look of such fury on him, but she'd been dismissive, as if she hadn't noticed how angry the captain was.

She'd merely patted his huge chest and joined Liam, smiling lovingly as she'd moved into his arms so he could lift them into the air.

His grandmother was certainly a princess, after all. She'd expressed needing to see him home safely, or at least to the Stones.

"How much trouble could we get in?" She'd reasoned. The captain was in command of all the Fae Warriors, and he had great magic. Lady Aileana hadn't even entertained an argument from his grandfather.

They'd exited the dungeons through long-forgotten tunnels that spilled out into the forest surrounding the king's palace. They'd gone in the cover of the pre-dawn hours and had encountered no one.

Their flight had been covered in an invisibility spell, and Daegus had assured Liam he could handle his Fae Warriors.

He didn't dare question the man, but it was the

second dangerous situation Liam had willingly entered into in less than two days, and the previous one hadn't gone his way.

Nerves skittered all over his body, but his grandfather was a man of great power—whether speaking of position, physical size, or magic, so he chided himself to trust him.

His grandmother he trusted without question.

Maroon-barked Acana trees and blue-barked Subh trees smattered the area, between them and the Field of Light. They were close enough to hear shouts of alarm from the winged soldiers guarding the Faery Stones.

In light of Liam's antics of the night before, two full Wings of twelve were posted to the Field of Light. So, his family would contend with twenty-four Fae Warriors the moment they stepped through the Stones. His grandfather had said the king had insisted. Along with a demand to bring Liam to him.

How Captain Daegus planned to get around that and stay alive hadn't been voiced either, but Liam prayed the man had a plan to save himself, too. He may not know his grandparents well, but he didn't want them in danger because of him, either.

Twenty-four Fae Warriors.

His heart slid to his gut.

"Stay on my flank, Liam. Aileana, stay here, my love," Daegus ordered. The endearment did not soften the command, nor did it stave off his grandmother's instant protest.

Liam wasn't about to contradict the captain. His

grandparents' bickering was reminiscent of his Aunt Alana and her laird husband when Alex had the audacity to forbid his wife from something. His father often had to step in as the voice of reason.

Was he going to have to do the same?

Liam wasn't afraid of his Uncle Alex, but his grandfather was another tale.

They didn't have time to argue, but again, it wasn't something he was brave enough to say aloud. He drew the dirk his grandfather had returned to him. It wasn't as good as the claymore he'd left at home, but any weapon was better than none.

Evidently Captain Daegus also assessed time was of the essence because he did not further address his wife. The largest Fae Warrior flexed his enormous wings and cursed under his breath, before whirling away from them both and drawing his huge magic sword.

Liam's head buzzed from one glance at the weapon, and he had to tear his eyes away from the glowing aura of the thing. He wanted to ask about the nature of the sword's magic, but it wasn't the time.

"Stay close to me then, wife," his grandfather barked.

Lady Aileana drew up the hood of her mantle and nodded.

She didn't have a weapon, but she did have significant magic. However, she was a healer and gentle by nature, so Liam wasn't convinced she'd inflict harm on any being. Hopefully she could defend herself if needed. Although, his human family wouldn't be a threat to either of his grandparents.

They made their way through the forest and foliage to the Field of Light quickly and silently.

Liam's gaze landed on his father, aunt, and cousin Angus. The three of them were hand-in-hand, next to the dais, chanting.

His stomach jumped with equal parts fear and relief that his clan had come for him. They were truly here, in the Fae Realm.

He was too far away to catch their words. The portal had already snapped shut.

Others huddled behind them, but he couldn't make out who. More MacLeods, no doubt.

Liam could join them in a mere glide.

"To the air!" His grandfather shouted, scooping his wife into his arms, and shooting up with one powerful flap of his wings.

He obeyed without question, pumping his own, and rising above the treetops, but he didn't look away from the scene before him.

Whatever spell his family cast was finally born.

The magic was a visible, bright pink hue, moving away from Angus, Alana, and his father in circular waves, each one wider, thicker, and more powerful than the last.

With a percussive boom that made Liam wince and his ears ring, all the Fae Warriors went flying back, or tossed away from whatever position they'd held. The surrounding foliage flattened in the shock wave, then dancing up, as if in a torrential gale.

He surveyed the damage from aloft above the

clearing.

None of the Fae Warriors were upright, now sprawled across the orange and blue grass, unmoving.

All twenty-four of them.

His family had stunned them all in one go?

Liam hovered over the trees in disbelief, moving his wings to keep himself airborne, his heart thundering in his ears. He sucked back a gulp. He'd never seen such magic in his life, but it'd taken three people to do it, so it wasn't a common quatrain.

Even now, and in the air, he could feel magical waves reverberating, but they weren't lethal anymore. Thank God and the Fae Goddess alike that his grandfather had recognized what was about to happen and they'd flown above the spell's power.

Liam caught his grandparents in his peripheral vision. They were already descending, Lady Aileana's purple cloak waving gently in the moving air. She was settled against Daegus' chest, with her slender arms around his neck. His grandmother looked so comfortable in her husband's grip. No doubt they'd flown together for years.

His heart gave a painful thump as he thought about Sienna. How he'd never been able to grant her wish of soaring into the night sky holding her close, except for that much too short flight home after the first time they'd made love.

He scanned the scene before him—a quiet chaos had settled over the Field of Light, with his human clan at its center, and unconscious Fae Warriors in various crumpled piles on the grasses.

His stomach flipped when he spotted familiar bright red tresses among the dark heads of his family.

Liam dove for the ground, landing so fast he continued into a jog to avoid plummeting to his face. He ignored the unbalanced sensation and closed the distance to his Fae healer, the woman who'd stolen his heart in a matter of weeks. His chest was tight, and he had to gulp to get air down. None of that mattered.

There was only Sienna.

When she turned that burnished bronze gaze on him, what little air remained in his lungs evaporated, but he didn't care.

"You're alive!" she sobbed.

Liam pulled her into his arms. He couldn't not touch her when she wore such a worried, destroyed expression.

Sienna came to him without delay, sliding shaking arms around his waist, and muffling a sob against his leine.

Her scent washed over him, the pleasant spice of herbs, mixed with the fresh air of the clear warm day. "Why're ye cryin'?" he whispered above the shell of her ear.

"I'm not," she retorted into his neck, but she wouldn't look up. She stifled a loud sniffle.

He smiled into her fiery locks, ordering himself to *not* kiss her right now. If he gave into the urge, he'd never hear the end of it from Lachlan and Rory.

The back of his neck tingled, becoming a row of fire down his spine from all the eyes on them. Even his grandparents watched, as if Liam and Sienna were traveling bards performing a show.

"I feared I'd never see you again." Her voice was low and muffled against the fabric of his leine, but he'd heard her clearly. "I thought...I thought the Fae Warriors had..." her voice wobbled again, and his heart skipped in tandem.

"Shhh. I'm hale. My grandparents helped me get free of the dungeons."

Sienna lifted her head, her gorgeous eyes wide. "Grandparents?"

Liam nodded. "My father's parents." He gestured to the huge captain and his tiny wife, who'd joined the rest of the MacLeods.

Her mouth was half-agape. Sienna's gaze skittered away from his and he felt her sudden nerves.

It had to be because of their audience, but he wasn't ready to let her go yet. Maybe he couldn't ever let her go.

Liam's previous regret of not telling her he loved her floated into his mind, but he couldn't do it now, from location alone, as well as his clan surrounding them. If she was uncomfortable with him holding her in front of them, Sienna wouldn't appreciate his declaration.

Besides, it still wouldn't change their fates. Their quest of undoing the agreement with Wardric still hung over them all. After they dealt with the evil mage, she would take her place in Fae society. There would be no place for him here.

His Aunt Alana embraced his grandmother, and Liam smiled.

Daegus was on the edge of the group, as if unsettled, and Liam couldn't imagine his grandfather hesitating over anything, but the huge, winged man certainly didn't seem eager to join the group of humans and Fae — despite not having seen his son in more than twenty years.

Liam's eyes landed on his father.

Xander, with wings.

A sight he'd never been privy to in his life. The iridescent appendages were larger than his own, and looked strong, as if they'd not been missing from his father's wide muscular back for the last several decades.

Xander's expression exuded joy and it stole Liam's breath all over again.

"Da..." he croaked, but it wasn't loud enough to carry beyond Sienna.

She'd slipped from his arms, but she clung to his hand, their fingers entwined.

Sienna squeezed to offer comfort, but Liam was torn between glancing at his love, and memorizing the freedom stamped all over his father's face.

Guilt swirled in his gut anew, and he had to swallow to stave off unwanted emotion. He felt incomplete when he was home in the Human Realm, without his wings, but Liam had never considered his father felt the same.

Never entertained the idea that Xander had had wings all his life, and strong magic that had been diminished by the realm he'd been forced to flee to. Liam had never contemplated how that had made the man who'd given him life *feel*.

He could sense his father's elation, Xander's *completeness* at being rejoined with his missing wings.

Liam's selfishness and his foolish childlike disregard hit him full in the chest, and almost doubled him over. "Da," he breathed again. Tears burned the corners of his eyes, but he wouldn't cry. "I'm sorry." He made this louder, so it would carry to the former Fae Warrior. More words pushed against his lips, but he couldn't voice them. He shook his head and frowned. His heart thumped, rebounding painfully against his ribs.

Xander's expression fell when their eyes met, but then his da closed the small distance to him. Instead of clasping his forearm, his father drew him in for a tight embrace.

"Da, I'm so sorry," Liam whispered, over and over. He clung to the man like he hadn't since he was a wee laddie, all his mixed emotions clogging in his chest and throat until he had to pant to breathe.

Xander was the one to end the embrace, but he held Liam by the shoulders, and shook him. "Lad, all is well." His voice was calm, but his face was a mask of concern.

Liam hadn't tried to hide his thoughts, so his father could no doubt hear the chaos in his head, too. He swallowed and inhaled, and this time the air went down smoothly. "Da..."

The corner of Xander's mouth lifted, and he cocked his head to one side. "'Tis good to see you, my lad."

Liam was able to smile, and took strength from Sienna beside him, as well as his father. He nodded. "Good ta see ye, too, Da."

Lady Aileana stood behind her son, her hand covering her mouth, and her violet eyes were wide and misty. A lone tear had slid down her alabaster cheek. "My two lads," she whispered.

"Mother," Xander said, whirling to face her, and wearing a warm smile. He opened his arms, and his mother rushed into his embrace.

Liam chuckled and exchanged a glance with Sienna when his father rose to his full height, lifting Lady Aileana from the ground because she was so petite.

She was crying and clinging to her only child, and Xander held his mother for a lot longer than he'd embraced Liam.

His grandfather watched the display, his large body taut, and his long dark hair swaying gently in the warm breeze. Although stoic and silent, his yellow eyes betrayed him, as did his locked jaw, as if trying to hold back the significance of his emotions.

The Fae Captain's feelings shone from his unusually hued eyes, and it made Liam's heart stutter. It was deeper than what he'd read from the man he'd met in the dungeon, and he hoped his father would notice what Liam could see.

The fierce winged man did love his wife and son, even if the whole realm only discussed his ruthlessness and prowess in battle or recall how he'd publicly disowned Xander.

Xander finally released his mother and glanced at Daegus.

Liam's gut told him his grandfather would not get closer to the group of MacLeods, so if his father wanted to greet the man, Xander would have to go to the captain.

His uncles and cousins clustered together in a defensive position, swords still drawn, and his Aunt Alana stood close to Alex.

Liam felt their sense of unease, despite the Fae Warriors still down and unconscious.

He understood—they did not have unlimited time in the Field of Light. They still needed to get to Sienna's family and break Wardric's spell.

His father went to his grandfather and thrust out his arm. "Father, 'tis good to see you."

Daegus cleared his throat, as if he couldn't speak without doing so. "My son."

Xander flashed a reassuring smile, and they clasped forearms with a loud clapping noise. The force translated the affection that neither man could give voice to.

Liam smiled to himself. He'd always considered his father the strong silent type, because compared to the raucous MacLeods, Xander tended to choose his words carefully and remain calm in disaster.

Seeing him next to the Fae captain told Liam his grandfather was much the same way. Even if they'd had a rocky relationship over the years, now all appeared forgiven, on both sides. Too bad they could not see each other regularly. His gut shouted if they could, his father would be as close to Daegus as he was to Liam's human uncles.

Lady Aileana stepped to her husband, and the huge man took her hand.

"Our stunning spell will not last much longer," Alana said, and all eyes shot to her.

"I need to go home," Sienna whispered.

"Liam has told me of the oath spell," his grandmother said.

Daegus grunted in obvious surprise and crossed his thick arms over his impossibly broad chest. He flexed his huge wings.

Liam swallowed, because he could feel the instant rage the man radiated, and Lady Aileana hadn't mentioned that she'd kept what he'd told her in the dungeon to herself.

His grandfather was angry because oath spells were illegal, something his grandmother had told him. The reason for the decree was her own magic of the same variety, the one that had bound her to the man she'd married. King Fillan had outlawed them after he'd discovered what they'd done.

Lady Aileana had also told Liam that Daegus had always hated Wardric. Maybe his grandfather would help Sienna's cause?

"We need to get to the exile camp," Xander said. "Father, we do not have time to explain."

"Go, my wife will reveal all," the captain barked. "Then I will meet up with you. Worry not about my Warriors. I will handle them when they awake."

Xander offered a curt nod.

His mother reached up and caressed his cheek. "Be careful, my lad."

He smiled and kissed her hand. "Aye, Mother, indeed."

Lady Aileana reached for Liam's hand, and he obeyed. She squeezed his fingers with her small slender ones. "You, too, my lad. Help your lass' family but take heed."

He nodded, leaning down to press a kiss to her cheek. "Thank ye fer all ye've done."

His grandmother smiled. "Do not say goodbye yet, my Liam." Her eyes turned misty again.

Liam smiled and had to swallow back a new wave of emotion. When he glanced back at Sienna, her bronze eyes were weepy, too, but he also read relief. He pressed a quick kiss to her mouth—couldn't help himself.

He scanned his human clan. People who loved him enough to endanger their lives by traversing to a strange realm with their definite disadvantage on full display, despite being trained warriors. He was grateful beyond words that they were willing to help a lass they didn't know, just because he cared for her.

Liam swallowed again. He made eye contact with both his uncles, each of his cousins, and lastly, his father. "Ready?" he croaked, then cleared his throat.

chapter twenty-three

Sienna wanted to jump into Liam's arms and cling to him, never let him go. Seeing him again had been a shocked relief to her heart and body. She'd sworn to herself that if she'd ever see him again, she'd shout her love at first sight. Now that the moment came, it was like her mind was a chaotic swirl of emotions, tasks to achieve and plans to sort. Words failed her.

Besides, they were surrounded by all the members of his family, and the timing didn't feel right. Truly, other than seeing him alive, nothing felt right. Her family was still in grave danger. Her focus needed to be getting to them and saving her *mórai*. She needed to see Amalie and Ealeric with her own eyes.

Despite having two winged men in their party now, they'd decided that navigating the forest on foot to get to Grànnda Falls and the exile camp would be safer and more efficient.

The MacLeods were big men, even Lachlan and Rory, so asking Xander and Liam to fly everyone to Sienna's home would take far too many trips.

She stayed close to her love's side as they moved through the trees, wishing she could entwine her hand in his. Sienna couldn't stop staring, as if her whole form was starved for him, and they'd only been separated twenty-four hours.

How would her heart survive when this was all over, and he had to walk away?

"Sienna?" Liam's voice was low and above her ear, close enough for his breath to kiss her skin.

A warm shiver slid down her spine. She swallowed to distract herself. She tripped over a rock and wobbled on her feet, crashing her shoulder into Liam's.

His large but gentle hand enclosed her upper arm to steady her.

After what felt like hours of watching Liam, suddenly, Sienna couldn't look at him. Her insides flipped and she glanced to her left. Her gaze collided with a very blue pair of eyes.

Angus offered a small smile, but concern was stamped all over his handsome face. "Are ye well, lass?"

Embarrassment shot into her cheeks and scorched up to her ears. "A-a-aye," she stuttered, looking at the greens and browns of the underbrush and ordering her feet one in front of the other. Twisting an ankle on a root in the forest she'd known her whole life would further humiliate her.

They'd crossed the border, moving into the exile's territory, where the muted colors similar to the Human Realm dominated. Hearing the Falls was moments away. The clearing she'd grown up in was only minutes over the hill.

What was wrong with her?

Sienna hadn't answered Liam, and she couldn't seem to speak full sentences to any of the MacLeods.

She should be able to tease Angus for referring to her as *lass*, considering she was older than him by a few years. She'd never look at him and think *lad*. He was a large attractive man, and a halfling just like Liam.

Of course, she didn't know him, but instinct told her she'd like her love's oldest cousin if she got to know him. He'd been nothing but kind to her, like all of Liam's family, and she would be forever grateful that they were all willing to help her *mórai*.

"Are ye sure yer okay?" Liam asked, worry wrapped around the question.

She nodded, so she wouldn't stutter out another answer.

The concern didn't fade from his eyes.

"I'm braw," she whispered.

He smirked. "Me, too."

Sienna allowed him to loop his arm in hers. Touching him felt right, and some of her anxiety eased. She tried to banish the constant awareness that their time together was coming to an end and focused on the heat of his arm against hers, even through their clothing.

A companionable silence fell. She concentrated on the crunching of the dead leaves and twigs under their boots.

She heard his chirruping keen before she saw him.

Her little bogle sounded frantic.

"Trioblóid!" Sienna called, rushing past large male bodies. She forced Rory and Lachlan to part to move between them, then Alex and Xander, who led their group.

Alana stood next to her husband, and Sienna threw an apologetic glance to the former princess, but she didn't slow.

Liam followed on her heels.

"Trioblóid!" she yelled again. She opened her arms right as they reached the edge of the clearing to the exile camp.

The bogle launched himself into her chest. His hairy coat shifted in colors, grays and blacks for fear and fright, as well as yellows of alarm. His round form shook uncontrollably in a way Sienna had never seen in him.

Something was very wrong.

Her heart slid to her gut.

"Trio," Sienna whispered. "What happened?" She wished he could tell her with words.

The MacLeods caught up, and like Liam when he'd seen her bogle for the first time, they stared and gaped. Except Alana and Xander, who looked on with concern.

"What is *tha'*?" Rory asked, his green eyes wide.

Liam hushed his cousin, making eye contact with her. Clearly, even he sensed Trioblóid was petrified. "Let's go home, love."

Emotion pricked her eyes when he referred to the tree she'd grown up in as *home*.

Her bogle calmed with every step, some of the darkness fading from his coat, but he wasn't the contented blues and purples he displayed most often. He went bright yellow and chirruped, then made a barking-growl.

Sienna nearly dropped him in front of her family's tree.

The door was ajar.

She took off, dashing into the dark home and ignoring shouts from her love's family to wait.

The rush of heavy male boots told her none of the MacLeods hesitated to follow her inside.

Sienna started her frantic search before her eyes had adjusted to the dimness. The treed home was unusually dark. Not even a single candle nor a magic globe Feneal had to recharge and light for them.

The kitchen was a mess, worse than the night the Fae Warriors had searched for Liam. The table was broken in half and overturned, and three out of the six chairs were smashed and splintered.

Firewood was strewn about, as was her grandmother's largest cooking pot, that usually lived over the hearth. Embers and ash from the fireplaces covered everything on the packed dirt floor.

Shattered glass from the small kitchen window that faced the clearing also littered the counter and the floor.

"Fan out. Search the dwelling," Alex whispered, sword drawn.

The other MacLeod men followed suit, slowly moving throughout Sienna's home.

Liam remained by her side, his small dirk in hand.

Alana was there, too, surveying from just inside the doorway.

Trio jumped from Sienna's arms, turning a frantic bright pink, hopping up and down. His chirruping sounded more like a screech or scream.

Sounds she'd never heard him make before.

He skittered toward the damaged table.

"Oh, Goddess!" Sienna breathed, scooting around a broken chair, and sliding to her knees in a move that made her thighs smart. "Ealeric!"

Her brother lay on his side, one leg bent and the other straight. His arms were limp, and his head was at an odd angle.

Her heart slid to her toes.

Trio nudged her brother to no avail.

Sienna scooted the bogle out of the way and shook Ealeric's shoulder. "Ealeric!" She rolled him to his back.

Blood trickled from his mouth, and an angry red and purple bruise bloomed on his forehead, disappearing into his hairline.

"Ealeric!" She shoved her knuckles into his chest, rubbing hard. The move caused pain, and should rouse him if he wasn't—

Sienna shut the thought down and surveyed his body for any other wounds. Nothing, other than his head, mouth, and swollen nose.

"No one else is here," Xander announced.

Blood drained from her face, and she bit her lip to stave off full body shakes.

Where were *Móraí* and Amalie?

Most of the MacLeods returned to the main living area, which suddenly felt tiny with the oversized men filling it. They murmured to each other and watched Sienna.

"Is he…alive?" Liam asked, taking a knee beside her.

"He has to be," she gritted out, not looking at her halfling. Tears filled her eyes and she tried to fight them, along with the fear for her missing grandmother and sister.

She couldn't lose any of them.

Sienna rubbed her brother's chest again, calling his name twice.

Ealeric's brow knitted, and then he frowned.

Alana joined them on the floor, moving closer.

"Thank the Goddess," Xander whispered. He, too, had taken a knee on the other side of Sienna and Liam.

Sienna blew out a breath. Of course, her love's father knew who Ealeric was, as she'd made no effort to hide her thoughts. She was too busy to concentrate on mind shields. "Ealeric, wake up, brother," she begged.

"I can heal him," the former princess said.

He reached for his head, groaning, and finally his dark eyes fluttered open. He tried to sit up, but she plastered a hand to his chest.

"Nay, brother. Slowly."

"Sienna?" he ground out, blinking a few times. "My head is killing me," he breathed.

"Aye, I'm here, as is Liam and his family."

Ealeric's midnight eyes flew open, wide, and very awake. He rushed to a sit, despite her urging to move slowly. Then he doubled over, grabbing his head with both hands and cursing colorfully in Fae.

That elicited a few chuckles from some of the

MacLeods.

Liam and Xander caught her brother's shoulders and helped him ease up against a carved wooden cabinet.

Sienna shot to her feet and opened a kitchen drawer, because she didn't want to waste time running to the medicine room. She grabbed a square of linen and squatted next to Ealeric.

He batted her hands away when she tried to dab the blood from his nose and mouth. "I'm fine. You have to go. Now."

"Go?"

Alana moved in and grabbed his face.

Ealeric stilled in the former princess' grip, and he didn't order her away from him, despite the fact she was a stranger.

Her hands glowed softly, but soon, the radiance faded, as did the bruise on his forehead and the swelling in his face.

He murmured thanks to Alana, then pinned Sienna with his eyes. "Find Amalie and *Móraí*. That bastard took them. In his rage at your absence, he changed his plans. He's going to marry our sister. Today. He said he would get what he was promised, no matter which sister."

"What?" Sienna shrieked. "How did this happen? Where's Feneal?" Her heart thundered so hard her chest ached. Her temples pulsed, and the room spun.

"Where did he take them?" Liam demanded. He made a fist, as if he was holding himself back from shaking her brother's shoulders.

Defeat and desperation dominated Ealeric's expression. "I don't know." His frown was full of despair.

"I do." The booming voice came from the doorway.

All eyes settled on Feneal.

"I am absolutely *not* staying here," Sienna gritted out, obviously trying not to shout in his face. Her slender body was taut and pitched forward, her tight fists white-knuckled at her sides.

"Neither am I," her brother piped up. Ealeric was now on his feet, and they all stood around the ruined kitchen.

Liam sighed. He didn't want to fight with her. He ran his hand through the long, tangled mess of his curls and resisted the urge to grab her and shake some sense into her.

"Don't make the argument that Ealeric and I have no magic," Sienna started, her gorgeous face flushed with pink. "Because neither do your uncles and cousins, except Angus. Alana is going, so you can't forbid females. You haven't the right to forbid me from *anything*, anyway."

There were a few murmurs from their audience, and Liam wanted to wince. He ignored someone's amused snort that MacLeods always picked troublesome lasses.

When the laird laughed at the comment, Aunt

Alana smacked Uncle Alex's chest.

"We don't have time for this," Feneal barked. All eyes landed on the former Fae Warrior, disheveled as always, and pacing near the front door.

"Exactly," Sienna snapped. "Let's go." She made a move to push past him, but Liam grabbed her.

"Love—" he whispered, hoping his cousins didn't hear the endearment. He didn't mind if they knew how he felt about her, after all, he'd kissed her in front of them at the Field of Light. He just didn't want to hear any jibes. This wasn't the time.

She narrowed her beautiful eyes. "Nay, Liam."

"I dinnae want anathin' ta happen ta ye."

Her expression softened. "I know. But this is my family."

Liam closed his eyes for a heartbeat and nodded. In her place he would do the same, he had to give her that. After all, his family surrounded them. Had come for him. He sucked in a breath. "Okay," he forced out.

Sienna offered a small smile, and he burned to kiss her.

She hadn't broken their physical contact and he wanted to pull her closer, wrap her in his wings, and keep her safe. Lock her away from what had to be done. He wished she'd stayed at Dunvegan.

A male throat cleared—probably his Uncle Alex—then the MacLeods filed out of the treed home.

Ealeric went, too, with obvious hesitation in his body, but Liam threw him a grateful look.

Feneal waggled a finger. "We must go."

"Aye," Liam said. "Give us a moment."

"Only one." With a curt nod, the former Fae Warrior also retreated.

"Liam, I—"

He shook his head when she turned her misty eyes on him. He pressed his forehead to Sienna's. She stifled a sob, sliding her arms around him.

"I ken it, love," he said the words into her hair, inhaling her scent, as familiar to him now as breathing. Liam burned to tell her he loved her but forced the notion to stay in his head and heart. There was no way they could end up together. Telling her now would only split her focus on rescuing her family from Wardric and breaking the oath spell.

"I'm sorry," Sienna whispered.

"Fer what?"

She pulled back from his chest and their gazes met. "For saying you don't have the right to forbid me. It was mean and unnecessary."

Pain speared into his gut, reinforcing that hiding his feelings was the right choice. "Why? 'Tis true."

Sienna blinked, and emotion darted across her gorgeous face, but she schooled her expression fast. She averted her eyes. Finally, she nodded. "Let's go." She slipped from his arms and whirled away so fast her hair nearly smacked him in the face.

What the hell had just happened?

Liam sucked in a fortifying breath and held it until his head spun. The burn in his lungs made the air whoosh from his mouth. It still wasn't nearly as painful as what he'd just had to say. With one last glance around the ruined home, he cursed himself to hell and forced his feet to move.

chapter twenty~four

"Now is not the time for matters of the heart, my lad." His aunt's low statement held regret, and her expression was full of comfort. Alana appeared at his side, reaching for his hand.

Liam glanced toward Sienna and Ealeric, but let the former princess grip his fingers.

His aunt offered a gentle smile when she'd followed his gaze back to the woman he loved.

She stood, head bent with her brother, away from the MacLeods. Her eyes had drifted toward Liam once or twice, only to be ripped away and land back on Ealeric. Sienna hadn't spared him another glance.

"I—" He tried to gather any kind of response, but it wasn't happening. He didn't want to talk about it with Alana, anyway. His aunt was an empath of significant power even in the Human Realm, so he didn't want to contemplate what the former princess could feel from him in the realm of her birth, where her magic was as strong as it was meant to be.

"Say no more. 'Twill be well in the end." She squeezed his hand. "You met your grandparents." She smiled. "It was good to see them again, even the captain."

He muttered something non-committal, because he didn't want to talk about his Fae grandparents, either.

Liam's father and uncles were huddled with Feneal, and his cousins were close to them, all expressions rapt on the former Fae Warrior's words, gestures, and instructions. There was some sort of diagram in the dirt at their feet.

He snorted. The exile hadn't shared a damn thing with him before they'd gone to the Field of Light. He should be grateful that this time they had a plan to go wherever the mage had Sienna's family.

The clearing was suspiciously empty of any other exile, which was odd, considering during most of the time Liam had spent there, he'd observed many day-to-day activities being completed outside, anything from tanning a hide to gardening near other treed homes, or even cooking over an open fire.

Perhaps they'd all fled because of Wardric's arrival, or they all watched from inside their homes. There was no doubt any exile with magic would know humans existed among them. Maybe they weren't curious, or maybe they were, but too afraid to investigate or ask questions.

"Can tha oath spell be broken?" Liam's words rushed out, because he desperately needed a distraction from more scattered emotions he didn't want to deal with.

His aunt's expression sobered. She nodded slowly. "'Tis possible, but 'twill not be easy."

"How?" he asked, just short of a demand.

"The easiest way is with Wardric's death."

"That is a path I'm willin' ta follow." Liam

gripped the hilt of his dirk, again wishing for his long-lost claymore. He should've asked why they'd neglected to bring it for him.

His aunt studied him, then gave a nod. "If it is necessary, it is well deserved."

He cocked his head to one side. "You know Wardric?"

"Aye, one of my father's mages for more years than I care to remember, and he's been the cause of many a death and at the root of many an evil deed."

The men's strategy session came to an end, and they broke apart.

Liam didn't regret missing it. He was a fast learner. Not to mention, he'd fought beside and sparred with his cousins and uncles for years, since his father had first handed him a sword at ten or eleven.

What he regretted was that Sienna wouldn't look at him. Shredded his heart piece by piece with every glance she didn't return.

Feneal clapped his hands and they all gathered around him. "We go. His lair is hidden in the foothills of the mountains." The exile gestured to the right, toward the Falls. "Beyond where Grànnda Falls ends, and beyond the lake and the largest royal Acana grove where the healers harvest the bark, to the west."

The area didn't sound familiar; Liam couldn't recall if he'd ever flown over it. However, it seemed far away. "How long is the journey?"

The former Fae Warrior smiled, which made his scraggly beard shift as if it was alive. "Seconds, if I can get some magical assistance."

He spoke in full sentences again, which signaled a good thing. It also solidified the notion for Liam that he wanted the others around him to leave him alone, so he played the role of a mad man.

Xander gestured for Angus, Alana, and Liam to move closer to the exile.

Feneal's dilapidated appearance was a startling difference from the former princess's fine purple trews and lavender tunic, as she took a place next to him. Although all Liam's family—save his da—wore plaids and leines, their garments were also of good quality, compared to the disintegrating clothing and filthy bare feet the former Fae Warrior displayed.

He looked out of place among them, but he was definitely in charge of this endeavor, whatever lay ahead. Liam chose to trust the man's crystal blue eyes, now lucid and determined.

Liam took Xander's hand when Feneal directed it, then Angus', as his cousin had settled on his other side.

The exile called for the MacLeods, Sienna and her brother to step into the middle of the circle they'd formed.

"I will project the place into your minds, then we will go," Feneal said.

"I dinnae be able ta *blink*," Liam said. Neither could his father, but Angus and Alana could.

"It matters not. We have enough magic, working together," Alana said. "Just ensure the picture in your mind's eye is clear." It was good that his aunt had gleaned Feneal's plan, too, and she must've agreed with the former Fae Warrior.

Magic tingled over his skin, palpable in the air. Liam shivered from it.

Sienna stood directly in front of him, but not nearly as close as he needed her.

Ealeric took her hand, and she shifted to her brother's side.

Somehow, Liam was jealous that someone other than him was beside her at this moment. He bit back a curse, chided himself to concentrate, and closed his eyes when he observed Feneal and his father doing the same.

A sensation like an itch made his nose twitch, but he didn't break either grip on his cousin or his da's hands.

Soon, a picture appeared in his mind, as if he'd called it up as clear as if he stood in front of it, or a memory of his own making.

Feneal was present in his mind, more thickly obvious than the times Liam had been the recipient of telepathic speech. It made him feel itchy again, and he wanted to shove the Fae man's consciousness away. Memorizing the image was important, so he ordered himself to calm and take in the hilly landscape.

The place was stark and sparse, and even one glance shouted that it was remote, secret, and had no evident signs of occupation. The blue and orange grasses around the boulders and cliffs were much longer than the Field of Light's, and Liam could picture them swaying in the warm, artificial breeze.

A large natural structure rose above them, the rock face ebony and startling in its darkness against the lighter pastels of the foliage and the pink and gold sky. It was foreboding and shot a tremor of warning down his spine.

There are a series of caves. Feneal's voice was in his head, not in his ears. *We will appear at a safe distance, here.*

The image sharpened and moved, as if Liam flew above it. When it finally stopped, a small group of boulders was centered in his mind.

This is as close as we can get without detection. Memorize this location. The former Fae Warrior's voice was clear and focused.

"Are you ready?" the exile asked aloud.

Liam opened his eyes to see the rest of their party had as well. A murmur of affirmatives floated across the group.

"Lay hands on us, and do not break the chain," Feneal instructed everyone inside their circle.

Liam offered a smile to Sienna when she bit her bottom lip, her hesitation to come to him obvious. He wanted to reassure her or beg her to touch him.

Eventually she closed the distance and rested her small hand on his left forearm. She didn't speak, but she finally met his eyes.

Ealeric took her free hand and placed his other one on Liam's right forearm. He didn't say anything, either.

Around the circle, everyone else followed the same motion. Alex and Duncan had gone to Alana, and Rory to Angus, Lachlan to Xander.

Liam smirked when he noted no one had chosen

Feneal.

Magic swirled up around them, moving faster and faster like a cyclone until it swallowed him whole. He couldn't feel Sienna's or Ealeric's hands on him, and blackness filled his vision. Blinking did nothing to clear the sensation.

Then he was falling.

He ordered his wings to pump, but he couldn't tell if they had obeyed.

Liam's feet slammed into something hard, and he opened his eyes. Blue and orange grasses swayed before him, like he'd imagined in the vision Feneal had projected. He was standing, but his legs wobbled, and no one was touching him anymore.

He'd *blinked* before, with his cousin Lexi, but this was something else.

His stomach inverted, and he fought the urge to vomit. Liam leaned over, resting his hands on his knees and reminded himself to breathe. Sweat beaded his forehead, and despite solid rock under his boots, the whole landscape spun.

The sounds of retching greeted his ears, but his neck was having trouble lifting his head so he could see who it was.

Small warm hands cupped his cheeks, and his gaze met a familiar bronze one. "Liam?"

He coughed and forced himself upright. "I'm braw." He didn't push away helpful hands from Sienna or her brother when they both steadied him. "Are ye well?" Liam forced out. He wanted her to keep her hands on him, but he couldn't tell her that.

"We are fine. It seems the journey was harder on those with human blood." Sienna grimaced.

Liam glanced around the hilly area, taking in the boulders Feneal had shown them. At least they'd ended up where they were supposed to. He scanned his family. Sienna hadn't been wrong.

Angus was upright, but he and Alana each stood by a twin, hands on their wide backs. Both his uncles were doubled over.

Rory and Lachlan helped each other stand with his father.

Xander watched, as if he would step in, if necessary.

Feneal stood on a rock, surveying as if he was ruler of the area, waiting for them to orient. If he felt like they wasted time, or was annoyed they hadn't come through hale, his expression didn't give anything away. The exile appeared stoic and strong.

Liam imagined him clean-shaven, his matted dirty hair long and shiny in a Warrior's braid. His broad shoulders and chest covered in a green chest-plate and large iridescent wings rising above his head, as he stood in that same position, his hand on the hilt of a sword.

Not for the first time, he felt for the Fae man. The reality before him seemed like a sad imposter, although the former Warrior had never been anything but kind to him, even saving his life with the spell he'd cast to hide his human blood. At least Feneal still had his magic, and it was strong. Their advent to Wardric's lair proved that.

Liam had never heard of such a way to travel, but he wasn't eager to do it again. Since he'd been raised in the Human Realm, he was ignorant of magic in so many ways. His father had always been reluctant to educate him fully. Aunt Alana had tended to be more open, but she shared the information only in small doses. He regretted that, as he did so many other things.

Many of the spells he'd learned over the years had been by pure chance, eavesdropping, or because his cousin Lexi had been involved. She had a keen instinct for magic and loved to experiment. He missed her greatly but was glad she was safely in the far future with the MacDonald man she'd fallen for. Lexi wouldn't have allowed her father to ban her from this adventure.

"Liam?" Sienna said his name again, her brow knitted tight.

He wanted to snatch her to him and kiss her. Why hadn't he kissed her in the treehouse when they were alone?

What if he never had the chance again?

Liam's heart stuttered. "I'm braw," he repeated with some intentional force, and flexed his wings for good measure. He mourned when she nodded and slid out of touching distance.

His uncles and cousins were finally upright, expressions less green, and everyone gathered around Feneal again. The tall, but filthy figure remained on the large rock.

"We must be quick and remain together. When

we get close, he will no doubt sense us."

"Are there protection spells on the cave?" Xander asked.

"I would assume so," Feneal said.

"I can sense them." Alana closed her eyes without waiting for a response. She spread her arms, as if for balance and took two steps toward the looming ebony caves.

Liam glanced around, cataloging the land before them, which matched Feneal's vision exactly. The mountainous caverns were likely only minutes away on foot, yet the boulders by them should shield their group from view, as long as Wardric had no aerial advantage.

The mage couldn't fly but had access to Fae Warriors. Would any of his grandfather's men willingly work with the bastard?

He glanced back at his aunt, who still probed for magic in the same position. His own powers were alert and tingling, as if separate from his body, and his wings had tensed of their own accord, readying him for a fight. Or a flight.

Finally, the former princess opened her eyes. "There is lethal magic surrounding the largest of the caves. It will blast anyone who enters. Strong enough to kill. Also, if the spell is tripped, it will alert Wardric." His aunt spat the mage's name, her disgust obvious.

"Magic as such is forbidden." Xander shook his head.

Feneal gave a bitter laugh. "As you know, brother, Wardric does not consider the law applicable to him."

Liam stared as the exiled Warrior's pale blue eyes flashed. This was the first hint of anger he'd seen from the man.

Shuffling sounds to the left made them all freeze. Claymores cleared their scabbards.

His heart stuttered and he shoved Sienna behind him, gripping his dirk in his sword hand.

She cut off her screeching protest when the movement caught her attention, too.

The MacLeods all shifted closer, and his uncle had also urged his wife behind the line of men. An inopportune instinct since Alana wielded more magic than anyone else in their party and could use it to defend them.

Three Fae Warriors landed hard, natural debris kicking up from the force.

Liam let out a tense breath and let his shoulders loosen when he recognized his grandfather at their lead.

But who are the other two?

He prayed they could be trusted.

Liam didn't recognize either Warrior from the many he'd seen since arriving in the Fae Realm. They weren't among the ones who'd beat him up and taken him to the dungeon.

Lady Aileana hopped down from her husband's grip, a smile on her pretty face as she joined Alana, then greeted Sienna and Ealeric.

Of course, his grandmother probably had refused to be left behind. Perhaps that was prudent. She was a healer, after all.

One of the Warriors strode forward, his expression implacable. He was tall and broad, as were most of the winged soldiers, and unlike the rank and file, his chest-plate was silver, not dark green. His Warrior braid of red hair fell past his hips. He gripped the hilt of his sword, sheathed at his waist.

"Eauan," Xander breathed, then a slow smile spread across his father's lips. He strode forward and clasped forearms with the Warrior.

"Xander." The man had wonder in his voice, and his eyes widened. He looked the former Fae Warrior up and down, and they exchanged low words.

Liam swallowed and couldn't tear his gaze away. If his da knew the man, that was good. Perhaps they could trust him after all.

The other Warrior his grandfather had brought also wore a silver chest-plate and had dark hair in a thick plait. He surveyed the group stoically before moving closer, then turned narrowed amber eyes on Liam. He paused, as if assessing him, before he moved on, looking at each of the MacLeods. He wasn't quite sneering, but it was obvious he would rather not deal with humans.

Would he be any help?

When his eyes landed on Feneal, his expression changed, sympathy and perhaps pain, darting over his sculpted face. The emotion was gone within a flash, but he averted his gaze from the former Fae Warrior, as if he could not stand to look at him.

Liam's magic tingled. Instinct told him there was something there, the way the winged soldier had gazed at the exile. True grief that went beyond empathy for Feneal losing his wings.

What did that mean?

Did the dark-haired Warrior know the man?

"My Seconds, Eauan and Caelan," Daegus said, gesturing to the two Warriors.

As if ordered, both winged men fell into formation behind his grandfather.

"Can we trust them?" Alex asked, no hesitation in his firm voice.

"Can we trust, you, *human?*" Caelan spat; insult wrapped around the word. He lifted his chin, a display of haughty pride.

Duncan, always the more hotheaded of Liam's uncles, took a menacing step forward. "Watch how ye talk ta my brother, Fae."

"We do not have time for this," Daegus boomed, his yellow eyes slits of irritation. "I trust these men with my life, Laird Alex. Did I not, they would not be here."

Liam rocked back on his heels at the respect in his grandfather's voice for his uncle, from leader to leader. It made him see the man in a different light. Perhaps the Fae captain was not all foreboding ruthlessness.

His aunt then stepped up, despite her husband's scowl. She quickly explained the magical protections on Wardric's lair.

Daegus listened raptly, his huge arms crossed over his massive gold chest-plate. He grunted occasionally but had no questions for the former princess. "Leave it with me," he ordered, and whirled toward the ebony rock face.

chapter twenty-five

The vast, dark cave loomed in front of them like a foreboding mountain beast, maw wide ready to devour them all whole.

Wardric's lair.

Sienna's earlier lanced heart at Liam's dismissal of her regard was now a dim ache in the back of her mind. Not that she'd wanted him to command her, but it was a keen reminder that he was not hers; she was not his.

They could never be.

Yet, as she stared into the darkness, she almost wished she would've permitted Liam to order her to stay home.

Coward.

Somewhere in this cave her grandmother and sister were being held captive. The MacLeod men flanked the Fae Warriors on either side, all with swords drawn and ready.

Captain Daegus moved forward from the center, huge, his black locks surrounding him like a sinister aura, instead of being captured in a neat braid down his back, like all of his men.

Again, a crush of protective male bodies surrounded her, making Sienna's head spin. She didn't want to be protected.

She wanted to get her grandmother and her sister back.

Liam was at her side, with her brother opposite him.

The former princess and the other woman, who'd introduced herself as Lady Aileana, were right in front of Sienna, although their husbands had urged them to stay by the boulders, but both had refused.

Their group had moved as one to the outside of the cave Alana had directed them to. She'd explained it was where the magic concealing Wardric's lair was coming from.

The place was well hidden out in the open, and since Sienna did not have magic, she couldn't sense the invisible forces protecting it, but wouldn't be fool enough to try entering until the barrier had been broken.

Captain Daegus had to be the largest Fae Warrior she'd ever seen. He was huge, and made Liam and his father, and Feneal, too, seem short in comparison. His face was handsome, as were all Fae, full of sculpted defined lines and high cheekbones.

She'd heard of him, of course, but seeing him in person, equating legend with reality was enough to make her want to flee back to the boulders and crouch behind them.

Sienna could not. She had to save her family.

"Wardric," The Fae captain boomed.

A tremor shot down her spine, and she shifted closer to Liam.

Two or three heartbeats passed, before Daegus shouted the evil mage's name again.

"Come out now, and we will go to the king

together to answer your charges. This does not have to end with your death."

Liam growled obvious disagreement with that sentiment, but Sienna didn't tear her eyes away from the cave's black entrance.

As with the first time, there was no response.

"Maybe he doesn't know we are here?" Ealeric murmured.

"He knows," Feneal threw over his shoulder.

Sienna shivered again.

"Very well," the largest winged man grumbled. Daegus straightened to his enormous height and inhaled a breath that seemed to float over their group. He gathered a ball of red light in his hands and threw it at the cave's entrance.

The offensive made the dark, empty doorway turn radiant, and merely appeared to absorb the magic, before disappearing and becoming transparent again.

Daegus cursed.

His Seconds broke formation, and fell in beside him, as did Xander and Feneal.

"Let us help," Caelan said.

The captain gave the barest nod, his ebony locks dancing around his big form.

As Liam's grandfather had done before, the men all conjured magical red balls in their palms, twisting and growing larger until about the size of their heads, then tossed them at once into the open portal.

This time the radiance wavered and crackled, but it still did not dissipate.

"Again," the captain yelled.

The second group-attempt resulted in a hissing protest from the cave entrance, and colored lights answered, blasting out from the invisible barrier.

The men scattered.

"One last time!" Feneal shouted, not waiting for his companions to gather their bright globes of light. He threw one, then another and another at the protection spell.

The Warriors soon joined the exile, lobbing bright red magic at the cave's entrance while dodging the shield's defensive blasts.

Hissing grew louder, and the radiance bulged before them, then winked out, as if unable to hold form.

Soon, a percussive boom knocked them all back. Everyone, including the MacLeods, Sienna, the other two women and Ealeric all landed hard on the ground. They scrambled to their feet.

Silence fell, and no one moved.

"It's gone!" Alana shouted. "I sense no magic."

They burst into the cave without delay, holding the protective formation like the trained fighting men they were, human and Fae alike.

Sienna stayed beside Alana and Lady Aileana, moving in step with both former princesses. Her brother was close, as well. He didn't have a weapon or magic, but he had always been a scrapper with the other exiled lads. Hopefully his hand-to-hand knowledge would protect him.

Those who possessed magic already had bright flashes of defenses ready.

The wide cavern came alive with radiance. Bright orb lights hung on the walls, and a high, jeweled chandelier dangled from above.

Unlike the rough natural appearance of the cave's exterior, the inside looked as if they'd stepped into an opulent room in the king's palace.

Decorative tiles covered smooth flat walls, complete with battle murals. Refined, expensive tiles patterned the floor in an alternating lavish pattern of gold and silver filagree designs on top of ivory.

Wardric's taste was too fine for such an evil man.

Sienna's eyes landed on a raised dais at the head of the room, and she gasped.

The evil mage stood in the center, dressed in fine white robes with gold stitching. His dark hair was slicked back as if he'd dipped his head in oil. Like the head of a snake.

The men around her fell into place, all swords at the ready.

Standing opposite Wardric, dressed in similar finery, was her sister. She wore a pale green elaborate gown with silver roses embroidered in the long train.

Wedding attire.

Sienna's throat closed in on itself from fear.

Amalie was not a willing bride.

Held prone and still with magic, her arms were plastered to her sides, and her mouth covered with some glowing spell.

She could not move or speak.

Even in the Fae Realm, law decreed consent of both parties into a marriage, so how was Wardric going to force her sister's acquiescence with her mouth blocked?

A short, portly Priest of the Goddess shivered before the two, the poor man's face shiny with sweat, including the top of his balding head. He, too, seemed as if held in place by magic.

The view worsened when Sienna spotted *Mórai*, also on the dais, seated and bound to a chair. With magic roping, no doubt, the fibers shining unnaturally in the light of the cave-turned-wedding-hall.

Fae law also required witnesses to all nuptials, so there was no doubt why her grandmother was bound there. Wardric had probably compelled the priest magically to perform the ceremony.

"I do not recall inviting you lot to my wedding," the mage spat, facing them. He grabbed Amalie up, plastering her to his chest, and pulled a small blade from somewhere inside his robes. He tilted her chin up with it, holding it at her throat.

"Release my sister," Ealeric demanded.

"Oh? Still alive, little magic-less lad?" Wardric drawled, cocking his oily dark head to one side. His upper lip curled, making him even uglier.

Amalie didn't fight him. Likely couldn't from whatever magic he'd used to paralyze her.

"Wardric, release the lass, and I won't kill you," Captain Daegus stalked closer to the dais, a huge glowing sword pointed in the direction of the mage.

Wardric threw his head back and laughed maniacally. "Well, well. This seems to be a day for the history scrolls. The great Captain Daegus storming my private domain with *humans*." His black eyes narrowed as he scanned their group. He straightened, shoving the short blade further into Amalie's slender neck.

Her sister whimpered but still didn't fight the evil man's grip.

Sienna's heart dropped to her toes when blood trickled from the cut at Amalie's throat.

Wardric's eyes flashed. "Feneal, too? How has life been without your wings?" he said conversationally, as if talking to an old friend. As he surveyed them again, obvious surprise darted across his narrow, ugly face. "Ah, Feneal, did you thank your former captain for bringing your son? Of course, I would very much be obliged to host your reunion. The poor lad overcame much to be disassociated with the likes of an exiled traitor of a sire. Dying together will be quite the relief for you both."

The bright ball of magic in the exile's palm *poofed* and shock rocked him back, until one of the MacLeods had to steady Feneal. His blue eyes darted to Captain Daegus and his Seconds.

Son?

Feneal had a son?

Sienna tore her eyes away from the mage who still had her sister trapped against his tall, gaunt form.

The Fae Warrior, Caelan's expression was fraught with pain before he schooled his handsome face with a clenched jaw.

Did Feneal not know or recognize the winged soldier?

Caelan did seem young. Perhaps he had been a bairn when his father had been exiled?

Sienna's heart ached for the former Warrior who had always been a friend to her family.

"I will kill you," Feneal spat.

Wardric threw his head back and cackled a malicious laugh. "Not likely. I have more magic than all of you combined. Oh, and it's nice to see you again, Princess Alana. Your father will welcome me back with open arms when I return to the palace with you, the traitor Xander and your *humans*." The mage said the last word as if it was the worst insult. "Not to mention news that his favored beloved captain has betrayed him because of supposedly disavowed blood ties!" As he spoke, he jostled Amalie against him.

"When King Fillan is informed of your use of illegal magic, not to mention trying to marry against your bride's will, you will be lucky to survive his wrath," Captain Daegus bellowed.

"You were never a worthy opponent, my dear captain," Wardric snarled. He slid his tiny blade into Amalie's throat. The mage tossed her away, as if she were refuse. She tumbled from the dais and crumpled hard to the floor.

"Noooo!" Sienna screamed.

She rushed forward, but one of Liam's cousins, Rory, beat her to Amalie and cradled her in his arms, his handsome face drawn with worry for a lass he did not know.

"What did you do to my sister!" Sienna demanded.

The mage laughed again, a bitter bark full of evil. "Poison." He tilted the glowing *sgian-dubh,* and it winked in the bright light of the wide cavern.

Then, from the top of the dais he attacked Captain Daegus with a blast spell.

The biggest Fae Warrior was ready for the onslaught, deflecting magic with his huge sword, and throwing bright red and green swirls of light back at the mage.

Both his Seconds, Xander and Liam all joined the fight, and bright flashes of magic surrounded them.

Sienna's grandmother struggled against her bindings, to no avail.

Feneal crafted a protection bubble and cast it at *Móraí*, the same one he'd used at the Field of Light.

Sienna breathed a sigh of relief, now that her grandmother was less exposed.

She rushed to her sister and Rory. The sight of angry, unnaturally bright pinkish blood on her sister's slender neck rocked her.

"No," she moaned.

Herbal poisons she could fight.

Magical poisons she could not.

Ealeric appeared on the other side of Rory, but the human lad refused to give Amalie over to her brother.

Sienna swallowed her gasp and shoved away the burn of tears.

Now was not the time.

Her sister's always pale complexion was even more pallid, with a gray tone that made her chest ache. She was starting to panic, and it was hard to get air down.

The cut on Amalie's throat still seeped, but it was a small wound that may not be mortal, from size alone.

She couldn't be…

"Let me through." A slender hand landed on her shoulder, urging her to move over.

Sienna glanced up to meet a pair of violet eyes and a calm, beautiful expression.

"All is not lost." Lady Aileana offered a small smile and shoved her long white locks from her face. She knelt, still the picture of royal elegance and cupped Amalie's cheeks.

Her hands glowed, and she closed her eyes.

The former princess pulled back in what seemed too short a time, but Amalie already moaned into awareness.

"The magic restraining her is gone, and she is hale."

Sienna released a breath, and Ealeric squeezed her hand.

Amalie's golden eyes fluttered open, and she looked up at the lad still holding her. Her cheeks went crimson, and if it had been another time, Sienna might've smiled.

Relief filled Rory's face and he helped Amalie sit up.

"Amalie!" Sienna and Ealeric exclaimed at the same time.

Their sister rushed forward, and Sienna snatched her close in a hug, and their brother wrapped his arms around them both.

A shout and a gargling noise pulled their attention to the dais.

Wardric stumbled back, his arms wide and flailing as he attempted to remain on his feet. Bright streaks of blood spread down his white robes like a sponge absorbing dye. The jeweled hilt of Liam's dirk protruded from his throat.

chapter twenty-six

Liam flexed his empty palm and blinked a few times. He'd been holding his dirk in one hand and flinging magic at Wardric with the other.

Feneal had called for his blade with a spellword, and Liam felt the weapon snatch away from his grip, only to land in the former Fae Warrior's hand, as if he'd tossed the dirk over.

All the spells everyone had been throwing at Wardric failed at penetrating his magical defenses, not even the ones from Aunt Alana or Captain Daegus.

The evil mage returned what he absorbed, as if possessing the powers of more than one person.

He truly wielded more magic than they, more than Liam had imagined.

They were all tiring, even his grandfather and the two powerful Seconds.

Sweat beaded Liam's forehead and ran into his eyes.

With a feral yell, Feneal threw Liam's dirk at Wardric, right as the mage changed positions on the dais.

The spell swirling in Wardric's hand popped like a bubble, disappearing in a bright blue light.

The long slender weapon pierced his throat, and blood spattered into the air, then ran onto his stark white clothing.

The evil man's dark eyes went wide, his mouth forming an "o."

Wardric collapsed to the dais in a pile of arms and legs.

He didn't move.

Blood spread out beneath him like a pool at the bottom of the waterfalls.

A whoosh of air burst through the room. The magical release from any spell he'd originated faded away, and now held no power.

"Eauan, make sure he's dead," Liam's grandfather barked, sheathing his enormous magical sword.

The redheaded Warrior scrambled to obey, swooping to the dais on a glide of his wings.

Liam also hopped onto the dais, helping Eilidh to her feet as the magic ropes fell away from her thin form.

The small Fae woman shot forward, wrapping her arms around him. "Thank you, Liam, thank you for bringing your family to save mine." Tears filled her green eyes when she met his gaze.

He nodded and smiled against the emotion in his throat. Liam couldn't find his voice to answer or tell her it was Sienna who'd brought them.

Eilidh joined the embrace of her grandchildren, and Lady Aileana was still at their sides.

Liam wanted to go to Sienna, but something held him back. He felt like an intruder watching her with her family, despite that his own grandmother was with them.

The two Fae healers spoke in low tones when the hug broke apart, and Sienna's *móraí* wore astonishment in her lined expression from whatever Lady Aileana had said.

"Alana, Xander, come assist me, please?" Liam's grandmother called.

His father and aunt obeyed, and Liam glanced around the sickeningly vast and fancy room.

Feneal spoke to his son, Caelan, tears streaming down both their faces. They held onto each other's arms, despite the exile's filthy attire.

A little smugness washed over Liam. He'd guessed right…Caelan's earlier emotions when he'd observed Feneal had indeed meant something. He was glad to see another family reunion. After all the former Fae Warrior had endured, he deserved some happiness, too.

Captain Daegus looked down at Wardric's body on the dais, Alex, and Angus beside him speaking together.

His cousins were with their father, watching the group of Fae assemble in a circle and joined hands.

"What're they doin'?" Liam whispered.

"I believe the Lady Aileana is helping them retrieve their lost magic. Now that Wardric is dead, it can be done without calling the Conclave of Mages."

He jumped at the voice to his right and glanced over to meet a pair of very green eyes, more vivid than Sienna's grandmother's.

The Fae Warrior, Eauan, offered a smile. "I did not mean to startle you, lad."

"'Tis fine, I'm braw," Liam said automatically, and made himself return the man's smile.

The winged soldier chuckled, but it was a warm, fond thing as if between friends. "You're just like your sire, lad."

He frowned. "I am?"

"Aye, I should say so. Xander and I trained together, even bunked together until he was chosen to protect the princess." The redheaded Warrior gestured to Alana. "I hate to admit it, I have missed him so over the years, but I am glad he is well."

Liam was able to smile genuinely. "My da dinnae discuss his days as a Fae Warrior much."

Eauan gave a sad nod. "That doesn't surprise me."

Whatever else the man said faded as Liam couldn't tear his eyes from the scene before him.

His grandmother, father, and aunt went radiant, their forms glowing with warm golden light, surrounding their bodies, and seeming to come from within them. A gale rose from the center of their circle, and hair and clothing whirled around with it.

One-by-one, first Eilidh, then Sienna, then Amalie, and lastly Ealeric also went brilliant, engulfed by the same glow of Liam's blood-kin.

It seemed to last forever but not long at all at the same time.

Soon, the wind died, and the glow faded.

Elation settled over Sienna's *mórai's* expression, and it was reflected in his love's pretty face as well, and both her siblings.

Then they were on their feet, embracing each other.

His father accepted a handshake from Ealeric and watched the group, wearing a proud smile.

Even as Liam observed his Fae healer's joy, his heart ached, before sliding to his stomach and down to his toes.

She was truly lost to him now.

Sienna had finally received her magic, her birthright, and would take her place in Fae society as the powerful healer she was destined to be.

Eauan beamed, but the look faded fast. "Lad, are you well?"

Liam shook himself and forced a nod. "If I dinnae be, now we've a room full of healers." He slipped away from his da's childhood friend, facing the corridor leading to the cave's entrance, without another word.

He needed to go. To get out of the cave and fly away. Anywhere other than here. There was no need for anyone, especially his family, to witness his heart being shredded the rest of the way.

"Liam."

He crushed his eyes shut. She'd said his name in her usual welcome way, the one that made him warm all over. Liam didn't have the bollocks to face her.

Instead, he envisioned his spine was made of steel and flexed his wings for good measure.

Sienna didn't wait for him to face her. She slid around to his front, a smile lighting her stunning face, her freckles and skin bright with what seemed to be an extra healthy glow.

His family and hers were in the periphery, their excitement even reaching the MacLeods with no magic. They all huddled together, talking enthusiastically.

The joy was contagious, but Liam couldn't share in it. He was in mourning. His pain simmered under the surface of his skin, fresh and alive, just like his magic.

"Liam," Sienna whispered his name this time, resting her dainty hand on his forearm.

He didn't know how he could bear to look into her face, but he made himself meet the burnished gaze he loved so much.

"What's wrong?" Her happy expression fell off, and her brows drew together in concern.

Liam shook his head and forced his lips to curve up. "Nothin'." He cupped her cheeks and didn't want to let her go. "Ye got what ye've always wanted. I'm pleased fer ye, an' yer family."

I'm just devastated for me.

Sienna's mouth quivered, but she nodded. "Look!" She offered him a raised palm, and a little ball of golden light was born. "I got my magic." Jubilation lit her eyes, but then something seemed to chase it away. Maybe guilt. The magic dissipated.

"Dinnae regret it," he said quickly. "'Tis fer the best."

"Is it?" she asked. So much sadness wrapped the two words, it made his chest ache.

He wanted to snatch her up, kiss that look off her face, then fly away with her.

Liam couldn't.

Captain Daegus' booming bellow caught his attention. He gladly let it snag his focus from the woman he loved, from the anguish engulfing his whole spirit.

From the woman he loved so completely but couldn't keep.

He ordered his hands to release her, even though he burned for the opposite.

"Caelan, Eauan, come. Take Wardric's body to the king, and I will see our human friends home. I will join you shortly."

Both Seconds went to their captain on the dais and coordinated their new mission.

Now, it was time to return Sienna home with her family, and Liam would go home, to the Human Realm.

How could he bear to let others witness him dying inside?

Getting to the Field of Light was a blur, for more than one reason. They'd parted ways with Sienna's family, and Liam kept telling himself it was for the best.

They hadn't really gotten to say goodbye.

Maybe that, too, was better.

His heart was already shattered. He didn't want to see the same reflected from those gorgeous bronze eyes.

His grandmother had stayed with them so she could help with getting them to the palace or in front of the king or follow whatever plan they'd made.

Liam hadn't caught it all, because it took all of him to maintain a placid expression for his family. The last thing he wanted them to know—especially his empathic aunt—was that he was dying inside.

They'd bid Lady Aileana farewell before they'd gone with his grandfather, but her words of encouragement and love had been lost on him. Liam had allowed her a long embrace and told her he was glad they'd met, and he had meant that.

They hadn't had to travel by the same spell they'd gone to Wardric's lair with—thank God and the Fae Goddess alike.

Alana and Angus had each *blinked* with a family member in tow, and he and his father had flown with the remainder.

His grandfather had come along, with no passengers this time.

Liam set his cousin Rory to his feet, and they didn't speak. Even in his haze of grief, it hadn't escaped his notice how his cousin had looked at Amalie.

The lad, only two years his junior, seemed to be hung up on a lass he couldn't have, just like Liam. Although Rory should count himself lucky that he hadn't had time to fall in love with Sienna's sister.

There were no Fae Warriors guarding the Faery Stones, thanks to the captain making them scarce, but they likely didn't have much time, or his grandfather would have to face the king's wrath at such an oversight—on top of everything else the large man would already have to defend.

Alana announced she would open the portal and darted onto the dais.

His laird uncle stepped forward and thanked Captain Daegus, and the MacLeods drifted to the dais.

His grandfather gripped his forearm and gave a small lift of his lips that Liam figured passed as a smile.

He swallowed and looked into the man's yellow eyes. Ordered his hand to return the captain's gesture.

"Take care of your parents, lad," the huge, winged man said, but emotion darted across his face before he schooled it away.

Liam nodded, because words failed him when he tried to speak. He had to clear his throat and try again. "Will ye…be well…with the king?"

Captain Daegus grunted but gave a nod. "Aye. I will report why the mission had to be secret. Wardric will take all the deserved blame. Caelan and Eauan will back me. Do not worry about the healer and her family. All has been righted. I will see to it."

"Thank ye. Fer everathin'."

Again, his grandfather grunted and offered an even curter nod.

Liam stepped back to allow Xander to offer goodbyes, his eyes instinctually looking for Sienna.

The memory that she was already gone burned anew and he turned away from his father and grandfather so they wouldn't see him lose it like a wee bairn.

They hadn't even been able to say a proper

goodbye.

He wanted to take to the air one last time.

No, not one last time.

Liam wanted to fly off and never return.

Going home meant losing his wings, again.

He'd already lost Sienna.

How could he bear the loss of both?

His father's large hand enclosed his upper arm, in a gentle, but firm grip.

Liam looked into the violet eyes that matched his own.

"Do not flee, my lad. Come home. Your mother is no doubt eager to see you."

His father didn't voice the reminder that he couldn't safely remain in the Fae Realm anyway, but somehow, Liam heard it nonetheless.

He bit the inside of his cheek to stave off the emotion. "Get outta my head, Da."

The ghost of a smile rippled across Xander's mouth. "Do not think so loudly, my son."

"If I leave, she's gone fere'er." Liam choked on the words.

Sympathy crossed his father's face, and he blew out a breath. "There are no words to comfort you now, my lad. I only urge you to return to your family. We love you. You belong with us." Xander squeezed his arm. "You and I…we will mourn our wings together, this time." His da's eyes went glossy.

Liam closed his own and nodded. Had to swallow against the lump in his throat.

He was, however, glad his da hadn't uttered any shite about time healing all wounds.

chapter twenty-seven

The smack echoed in the great hall of the castle Liam had been born in. His cheek stung to a matching, reverberating throb.

All the males in his family standing around him winced.

His mother was generally known as the gentle one amongst hotheaded MacLeods, but evidently not when her only child disappeared to the Fae Realm for a fortnight.

He didn't dare flinch.

The tears in her sapphire eyes slayed him worse than the slap.

She threw her arms around him and squeezed tight.

Liam hugged her back. Even though he was a profound idiot, he *had* missed his mother.

She was tall for a woman, much taller than his Fae healer.

Holding onto her became clinging. A single thought about Sienna reminded him of his loss all over again, and there was no helping it.

Liam didn't want to deal with that.

Now or ever.

Janet MacLeod clung right back, before abruptly leaning away. "If ye e'er dare…" she trailed off on a sob and buried her face against his shoulder, burrowing into his neck.

He was suddenly grateful his grandmother had healed him completely. His sword wound would never have tolerated the way his mother crushed his waist.

However, he didn't care overmuch about that at the moment.

His mother's feelings were a great distraction from his own.

"I'm a sodding fool," Liam whispered.

"Ye'll get nay an argument from me," she returned. She wore a smirk when she leaned away again, but her eyes were still misty.

"Nor from the rest a' my clan, I'd imagine."

His closest cousin snickered.

His father was hovering, pacing, obviously eager to speak as well. Probably wanted to comfort the woman who'd fallen apart in front of them all.

They'd made it back to Dunvegan without incident, meeting his mother, Angus' wife, Iain, and Aunt Claire in the great hall.

They'd prepared hot meals on laden trenchers, resting invitingly on the head table his family always sat at, but Liam had little appetite.

"*Mò aingeal*, let the lad breathe." His father stepped forward, with a soft hand on his mother's shoulder.

Liam kissed her cheek. "*Mamaidh*, I'm sorry I worried ye. I'm home now, I dinnae intend ta repeat my follies."

Her mouth wobbled, as if she was too emotional

to speak. Which made him feel as bad as when the Fae Warriors had run him through, or even the second set that had beaten him and dragged him to the little dungeon.

He should hand her his claymore to finish him off.

As soon as he'd released her, his father pulled his mother into his arms, and Liam had to look away from the obvious love between them.

Xander never could stand the sight of his wife upset.

Janet held her husband tight.

Liam's gaze collided with Angus' over his wife, Lila's, dark head. He held her in his arms, just like his parents were embracing.

His cousin offered a wink, and Liam had to again look away from another happy couple, only for his eyes to land on Uncle Duncan and Aunt Claire's mirroring tight hug.

Liam couldn't take it. He cleared his throat. "I'm goin' ta retire. I need ta bathe."

His mother frowned. "Have somethin' warm ta eat, first." She gestured to the food piled high on the nearby table.

"Nay, I will eat later."

Her sapphire eyes scanned his face. "Verra well, I'll order ye a bath."

"Nay, nay, dinnae be necessary." He shook his head and gestured for effect. He needed to go.

Now.

Liam fled the great hall without another word.

No doubt his father would explain to his mother

that not only had he acted like a wee selfish bairn and had wanted to fly, but he'd also been foolish enough to leave his heart in the Fae Realm.

He let his feet wander, making his way outside, across the bailey and the large courtyard.

None of his meddlesome family followed, thank God and the Fae Goddess alike.

Liam eventually found himself standing on the ridge above the cave of the Faery Stones, high above the beach.

Night had fallen, and his eyes adjusted to the moonlight.

It was a cold, clear evening, and he shivered without the warm, magically induced air of his realm's counterpart.

Liam took a step forward, intending to glide down to the beach, then startled in his boots.

His wings were gone, and two more steps would lead to a long painful tumble, and probably broken bones.

He crushed his eyes shut and his head spun in a chaos of loss. His back tingled where his wings should be.

Liam scrambled down the cliff face, cursing all the way until his boots hit the loamy beach.

Screaming the MacLeod war cry, he plunged into the cold sea, wading until the frigid water smacked his calves, then his thighs, and he pushed past the resistance of his plaid and leine, fighting the waves.

Liam kept going, until the cold seeped into his bones and he had to kick his water-logged boots to stay above the surface.

He could let the water take him deeper, let it all go. It was probably the fastest way to end all this pain. That wasn't him, wasn't a thought he'd ever had, and it shocked him back into his skin.

Liam had loved and lost.

Many a time, from his elders, he'd heard that was just a part of life.

He didn't regret meeting Sienna. Or loving her.

He only regretted losing her.

They'd both understood from the start that they couldn't be together permanently. They came from literal different worlds.

She'd always wanted her magic, and she finally had it.

It wasn't her fault he couldn't keep his wings.

Liam floated in the water on his back, his arms and legs spread like a star until he couldn't feel his fingers or toes.

He remained in the sea until his body matched his heart—frozen and numb all over.

Sienna rolled over on the unfamiliar bed, wishing for the tiny room in her treed home in the exile camp, far from the palace. Grànnda Falls felt like a million miles from where she was tonight.

She had her magic.

Something she'd always wanted.

Her family had their magic too, and they'd been

reinstated by the king. Returned to their bloodline's legacy, and the prestige that accompanied the most powerful healing powers in their realm, or so they'd been told.

It was all surreal.

The current head healer, a man named Leighiche, not only bowed when he'd seen her grandmother, but he'd kissed *Móraí's* hands, and prostrated to the floor weeping in joy, and muttering how he was not worthy.

Sienna had exchanged wide-eyed glances with her siblings, but *Móraí* had leaned down, comforted the man, and urged him to his feet, as if people cried all over her daily because of her healing magic.

The woman who'd raised her had been so…regal.

Then there had been a flurry of plans, from *Móraí*, Lady Aileana, Leighiche, and several other healers considered masters of their magic.

Sienna had met so many healers, she hadn't retained their names, and her mind swirled with all they discussed, but the most important things she'd noted regarded her and her siblings. Where they would live, how the three of them would continue their training.

She and her siblings had been brought up in the ways of herbal healing, but they needed to learn to use their magic to heal.

Because of that, *Móraí* would be interim head healer, until Sienna was ready to take over.

She'd gulped then, and now at the memory.

When would that be?

Leighiche had insisted on deferring to her

grandmother, even though *Móraí* had expressed he could stay in the position. He'd flatly refused. However, that melded into delight as *Móraí* named him her Second, which had been heartily approved by the attending council of healers.

Per Liam's grandfather, they would be presented to the king in the morning, and it was something Sienna could have lived without. Everything she'd heard about the Scottish Fae ruler was negative. She did not want to put a face to the name, nor the sentiments.

Liam…

She shouldn't have let his name loose, even in her own mind. Thinking it made the pain in her gut spread up and out, until her limbs hurt, and her fingers and toes ached.

Sienna winced when his gorgeous smiling face popped into her head.

His departure to the Human Realm felt like days ago, instead of mere hours.

It didn't dull the agony in her heart.

"Rory…" Amalie moaned the lad's name, but her sister was asleep.

"*Soillsich,*" Sienna whispered the spellword she'd heard Feneal say a thousand times when he'd recharged the magic lights in their treed home.

The globe on the wall between the beds in their guest room obeyed, offering a dim ambiance, as if it knew it was late at night.

She gasped.

I have…magic.

Sienna could make the lights work herself.

How would she ever truly get used to that?

Tears sprung to her eyes for so many reasons.

Liam had uttered the same spellword in the cave behind the Falls, where she'd given herself to him for the first time.

Would she think of him every time that spellword was spoken?

Sienna swallowed a sob and banished the memories.

Liam was gone.

He'd gone home, where he belonged, in the Human Realm, and she'd gotten her magic back.

He hadn't even said goodbye, beyond the few words they'd exchanged in Wardric's cave.

A tiny voice in the back of her mind whispered that he hadn't wanted to look at her, or touch her, or…fight for her.

Sienna shoved it away because it was wrong and selfish.

He couldn't have changed their fates if he'd battled a thousand evil mages or Fae Warriors. Remaining in the Fae Realm was not only dangerous for Liam, it was a death sentence. Even if his grandfather was the king's captain, it wouldn't have helped.

She was in the king's palace, for the Goddess' sake, and she had what she'd always wanted. She was about to receive her birthright, and she was proof of her father's legacy, as were her siblings.

This was what *Mórai* had always wanted for her —

for them.

Her parents would be proud.

Sienna forced her focus on her sleeping sister.

Amalie was out, a small smile curving her lips, and she clutched a pillow to her breasts.

They shared a room, like they always had, and that made her feel better about being in the palace. However, it was only temporary, and because the meeting of the healers had ended so late. In the morning, their proper quarters would be ready, and they would all get their own. No more living together in a small space.

Sienna swallowed, because the idea was so foreign, she didn't want to see it to fruition, despite her current surroundings being large and magnificent. The room they were in could've held the whole interior of the treehouse. She was able to smirk. "Amalie," she whispered loudly.

Her sister's golden eyes flew open. "What?" She rushed to a sit, and the pillow she'd been hugging flopped to the floor.

Sienna giggled. "Nothing. I'm sorry I scared you."

Amalie looked around, as if she, too, had forgotten where they were. "I can't believe any of this." She leaned heavily into the carved, jeweled decorative headboard and smiled.

It was a sweet thing that—almost—made Sienna feel better.

"Me either."

Her sister held out a hand, concentrated and her skin started to glow. "Magic. *My* magic. I can't believe it," she repeated.

"I know, but it will sink in soon, and we will do well here."

Amalie's smile went sad. She wasn't the kind of lass to call Sienna on her nonsense, but her eyes asked, *"Are you trying to convince you or me?"*

Sienna swallowed and averted her gaze, so she wouldn't blurt anything about Liam or start to sob. As she fell into her new routine, she would heal. She would forget her halfling Warrior. She would move on.

She didn't have a choice.

"All will be well," her sister whispered.

The room was too large, and the beds were too far apart to grab her sister's hand, but Sienna wanted to.

She met her eyes and was able to smile. "Thank you. I needed to hear that."

"Why did you wake me?" Amalie demanded, cocking her head and making her rich blonde hair fall over one chemise-covered shoulder.

Sienna grinned wickedly. "What were you dreaming about?"

Her sister's cheeks lit up bright pink. "I..I don't remember. Why?"

"You were calling Rory's name in your sleep."

"Was not!" Amalie snatched the pillow off the floor and hid her face.

"You were, I promise you."

"I.." She let the pillow slip down, and a morose set in her pretty expression. "It matters not." Amalie swallowed audibly.

Sienna's heart skipped. She slipped out of her bed

and joined her sister, reaching for her.

Amalie let Sienna hug her.

"He…saved me. Rory MacLeod."

She smiled into her sister's soft golden locks. "I know it." She didn't correct Amalie that Liam's grandmother had healed her. It wouldn't shut down the lass' infatuation for Sienna's lost love's handsome human cousin.

She pressed a kiss to Amalie's cheek. "We have a big day tomorrow; we should sleep."

Her sister nodded and Sienna tucked her in, like she had many times when Amalie had been wee. She still smiled to herself when she crawled back into her bed.

"Sienna?"

"Aye?"

"You love him, don't you?"

There was no doubt who the *him* was.

Sienna's heart stuttered and slid to her toes, like it had multiple times that day. "Aye, I do." The truth fell out and clouded her eyes with more tears she wanted nothing to do with.

"What does being in love feel like?" The heaviness of sleep infused in her sister's question blessed Sienna with the opportunity to not answer.

Amalie wouldn't want to hear her honesty, anyway. The lass was starry-eyed for a lad she'd met only once, and Sienna didn't want to ruin that.

Because being in love was nothing but pain.

chapter twenty-eight

iam cursed as the breath fled his lungs, leaving an aching burn in its wake. The discomfort matched the one in his backside, as well as the stretched throb in his thighs. He glared up into Lachlan's dancing, triumphant blue eyes. "What are ye laughin' at?" he demanded in a pant.

"Ye, on yer arse." His cousin smirked. He stood over him, clutching his sword in his hand.

He didn't miss that his father and his Uncle Duncan—Lachlan's da—stood not far on the fighting yard, both with arched eyebrows and an identical look of shock on their faces.

His cousin was good with a sword, but Liam had always been better. He, too, was stunned that his cousin, older by two summers, had bested him.

"I notice ye dinnae be offerin' ta help me up," Liam grumbled, struggling to his feet and snatching his claymore from the dirt.

Lachlan chuckled and shook his dark head.

Rory and Iain rushed over, chattering like lasses about the sparring match, and demanding to know how Lan had beat him.

Liam rolled his eyes.

He'd been distracted, but it wasn't like he'd admit that aloud.

Even if he didn't close his eyes, all he could see

was her face. When he did close them, it was even more unpleasant. A physical pain ten times worse than his healed sword wound, and always seeping, aching, never healing.

Concern darted across Xander's face, as his da closed the distance to him and his cousins. "Are ye well, lad?" He handed him a skin of water.

Liam took a swig before handing it back. He forced a nod and looked away because even if his father didn't read minds, he would no doubt read his expression. "I'm braw, Da. My pride hurts more an' my arse." He brushed the back of his plaid off for good measure.

His quip didn't affect the amusement he'd expected.

Xander squeezed his forearm, as if he had admitted what he was really feeling.

His gaze skimmed the former Fae Warrior's.

"Well, you usually dodge much better than you did, especially since Lan's strikes are so predictable." His da smirked. He'd raised his voice with the latter part of his statement, so his cousin could hear the censure and be reminded of the danger of always attacking in the same position.

It was Liam's turn to smirk when Lachlan threw a glare at Xander.

"Go again?" his cousin asked.

Liam shook his head. "Rory's eager ta try ye in yer victory. I defer ta yer greatness." He gave a mocking half-bow.

His da snorted.

Instead of being insulted, Lachlan beamed, and Liam let him revel in the rare win.

As lads all growing up together, they'd played, trained, sparred, and argued more like siblings than cousins, even Iain, who was younger by quite a few years than the rest of them.

Lexi, too, had never been left out, although she had not been permitted to train with a sword, much to her dismay. In everything else, the sole female among them always held her own—or cheated with magic.

He scanned the fighting yard, and despite the normality of everything, it exhausted and disinterested him.

Liam wanted to flee it all.

Rory and Lachlan circled each other, their swords at the ready, with Iain eagerly waiting for his turn. MacLeod men-at-arms, whether by blood or fealty, also scattered the grounds, some talking, some sparring.

Angus spoke to Cormac, the large MacLeod cousin in charge of the castle men, and Uncle Duncan, as the laird's war chief oversaw it all. His father was Uncle Duncan's second, but really, he was like another war chief because Alex respected Xander so much.

Liam had spent a great deal of time on these grounds, eager to learn the art of the sword, and how he could protect his clan. Not only that, his uncles, and even his father, had instilled in him and his cousins what it meant to be a MacLeod and what was expected.

He'd always wanted to be recognized as a contributing member of his clan, a man of honor. A

Warrior like his da, even without wings.

A man who fought for what was right and what he loved.

"Then why don't you, my lad?"

Liam jumped.

His father's voice was low and close, but it had the effect of a shout.

The stupid mind reading...

"Wh-wh-what?" he stammered out. A glance at his da became a locked gaze, and his tongue glued to the roof of his mouth.

"Your lass."

Liam blinked, unable to reaffirm he had no lass. Because even if it was the truth, it hurt too much.

"Come, my lad." Xander gestured, maintaining the same low tone, but it was a command, nonetheless.

Numbly, and mutely, he trailed the tall fair-haired man he'd always loved and respected, letting his father lead them to the wooden spectator tiers outside the fence that lined the fighting yard.

The seating area was used primarily for contests or games, so today the benches were empty, and they would be out of earshot of any of the other men.

Liam could contemplate later what he would do to answer the inevitable questions.

The MacLeods were made up of meddlers.

"Dinnae ask what's botherin' me," he muttered when his father urged him to take a seat. He felt as if he was a wee laddie ripe for a lecture.

Xander's rich chuckle had their gazes meeting again. "Even if I didn't have the curse of reading minds, I know heartbreak when I see it."

"I dinnae wanna gossip like lasses," he complained.

His father had always been quiet by nature and didn't remark.

Perhaps the man knew him better than Liam had ever wanted to acknowledge. He couldn't find the words to affirm that now, either.

However, Xander's presence was calming, too, and he needed it. He took a breath and fought the urge to close his eyes.

"You've been trailing the halls like a ghost for the better part of a fortnight, lad. Then today's folly on the yard. It's not like you, Liam. Your mother is worried about you. I'm worried about you. So is Alana."

Liam swallowed and averted his gaze. He didn't want to have this conversation with his father. None of it mattered. It wasn't Sienna's fault he fell in love with her. She was where she belonged, doing what she always wanted.

"Are you sure about that, my lad?"

This time he did close his eyes, and the back of his neck burned with embarrassment, hot enough to leave scorch marks on his leine and make his spine tingle. "Aye," he forced the word out, again not able to holler at his da for plucking the thoughts from his head.

"Sometimes, we come to learn what we thought we've always wanted wasn't what we wanted — or needed — after all."

"Sienna always wanted her magic."

"Aye, before she met you."

"So, I'm ta demand she give it all up?" Liam snapped. "Because of what *I* want?" He'd already been a selfish sod. His father wanted him to do it again?

"Nay, lad. Not *demand*, as you say. Present her the choice."

When he mustered the bollocks to look at the man, he had to swallow again, and his heart stuttered.

Xander peered at him with love and concern, but also bolstered him with something dangerous, and it made him ache all over.

Hope.

Hope that warred with doubt.

"Do ye regret it?" Liam blurted.

Xander had given up his life as a revered Fae Warrior and bodyguard to the crown princess. He'd exiled himself to stay at Alana's side so she could be with Alex. Then he'd met Liam's mother, and they'd discovered they were fated mates.

Janet MacLeod often touted that everything happened for a reason.

Could that be true?

His father studied him for a long moment before he spoke. "Nay, my lad."

"But ye had ta give up yer life."

"Because I did, yours exists."

Liam fell quiet and studied his boots. In that moment, perhaps he understood the man who'd given him life more than he ever had in the past, despite the short answer. "I love ye, too, Da." He met his father's eyes again.

The corners of the man's mouth curved up, if only

a little. "I'm glad to hear you say it, lad."

"I'm sorry fer e'erythin', Da, except Sienna. I could ne'er regret her."

Xander's smile widened. It was soft and he offered a curt nod. "And you should never regret the woman you love."

Liam cursed how his cheeks heated all over again like a bairn when the former Fae Warrior spoke so frankly of feelings he'd never given voice to. "Get outta my head, Da," he complained, finally chiding the man, despite multiple invasions in the last moments, alone.

Xander chuckled. "Oh, lad, I did not need to read your thoughts to know that. Remember, I saw you two together." His father ruffled his hair, as he had many times when Liam was wee, no matter that they were mostly equal in height and build, and he was a grown man. "I like your hair like this. Your mother is fond of your curls, too."

He whirled away, like he had as a child, scooting further down the bench they were seated on, in the lowest tier of the wooden structure. "Really, Da? Ye sound like an ol' woman."

Xander laughed again. "It's good to have you home, lad. I missed you."

Liam grudgingly smiled. "I missed ye, too."

Then his father's expression sobered. "However, your mood of the last two weeks must be resolved."

"What if she dinnae want me?" he breathed, trying not to focus on the frankness of the question, its gravity or to whom he spoke.

Since Xander could read minds whether he

wanted to or not, it was very likely his da already knew how Sienna felt about Liam.

He didn't have the bollocks to ask straight out.

"What if she does?" his father retorted judiciously.

Sienna let her eyes move slowly over the opulence surrounding her. A jewel-encrusted chandelier hung large and low from the high ceiling; the magical orbs secured throughout giving off a soft ambient glow.

The hearth dominated the wall across from the huge bed, with two large jewels glinting in the light, one blue and one red, forming around carvings in the bricked surface in a shallow u-shape. The finest craftsmage had etched an embossed unicorn in the center. She'd run her fingers over it many times. It was a beauty like nothing she'd ever seen.

Richly colored tapestries hung from the walls, depicting battles and flying Fae Warriors, each so intricate they almost appeared alive. The furniture in the vast sitting area was so fine, she was too afraid to use it. A worktable in the opposite corner housed all the parchment, quills, and ink she could ever use. All supposed to be hers.

When Sienna had refused to leave Triobloid behind, the maid she'd been assigned had retrieved a small bed for her bogle, in carved dark wood in the shape of an elaborate mini sleigh, complete with cushions in finer fabrics than she'd ever laid eyes on.

The thing rested on the tiled floor, next to the hearth.

Trioblóid lay sleeping on it now, with rolling contented blues and purples traversing his hairy coat.

Sienna shook her head and smirked. When her gaze met her own reflection in the large looking glass hung over the hearth, it quickly melded into a frown.

She barely recognized herself.

Her bright red hair was elaborately braided up, with flowers weaved in. Because she'd had to meet with nobles today, she was still wearing a rust-colored gown that had been selected for her because it brought out the color of her eyes.

Although the gown was form-fitting and made her look fantastic, she didn't like it. Nor want it. Sienna much preferred the trews she always wore, or the comfortable loose skirts that she was told were now a part of her past. She also missed her ratty old ever-present apron that had been mended many times over.

How could she be surrounded by such splendor and be so miserable?

Sienna cursed herself and shook her head, taking a few steps toward the massive fireplace. She stared into the colors of the fire dancing over the sweetwoods burning there. Greens and yellows, entwining with purples and blues, and since the tender woods had been mixed, the scents were too. She could smell flowers and citruses, berries, and something clean that reminded her of Liam's sandalwood and leather.

Goddess, how she *loved* that scent.

Her heart plummeted to her toes.

Again.

Sienna crushed her eyes shut and took a deep breath, then pushed it back out, wincing when her breasts were squeezed in the constricting corset. She wanted out of the stupid gown, but she couldn't unlace it herself, and she didn't want to call for Michela, the lady's maid she'd been assigned.

She looked at her palms, turning them over, mapping the back of her hands. She stared again into the fire, said a spellword, and watched the flames rise, larger, hotter and the colors brightened.

Perhaps she could use magic to loosen her dress?

Even after a full fortnight since her family had received their powers, the unfamiliarity of the power beheld in her hands still startled.

Sienna plopped down on the floor next to Trio. Her grandmother had brought her up as a healer. She could recite any herb and its use, any plant with even a remote medicinal application. She could stitch flesh and bring down a fever with teas, and sooth bruises with salves.

Only now, she could do all of that with a thought, a whim, all from the power inside her. She could heal with her hands in a different way than she'd ever imagined.

She could've whisked Liam's bruises away with a touch and a thought. She could've sealed his sword wound by running her hands over it.

If she'd had magic when she'd found him on the burn, he would've been healed the same day.

He would've left her faster.

"He left me anyway." The whisper was miserable

to her ears. Tears pricked her eyes and welled, until the quarters that had once belonged to her parents blurred.

Sienna had always wanted her magic, and she'd finally gotten it.

Trouble was, she wanted Liam more.

It would've been better if she'd had her magic and been able to heal him the day she'd found him. Because that way, she wouldn't have fallen in love with him.

She swallowed against the lump in her throat and one hot tear was born, followed by a few others. Everything hurt.

Sienna grabbed her middle and barreled over, giving into the sob clawing up and out, and ignoring the stabs of pain from the corset's boning digging into her sides.

Trio opened one large eye, then the other, keening a whimper when their gazes met. The contented colors of his fur faded, and he changed to pastels of concern and comfort.

She stroked his round body and he chirruped, but it didn't make her feel better.

After everything, Sienna was glad she didn't have her magic when she'd met Liam. It had given her more time with him. She was even glad she'd fallen in love with him and taken him for her first lover. She would cherish the memories for the rest of her life.

Sienna just wished the aftermath didn't hurt so horribly.

Because she would always love Liam MacLeod.

There was noise at the door, pulling her gaze. Someone was coming into her rooms.

Sienna hastily swiped at her cheeks. The last thing she needed was for someone to catch her crying.

"Sienna, *mò ghràdh*—" Mórai froze in her tracks, and blinked. "Why are you sitting on the floor?" She wore a simple but refined white gown with a wide green belt encircling her slender waist. Her long white tresses were gathered in a knot common among women her age.

Her grandmother looked happy and lighter than Sienna had seen her in years. Elegant and unburdened, with a side of appreciation for anything prestigious.

That just made guilt and ungratefulness swirl in her tummy.

Sienna was a selfish bairn.

Her *mórai* narrowed green eyes on her and studied her face. Worry dominated her expression, and the elderly healer crossed the distance to her, hands outstretched. "Whatever is wrong, my love?"

She sucked back a wince when her grandmother didn't say her normal endearment in Fae. Liam had called her *love* and she didn't want to hear that word.

Sienna shrugged, because she didn't dare try to speak, but her grandmother shook her head.

"Talk to me, please." Despite the politeness tacked onto the end of the statement, *Mórai* had issued an order.

She allowed the woman who'd raised her to take her hands and help Sienna to her feet. The elderly healer was petite, but deceptively strong.

Mórai led them to the fancy bright red chaise to the right of the fireplace, that had elaborate gold trim carved in a decorative filagree. Her grandmother sat first.

When Sienna didn't immediately sit beside her, *mórai's* lined hand tapped the rich fabric with a touch of irritation.

She smoothed the back of her gown. The soft cushion enveloped her, as if infused in magic to fit each sitter's personal preferences.

Sienna dug down deep and avoided her grandmother's open, concerned expression. "*Mórai*, I—"

"'Tis only I, *mò ghràdh*." *Mórai's* eyes were impossibly compassionate. "You and I have always been able to talk. There was a time you kept not a thing from me." Her grandmother looked down. "I am sad that has changed."

Sienna's eyes stung all over with an extra touch of guilt, but her *mórai* wore a soft smile to ease the admonition.

She hadn't told the elderly healer how she felt about Liam, true—or that they had been lovers—but who wanted to tell their grandparent those details?

Sienna had to clear her throat before she could speak. She looked around the rich rooms, then gestured. "*Mórai*, this is more than I could've ever dreamed, and—" she couldn't put voice to the truth. She didn't want to hurt the woman who'd been stuck with raising her and her siblings.

"Go on," her grandmother urged, patting the back of her hand.

"It's nothing I ever wanted." Her confession came

out the barest whisper, and she had to swallow against the lump in her throat.

Silence fell, and her heart beat in tandem with her building stress from crushing the elderly woman she loved so much. Sienna had to avert her eyes because her guts had torn through her courage.

"What do you want, *mò ghràdh?*" Her grandmother's voice was equally low but didn't betray the hurt she'd expected.

"Liam." His name tumbled out of her mouth without another thought.

"Very well." Her grandmother's smile was sad, contradicting her acquiescence.

"It is?"

Móraí nodded. "If you want Liam MacLeod, *mò ghràdh,* I know just who to see to make it happen."

A sob caught in her throat, but Sienna tried to compose herself. "But *Móraí,* I can't leave you."

"Aye, my lass you can." Her grandmother caressed her cheek with a warm, loving touch. "I believe I was wrong."

"What do you mean?"

Her *móraí* sighed. "From the moment Liam MacLeod entered our lives, the Goddess has been whispering to me of changing fates, and I'd refused to see it. Your place is in the Human Realm, *mò ghràdh,* as I suspect is Amalie's. Since we've come here, you and your sister have wilted, which is not what I wanted. Perhaps I was the selfish one, and it is I who owe you both an apology."

Sienna gasped and shook her head. "Nay, *Móraí.*"

"Aye." Her green eyes were so melancholy, but her expression was determined. "I love you, and I always will."

Sienna bit her bottom lip. "I love you, too."

Her grandmother flashed a smile and patted her thigh. "We have to tell your brother he will take over your place, training for head healer, and that you and your sister are to go to yet another new home. A permanent one. Then we need to speak with Captain Daegus and Lady Aileana."

Sienna's heart thumped at the idea of going to the Human Realm. There was no stopping her genuine smile, but her grandmother was concerned with Ealeric. "I know he wants it."

Móraí nodded. "As do I. He has taken to palace living quite well as I had hoped you all would."

Since they'd gotten their magic back and come into Fae society, Ealeric had thrived. It was as if they'd always lived and worked there and spent all their time with nobles. It figured. Her brother had always been a haughty brat.

Ealeric would excel in his duties with the care and enthusiasm the palace deserved. He had an equal knowledge of healing as her, and he was very good. Perhaps, like Sienna, he'd only needed to find his place to motivate him. Not to mention, noble lasses were all vying for his attention.

"Gather your things, my lass. I will get started on our plans." With a kiss to her cheek, her *móraí* rose from the chaise and disappeared from the room.

Sienna sat dumbfounded for a moment, unable to

move, her pulse thundering in her temples.

What just happened?

Her grandmother had just given her blessing for Sienna to join Liam…forever.

Her tummy wobbled, and she denied the doubts churning there that he wouldn't want her. He had never confessed love, but Liam MacLeod cared for her.

If he didn't love her, as she loved him, Sienna would just wait until he did.

He might've left her because it wasn't safe for him to remain in the Fae Realm, but there was nothing stopping her from remaining in *his* realm.

Liam had said magic was diminished there, but what did she care?

Sienna had lived all her life up to the last two weeks without her powers. His human clan had a healer already, and she could apply her duties in that area.

So could her sister.

Three healers were better than one, right?

Trioblóid chirruped from his couch.

She sucked in a silent gasp.

Sadness suffused her again. "Oh, Trio," Sienna breathed out a tear, and opened her arms.

Her bogle skittered across the decorative tile and launched himself into her embrace, crooning softly as if he already understood what was to happen.

"You can't go with me," she whispered. "You have to stay here and care for *Mórai* and Ealeric. They will need you." She closed her eyes against the newest round of tears—this time for her beloved companion.

Trioblóid burrowed his little round body into her, and Sienna held him in mutual silence for a long time.

When she released him, the bogle remained glued to her, even as she flitted around the large suite stuffing her belongings into a brown satchel.

chapter twenty-nine

S ienna looked around the Field of Light, startlingly empty of any winged soldiers, and she swallowed. Her whole body was lit with a nervous energy and no matter how many times she'd ordered herself to calm, she couldn't release the jitters.

Amalie squeezed her hand, and she squeezed right back.

They exchanged a smile, and her sister shifted in the fine brown boots she wore. Amalie's mantle was short and hunter green, which made her hair and eyes even more striking. Her travel clothing consisted of dark brown trews and an olive green leine. Despite its simplicity and lack of femininity, her sister was stunning.

She'd always been envious that Amalie's alabaster skin was clear of the freckles Sienna had, and she couldn't deny her youngest sibling's beauty. Rory MacLeod would be a fool if he didn't see it, but she suspected the lad was as infatuated as Amalie.

Sienna couldn't bear to discuss the seriousness of her sister giving up her life in the only realm they'd ever known for a lad she'd met once. Amalie hadn't stated any other reasons for her decision to leave home with her. Like her situation with Liam, she could only pray Amalie's heart would not end up shattered.

"Lasses, are you ready?"

Sienna met Lady Aileana's violet eyes and nodded.

They'd had to say their goodbyes to *Mórai* and Ealeric at the palace, for practical reasons—they hadn't much time for the Faery Stones to remain unguarded, and Captain Daegus couldn't travel with more than two passengers.

Lady Aileana had *blinked* to the Field of Light and met them there.

Allowing the huge, winged man to hold her and Amalie close had been disconcerting, but Sienna had finally been able to soar through the pink and gold skies of the Fae Realm. She only regretted it was not the halfling she loved flying with her.

Her brother had taken the news in stride—he'd only threatened to pulverize Liam if he hurt Sienna, but he couldn't hide his glee at his new destiny as head healer. Sienna was happy for him and had told him so.

Suddenly, another Fae Warrior appeared above them, making all four of them tense.

Captain Daegus gripped the hilt of his magic sword, ready to draw.

When the Warrior landed, it was evident that he had a passenger, as well.

As soon as his silver chest-plate came into view, Captain Daegus relaxed his grip.

The two men closed the small stretch of distance on foot.

The Fae Warrior was Caelan, one of the captain's Seconds, and the other man with him Sienna didn't recognize. He wore a palace guard uniform, a royal blue overtunic with fine silver trim, and matching blue trews and boots. Two swords were strapped to his back, common for the men-at-arms. His dark locks were shorn, and his face clean-shaven.

The moment familiar blue eyes met her own, Sienna gasped.

"Feneal?"

The man she'd always known as a bit mad, beamed. "I had to see you lasses off when your *móraí* told me of your plans. My son was nice enough to oblige." He gestured to Caelan.

The Fae Warrior offered a nod, then bowed to the Lady Aileana.

Amalie rushed to the Fae man they'd both known all their lives and threw her arms around him.

Feneal chuckled and pulled her sister into a warm embrace.

Sienna stared, unable to process the man before her, not an ounce of filth in sight. Not only was he clean, but without the beard and messy long hair, Feneal was wickedly handsome, and looked decades younger.

"Close your mouth, dearheart," Lady Aileana whispered, tapping her arm. Her violet eyes twinkled when Sienna spared her a glance.

"I don't…understand," she whispered.

Feneal released her sister, and his smile was kind. "I can't get my wings back, but the king has restored me and given me a position." He indicated the uniform. "It is not what I was, but it is duty, and duty feels good. And I have my lad back." He threw a look at the tall Fae Warrior beside him.

Caelan cleared his throat, his amber eyes shiny. He didn't speak, but his expression was equally grateful.

Seeing them side-by-side marked their relationship, which had been much less obvious with Feneal's overgrown, untamed beard. Despite the eye color difference, they looked very much alike, and more like siblings than father and son.

"Well, do not let us delay your mission," Feneal said, falling into a polite bow that seemed below his station, somehow. "Live well, Sienna, and take care of your sister." He flashed a fatherly smile that warmed her heart and stirred her emotions all over again.

"I'll miss you, Feneal. Thank you for always caring for my family." Sienna stepped into the former exile and hugged him. "Don't stop that now, please. Look after my grandmother and brother for me."

"I will. Take care of Liam MacLeod, too. Tell him I enjoyed our adventures." His grin was impish and had her grinning back. "I owe your lad everything. Had he not come here, I would not be where I am. Back at the palace with my lad."

Sienna nodded, because her words evaporated at Feneal's sincerity.

Liam changed multiple lives for the better.

Did he know that?

Her sister tugged her wrist and Sienna stepped back from the former exile and nodded to Caelan.

Captain Daegus moved to the dais, tapping each of the crystals that made up the Faery Stones.

Lady Aileana indicated for Amalie to climb the three steps to the dais, then she reached for Sienna.

Sienna paused and gripped the healer's smaller hands and was compelled to meet the violet gaze that matched Liam's. Her heart skipped.

The former princess' countenance was kind and loving. "This is what you want, my lass?"

Sienna's body warmed at the care the woman showed. They didn't know each other well but had spent a great deal of time together since her family had returned to the palace. She liked Liam's grandmother very much. Lady Aileana had been one of her teachers.

"Aye, I want Liam very much."

I just hope he feels the same.

"Don't you fash over that." Liam's grandmother squeezed her fingers.

Sienna wanted to crush her eyes shut. She'd almost forgotten the healer was a mind reader, too. Embarrassment kissed the back of her neck and burned into her cheeks.

"My lad's lad is nay a fool." The older woman's expression was amused and sly. "I've no doubt you'll handle him."

The captain called for them; the portal was starting to open.

She couldn't control the thunder of her heart as she trudged up the stairs.

Amalie reached for her, and Sienna entwined their fingers.

With her free hand, she tossed her satchel over one shoulder.

They exchanged one last look, took an identical breath, and without a backward glance, stepped through the magic doorway.

Liam sheathed his dirk in his boot, his head spinning, and it had nothing to do with straightening too fast.

Was he mad to attempt this again?

Of course, this time he had his family's blessing, and his father had even offered to go with him. This was something he needed to do on his own. Convincing the love of his life to come back to his realm and give up everything she'd ever wanted…to be with him.

He wouldn't contemplate that Sienna might want her magic more.

Liam would give up his wings a thousand times if she wanted to be at his side for the rest of his life. If she loved him as much as he loved her.

He donned a short brown mantel, because the ride down to the beach would be chilly, but he could leave it in the cave of the Faery Stones, since the other realm was always so warm.

Liam's smaller-scale stunning spell wasn't nearly as strong as his father's, aunt's, and cousin's when they'd come to rescue him, and he only prayed that he could quickly deploy it and fly away unscathed.

The door to his quarters was wrenched open, and Angus' large frame filled the doorway, as if Liam's thoughts had conjured him.

"The Faery Stones," the man panted, as if he couldn't catch his breath. It wasn't often his very physically fit cousin overexerted himself.

What could have him so riled?

"I'm comin'," Liam drawled. "I dinnae need ye ta open them, remember?"

"Nay, nay." Angus shook his head, scattering his dark hair over his shoulders.

Liam's heart skipped and he stared his eldest cousin down. "What is it?"

The laird's son blew out a breath and flashed a much-too-knowing smirk. "Someone opened the Faery Stones."

He startled. "What?" floated out of his mouth on a breath instead of the intended demand.

"Aye, come. We're ta go down ta the beach."

"We?" Liam's adventure was supposed to be solo.

Angus' grin was wry. "My father an' Duncan insist upon it, in case of danger. The lads want ta go as well."

"Nothin' but meddlers," he muttered.

His cousin chuckled. "Ye'll nay be permitted ta go alone."

Liam rolled his eyes. "A course no'." He gestured for Angus to precede his exit, and he wasn't shy about slamming the door behind him.

He ignored his cousin's second chuckle.

Everyone was already mounted up when he and Angus made it down to the bailey, and one of the stable lads handed Treun's reins over.

Liam's roan stallion whinnied a welcome, and he spared his beloved horse a stroke to his soft nose before he swung himself up on the wide back.

The short ride to the ridge above the cave of the Faery Stones was surrounded in an undercurrent of *"expect anything,"* and his heartrate increased with every inch of ground Treun's hooves gained, and soon it was so loud in his ears, it drowned out the voices of his family.

"Amalie," Rory breathed beside him, leaning up in his saddle and pointing to the beach.

Liam swallowed and followed his cousin's gesture.

Two lasses stood hand-in-hand and looked up to the MacLeods on horseback.

One wore a short green mantel, and she removed her hood, revealing fine golden locks.

The other stood with her fiery tresses visible, wild, and free. Her body language screamed uncertainty, and she clung to her sister's hand.

A chilly gale whipped their cloaks and hair around, but they made no move to ascend the cliff face.

Liam threw his leg over Treun's back and slid down too fast, almost falling on his arse. He ignored answering chuckles and righted himself, then dashed for the ridge.

Rory was already three paces ahead of him and led their descent.

None of the other men attempted to join them, and Liam was grateful. He wished his magic worked in this realm and he could whisk them back to

Dunvegan with a mere thought.

Amalie broke away from Sienna and rushed to his cousin.

Rory and his love's sister stopped short of grabbing each other, as if both instantly shy.

Liam smirked.

His cousin was no womanizing letch, but nor was Rory an untried virgin. There had been lasses. To see him react such a way toward this Fae lass was telling.

They stared at each other, before Rory awkwardly closed the distance, and pulled her into his chest.

Amalie, with bright pink cheeks, allowed the embrace, wrapping her arms around his cousin.

One look at Sienna drowned out the rest of the world, including Rory and Amalie's low voices.

She stood in the same spot, gnawing on her full bottom lip, her whole body seeping insecurity.

Liam had to touch her.

Without a word, he tugged her to him, squeezing her against him. A sigh floated out of his mouth as the sense of rightness washed over him.

Now that he held her again, he wouldn't let her go.

Ever.

Sienna slid her arms around his neck and snuggled in, as if she too couldn't get close enough.

He closed his eyes and rested his cheek against her soft hair. Liam breathed her in, the familiar floral-mixed-with-herbs scent tickling his nose, as well as the sea air.

"Liam," Sienna breathed.

He swallowed because there was no way he could speak.

"Sienna?" The sound of Amalie's voice broke their spell.

Liam cursed, earning a smirk from Rory, when he met his cousin's green eyes over Sienna's head.

Unfortunately, his love gently pulled away and glanced at her sister.

Rory had Amalie's hand entwined with his, as if his cousin had also made a decision to keep the Fae lass.

"Go back to Dunvegan with Rory. Would that be okay, Liam?" Sienna's voice was wrapped in the same uncertainty, and he wanted to banish it.

"Aye." He nodded to his cousin. "We'll be along soon. Get her warm an' fed." Liam gestured to Amalie.

Sienna glued herself to his side and they watched Rory help Amalie up the cliff face, holding her close when she slipped.

Soon they were astride Rory's bay mare.

Liam caught Xander's eye up on the ridge.

His father gave him a curt nod, then the group of MacLeod's departed.

"I'll kill him if he breaks her heart," Sienna whispered.

He arched an eyebrow at the menace in his love's tone and smirked. "Nay, love, I'll kill him fer ye."

Her burnished bronze eyes flashed. "You need not fight my battles, Liam MacLeod."

Liam fought a smile as she turned her ire on him. He wasn't about to bring up Wardric or what'd happened in the Fae Realm. He cupped her cheeks and stroked her soft skin with his thumbs. "I was comin' fer ye, love. Headed down ta the Faery Stones today."

"You were?" Sienna leaned into his touch and closed her eyes for a heartbeat.

He nodded. "Seems ye beat me."

"How did you know we were here?" Her face was stained adorably pink, and her insecurity was back, as she sucked her bottom lip into her mouth.

The move stirred his libido. He wanted to taste her again, but he needed to tell her how he felt, first.

Liam made himself focus on her question. "Alana. She always kens when the Stones open."

"Oh," Sienna whispered.

Silence fell, and he fought the urge to squirm in his boots, then chided himself.

She'd come to him.

That had to mean something, right?

"Sienna, I love ye," Liam blurted.

Large tears rolled down her cheeks, but she didn't say anything.

"Sienna?" he whispered, trying to keep sudden panic at bay.

"I love you, too, Liam." She threw her arms around his neck and pushed to her tiptoes to crash her mouth into his.

Liam didn't deny her. He met her seeking tongue and deepened their lip-lock, kissing her with all the desperation and love he felt, as well as the regret he'd experienced over the fortnight without her.

Sienna kissed him back with the same fierceness.

He was hard and aching in seconds.

They panted against each other when they finally parted, forehead to forehead, and he fought the urge to throw her down to the beach and take her.

"I've been miserable without you," she confessed, her lips already swollen from his and her gorgeous face flushed. "I came to beg you to have me. I want to stay here with you."

His heart stuttered and Liam flashed a grin. "I was dyin' without ye. I was comin' ta beg ye ta return home wit' me."

They leaned back, locked eyes, and laughed.

Elation washed over him, and he let out a relieved breath.

Sienna *loved* him. She'd come back to him.

"How'd ye get past the Fae Warriors? Are the Stones not guarded?" he breathed, urging her back into his arms.

"Your grandparents. They helped without hesitation."

Liam smiled. Then he studied her face. "What…what about yer station? Yer magic?"

"I want you more than I ever wanted my magic." Sienna's eyes misted over again.

He caressed her cheeks because he didn't know what to say. Liam had been prepared to beg her to give everything up. Intended to do whatever it took to convince her, to show her how much he loved her.

Yet his love had made the huge decision all on her own and had made her way back to him. Risking the rest of her life without knowing if he felt the same.

"I love ye," he breathed, in wonder of this Fae lass, the strongest woman he'd ever met.

Sienna's face lit up, making her freckles stand out.

Liam wanted to kiss each one. He'd have the chance because she was now his forever. "Marry me?" he blurted.

She blinked.

Her loud swallow made him want to kiss her throat.

"Truly?" she whispered.

He smirked. "Ye doubt me, e'en after I bare my heart?"

She shook her head, making her bright red hair shift. "Nay, but I didn't let myself hope beyond—"

Liam dipped down and forced her silence. He kissed her deeply, until Sienna sagged against him, clinging. "How I want ye. I ache fer ye. 'Tis been way too long," he pushed the words into her lips.

"Then we'll have to marry," she whispered back, one corner of her delicious mouth up.

"Aye?"

"Aye." She nodded. "I've heard in the Human Realm 'tis improper to be lovers without the benefit of vows."

He chuckled and kissed her again. "Yer already my lover. Now, ye will be my wife."

"And you, my husband." Sienna grinned and nodded. Then her mirth fell off, and she stared, a sudden sadness stamped all over her beautiful face. "Your wings…" her voice went thick with regret.

Liam shook his head. "Nay, love. Dinnae fash o'er

them. I've lived most a' my life wit'out them."

Her brow knotted and she frowned.

"As ye say regardin' yer magic, I want ye more."

Sienna smiled softly and nodded, reaching for his face and cupping his cheeks. "I'm glad you do, because I had an elaborate plan to convince you if I needed to."

Liam arched an eyebrow and fought a smile. "Aye?"

Her face brightened with a crimson flush too appealing to resist.

He kissed her again, until Sienna writhed against him, and his cock was throbbing into her belly. "Will ye…show me, when we get home?"

"Home?" Sienna panted, her face hazy with passion, and her burnished eyes glowing with desire.

A singe of want slid down his spine and made his bollocks tingle. "Aye, I vow ta sneak inta yer room tonight."

She flashed an impish grin. "You will?"

"I'll have ta. My mother will insist ye dinnae stay with me until we're wed, an' I've nay intention ta wait that long ta have ye again."

"Then let's wed tomorrow."

Liam grinned and nodded. "Whate'er my wife desires."

Sienna beamed and pressed a much-too-fast kiss on his mouth. "Take me home, Liam. Then just take me."

He swung her up into his arms and headed

toward the ridge where Treun waited.
    Dunvegan was home for them, indeed.

the end

about the author

USA Today Bestselling, award winning author of romantic suspense, epic and historical fantasy romance, C.A. loves to dabble in different genres. If it's a good story, she'll write it, no matter where it seems to fit!

She's a hopeless romantic and always will be. Risking it all for Happily Ever After is what she lives by!

C.A. is originally from Ohio but got to Texas as soon as she could. She's happily married and has a bachelor's degree in criminal justice.

She's always writing, and helps small business owners by writing their websites, and she loves it!

WEBSITE: http://www.caszarek.com
EBOOK STORE:
https://www.caszarek.com/ebook-store
PAPERBACK STORE:
https://www.caszarek.com/paperback-store
FACEBOOK:
http://www.facebook.com/caszarek
INSTAGRAM:
https://www.instagram.com/caszarek/
TWITTER: https://twitter.com/caszarek
BOOKBUB:
https://www.bookbub.com/profile/c-a-szarek
GOODREADS:
https://www.goodreads.com/author/show/58
15085.C_A_Szarek
EMAIL: ca@caszarek.com

You can sign up for C.A.'s newsletter on her website, as well as buy all her books!